PRAISE FOR ELLE MARR

Strangers We Know

"Elle Marr is an author to know. Just when you think you understand the motives behind her characters and the way their story lines are being presented—bam!—Elle will hit you with twists you won't see coming. Told from multiple points of view, *Strangers We Know* is about more than Ivy learning of her past and, shockingly, the serial killer within her family; it's also about knowing who to trust and how to discern who's telling the complete story. Because if everyone has secrets, are they truly family or only strangers? Read *Strangers We Know* to find out."

—Georgina Cross, bestselling author of *The Stepdaughter*

"Elle Marr burst onto the suspense scene in 2020 with her bestselling debut, *The Missing Sister*, and followed up a year later with *Lies We Bury*, another trust-no-one murder mystery. With her third novel, *Strangers We Know*, Marr firmly establishes herself as a master of 'did that really just happen?' thrillers. *Strangers We Know* has plot twists so unexpected and characters so creepy you won't want to turn out the lights, and the ending is surprising in multiple ways. Who knew a deranged-serial-killer whodunit could leave you with all the feels?"

—A.H. Kim, author of *A Good Family*

"Dark family secrets, serial murder, and a cult? Yes, please. Twisty and a little twisted, the highly addictive and surprise-packed *Strangers We Know* will have you pulling an all-nighter."

—Heather Chavez, author of *No Bad Deed*

"From the first page I was gripped by *Strangers We Know* and read through the night till the end. The novel is thrilling beyond belief, with suspense and twists ratcheting up on each page. Elle Marr is brilliant at delving into the darkness of a seemingly normal family, and by the time she pulls back the curtains on each character, the terror has built so excruciatingly, you just have to keep going till you find out every single thing—you're afraid to know, but you have to know. This is the year's must read."

—Luanne Rice, bestselling author of *The Shadow Box*

Lies We Bury

"A deep, deep dive into unspeakable memories and their unimaginably shocking legacy."

—*Kirkus Reviews* (starred review)

"The suspenseful plot is matched by the convincing portrayal of the vulnerable Claire, who just wants to lead a normal life. Marr is a writer to watch."

—*Publishers Weekly*

"Marr's #OwnVoices, trust-no-one thriller unravels with horrifying 'THEN' interruptions, producing a jolting creepfest of twisted revenge."

—*Booklist*

"In *Lies We Bury*, Elle Marr (bestselling author of *The Missing Sister*) has brought a cleverly plotted and compelling new mystery with unique characters and truly surprising twists."

—The Nerd Daily

"A deep, thrilling dive into the painful memories that haunt us and the fight between moving on or digging in and seeking revenge."

—Medium

"A twisted mash-up of *Room* and a murder mystery, Marr's *Lies We Bury* is a story that creeps into your bones, a sneaky tale about the danger of secrets and the power the past holds to lead us into a deliciously devious present. Say goodbye to sleep and read it like I did, in one breathless sitting."

—Kimberly Belle, international bestselling author of *Dear Wife* and *Stranger in the Lake*

"Dark and compelling, Elle Marr has written another atmospheric and twisted thriller that you don't want to miss. *Lies We Bury* delves into the darkest of pasts and explores the fascinating tension between moving on and revenge. This is a fly-through-the-pages thriller."

—Vanessa Lillie, Amazon bestselling author of *Little Voices* and *For the Best*

"This haunting and emotional thriller will keep you up at night looking for answers."

—Dea Poirier, international bestselling author of *Next Girl to Die*

"A clever, twisty murder mystery packed full of secrets and lies that will keep you turning the pages way past bedtime. *Lies We Bury* hooked me from page one and kept me guessing until its dramatic conclusion."

—Lisa Gray, bestselling author of *Thin Air*

The Missing Sister

"Marr's debut novel follows a San Diego medical student to, around, and ultimately beneath Paris in search of the twin sister she'd been drifting away from. Notable for its exploration of the uncanny bonds twins share and the killer's memorably macabre motive."

—*Kirkus Reviews*

"[A] gritty debut . . . The intriguing premise, along with a few twists, lend this psychological thriller some weight."

—*Publishers Weekly*

"Elle Marr's first novel has an intriguing premise . . . The characters are well drawn and complex, and Marr's prose offers some surprising twists."

—New York Journal of Books

"A promising plotline."

—*Library Journal*

"*The Missing Sister* is a very promising debut—atmospheric, gripping, and set in Paris. In other words, the perfect ingredients for a satisfying result."

—Criminal Element

"Brimming with eerie mystery and hair-raising details . . . A chilling read that shows the unique bond of twins."

—*Woman's World*

"This thrilling debut novel from Elle Marr is a look into the importance of identity and the strength of sisterhood."

—*Brooklyn Digest*

STRANGERS
WE KNOW

OTHER TITLES BY ELLE MARR

Lies We Bury
The Missing Sister

STRANGERS
WE KNOW

ELLE
MARR

THOMAS & MERCER

Text copyright © 2022 by Elle Marr
All rights reserved.

Published by Thomas & Mercer, Seattle

www.apub.com

Amazon, the Amazon logo, and Thomas & Mercer are trademarks of Amazon.com, Inc., or its affiliates.

ISBN-13: 9781542032773
ISBN-10: 1542032776

Cover design by Shasti O'Leary Soudant

Printed in the United States of America

For Liana

One

IVY

Blood doesn't lie, or so the saying goes. I just wish I knew whether that applies to adopted blood. Does adopted blood most closely identify with those who gave it life? Or does the family who raised the adopted blood have the most influence? Nature or nurture—I'd love to know what's responsible for the splitting headache burrowing into my skull.

I slide into a corner booth, then scan the café. A lone man sits at a table on the other side of the room, scrolling on his phone, while a barista checks her manicure from behind a silver counter at the front. The gurgling of a coffee machine fills the shop. It's as good a spot as any to work outside my apartment for the first time in weeks, while I wait for the results of my genetics test.

Before my symptoms began six months ago, I used to edit all the time in this café. But then piercing headaches, a low-grade fever, all-over muscle aches fit for a retiree, and fatigue that left me lying in bed for hours at a time made it a challenge to go grocery shopping, let alone walk seven blocks. It's nice to be out in the world again—among people but not directly next to them.

I open my laptop. The reflection of the painted script on the glass wall beside me—GINNY'S JOE—covers my screen until I angle it toward my face. Black hair pulled back in a crown braid emphasizes the eyes I've always considered strangely large and the bump in my nose that shows I'm not full Chinese.

The cursor returns my stare from a page filled with text. Marketing copy I need to copyedit, from a client whose deadline I've already pushed out twice.

A scone would be nice. Maybe another coffee.

At the counter, I pay for both items, then return to my seat. Settled back in front of the document, I watch the blinking cursor. The steady rhythm is almost hypnotizing, and the truth hits me: I don't want to work. Despite residual pain in my shins, today is the first day I've had the energy to venture to a café, and I want to enjoy it.

One of San Francisco's iconic cable cars turns onto the street. People clutch the brass bars, skin of all colors on display in the shorts and tank tops that tourists wear in August. I smile, then reach into the oversize shoulder bag that doubles as a laptop carrier and withdraw the crossword I've nearly finished. Twenty-two down is the final clue needed.

"What is a three-letter word for regret?" I mutter out loud.

"Rue."

I look up. A man in a suit jacket and tie stands before me. Sweat glistens across his forehead.

"Ivy Hon?" He flashes a badge from the inside of his jacket. "Special Agent Ballo. Mind if I join?"

He waits for me to reply, knobby knuckles resting on the back of a chair. Thick eyebrows balance out a broad nose and grizzled jawline. His ears were pierced at one point. He's probably in his late fifties.

I nod, too startled to decline. "Up to you."

Is this guy really FBI? How would the FBI know what café I visit— or used to?

He takes a seat. Signals to the barista for a black coffee with oat milk. Very San Francisco.

"It is, isn't it? Rue?"

I look at the crossword. "Yeah. Good pull."

He smiles. "Sorry to surprise you like this. I planned to catch you at home, but you were on your way out when I arrived. These conversations are always easier in person. Have you ever been to the Pacific Northwest?"

"No. I don't travel much."

"Okay. Have you ever heard of the Full Moon Killer?"

A pot falls behind the counter, hitting the tile with a clang that scrapes my ears. "No. Should I have?"

Ballo presses his lips together. "Not exactly, Ivy. Just trying to get a baseline here. The Full Moon Killer was primarily active in the Pacific Northwest from the late eighties to the early aughts. His target was young women—teenagers and twentysomethings. Eight victims have been ID'd as his over the years. His MO was to kill during the full moon."

Ballo leans back in his chair, the cheap plastic creaking dangerously. "Any of this ring a bell?"

"Should it?" I take a sip from my cup, wondering more than ever why he's approached me—why me?

"The first girl murdered was seventeen-year-old Stacey Perez," he continues. "High school cheerleader, honor-roll student. She was killed under a full moon while running out for a jug of milk so her mother could make horchata. Her body was found in the Columbia River, poisoned, then strangled."

I shudder. "That's horrible."

The barista drops off a white ceramic mug filled to the brim. Agent Ballo selects a sugar packet from a ramekin at the side of the table.

"The second victim was Geri Hauser, a college student home from Washington State for the summer. Also discovered in the Columbia after the full moon, poisoned and bludgeoned."

My stomach twists as I imagine the scene. "How awful." I imitate him, grabbing a sugar packet, then adding sweetener to my latte for something to do. "But what can I help you with?"

"More victims followed, but the Full Moon Killer took a break for several years. From 2006 on, no one else was killed in Washington or Oregon according to this pattern until last month—Katrina Oates, a day-care provider."

I tap the paper wrapper of the fake sugar with my finger. Make the crystals bounce on the tabletop. "But why was Stacey strangled, and Geri bludgeoned?"

He raises both eyebrows, as if impressed that I'm paying attention.

"I'm a copyeditor," I add. "I notice details for a living."

"Stacey and Geri were likely his first, when he was still getting the hang of things. Serial killers tend to experiment before settling into a consistent routine."

"Okay. If the bodies were found after the full moon, and the timing isn't exact, why the nickname the 'Full Moon Killer'?"

Ballo waves a hand. "Forensics confirmed that's when they died, and both women disappeared on the night of a full moon."

"And when is the next full moon?"

He narrows his brown eyes on mine. "Thirteen days."

Air-conditioning kicks on from the vent above. I hug my elbows, wishing I'd brought a jacket for warmth. "Look, Agent Ballo, I'm sure you're very busy. I'm still not grasping why you approached me."

"You recently submitted your DNA for genetic analysis. You're adopted."

A chill kisses the back of my neck, independent of the AC.

"You signed a privacy waiver that uploads your results to a national database," he continues. "The bureau searches that database for links to major crimes."

"I'm sorry. I don't understand." I shake my head, genuinely confused by his train of thought. He's not suggesting . . . What is he suggesting?

I stare at this man. This FBI agent. At his fist now tapping the table, punctuating words that don't make sense. His pursed mouth and the stubble along his jaw.

"You're saying I haven't received my results yet, but the FBI has? How did you know I'm adopted?"

Agent Ballo takes a sip of coffee. "Tell me, Ivy. What do you know about your birth family?"

I glance past him to the blonde, plucky barista counting mugs and lining up ramekins to refill. She laughs at something someone out of sight in the kitchen says—both of them are blissfully ignorant of our conversation. My shoulders sag forward and new fatigue coats my frame. Visiting this café while I was just getting past a flare-up was a risk. Energy seems to leach from my fingertips the longer I sit idle. "Not much."

Agent Ballo sets his cup down. "You've never had any contact with them? Have you ever wanted any?"

"No. None." I first learned I was adopted when I was seven and old enough to understand what that meant: my birth mother couldn't raise me, but my adoptive parents were ecstatic to round out their family with a baby girl; I was loved deeply, almost from day one. And though I sometimes felt at odds with my laser-focused parents and brother, I never contacted my birth family. Nor they me.

"Any letters from your relatives? Any belongings, sentimental items, or paperwork from them?"

Beside us outside, two teenage girls chatter excitedly on the sidewalk. The taller one holds a cell phone up at an angle high enough to pop a vertebra loose. They selfie. When was the last time I pressed my cheek to someone else's, besides my cat's? Or shared a coffee in a café? And now, when I leave my apartment for the first time in weeks, some federal agent tracks me down.

After my mom passed away two years ago, I stopped returning friends' calls; I couldn't handle someone else eventually letting me down—leaving me like she had, like my dad did. The mysterious flare-ups that no doctor has been able to diagnose have given me justification to withdraw even further.

Agent Ballo leans closer. "Your DNA is like a blueprint, unique to you, right? When people add their test results to the national database, sometimes there's overlap between two individuals—some matching DNA segments that suggest two people share a common ancestor. When these segments are compellingly long, we start thinking—maybe these people share a closer ancestor than anyone realized."

"Are you saying you found my birth parents?" I wince against the new ache in my temples. Half-formed thoughts and fears spark in my mind, but I can't make sense of Agent Ballo's words.

He doesn't reply. Instead, he withdraws a business card from his jacket's inner pocket. A handwritten phone number is on one side.

"I'd appreciate it if you kept our visit to yourself, Ivy. And if you think of anything about your relatives—or find anything from them—please reach out."

Cutlery clangs together behind the counter, and the lone man four tables over slams his laptop shut, each noise stabbing my nerves. I lick my lips and taste the coffee's acidity once more. "What's so interesting about them?"

Agent Ballo folds his hands on the tabletop. "It's more about you and your test results, Ivy. We've been hunting the Full Moon Killer for decades now. Comparing the genetic database with partial samples left behind at crime scenes, we've been able to identify a segment of DNA that the two of you share."

I gape at him, openmouthed. "So you're saying . . . What are you saying?"

"We believe that you may be related to the Full Moon Killer. And we need your help to finally find the bastard."

Two

Samson

The Past

Goddamn Debbie Dawson.

Dust kicks up on this backwoods road like all of them in this shit-hole, and I step on the gas. My headlights catch on the dirt clouds, and for a second I can't see anything.

"Sam! What the hell!" Debbie Dawson screams.

What a stupid name. *Debbie Dawson.*

"Relax, baby, we're good." I take the turn in the road sharply and feel the wheels of my pickup lift a few inches before we slam back down. "You turning into one of those Reagan crybabies?"

"What the hell does that mean?" She smooths back kinky brown curls that I'm dying to twist my fingers in.

Burrel, the elbow lint of California, a town just south of Fresno, still holds a torch for Reagan even though it's been a solid while since he was in office. Bumper stickers everywhere. Someone'll have to pry them from all these idiots' cold dead hands at some point.

"Everyone talks about the good old days, where people drove slow and gas was cheap and kids behaved," I say.

Debbie sits up, unbuckled in my passenger seat. She drapes her arm across my neck, her breast pressing against me. "Well, if that's the good old days, I don't want them. No behaving for us, Samson."

Her tongue slides along my earlobe, but I'm still annoyed at her reprimand a few moments ago. I see a pothole and accelerate before slamming into it. The truck rears up like a bronco, and for a second it feels like flying. "Boom! We got our own rodeo, baby!"

Debbie slouches off, bitching about me being no fun. She leans against the door, spindly legs pressed together in her skirt like a Venus flytrap; the half-open window gnashes at her hair, making her seem wild, the way I wanted her to act at the movies earlier, but she wouldn't take off her underwear. Teenage girls are so prissy.

I've got to get out of Burrel. It's sucking me dry. The hot stench of cow manure in May alone is a moist blanket stifling my true blood-thirsty self—my exploration of who I am. As soon as graduation hits, I'm leaving Mrs. Rayvin's and getting the fuck out. Mama Rayvin is fine, I guess, and she's a hell of a better foster parent than grabby-hands Gerald Gilpin, but it's time to leave. Too many busybodies in this town, too many prying eyes. Even if Burrel's dairy farms attract lots of unsuspecting migrant workers who can be fun to play with, I gotta move on. Stretch my legs. See the sights. See how far I can go.

Northern California might be nice. All that green, the redwoods, the national parks filled with campers. Some hitchhikers too, I'll bet.

One more month until grad. One more month and I am gone.

"What are you thinking about?" Debbie sidles up to me again, apparently too needy to cold-shoulder me any longer. The night is black on this shortcut home from Fresno, and the city lights become smaller in my rearview until they're like fireflies. Nothing but my headlights and the stars to escort us. We are alone.

"Thinking about you and how hot you looked tonight," I say. I slide a hand onto her knee, but she slaps it away.

"Samson, I already told you, I'm not messing around in your truck."

"God, what a fucking buzzkill you are!" I roar, then turn to catch her expression, relish her fear a bit, but she's staring straight ahead.

"Watch out!"

An owl smashes into my windshield, a big one, cracking the glass. I slam on the brakes, swerving into a ditch I know leads to the river nearby. Lucky this happened now.

"What the fuck, Samson! You hit a hawk!" Breathless and accusatory, Debbie stares at me like I did it on purpose.

"Barn owl. And I didn't see it—it was an accident, obviously!" God, I hate raising my voice. I sound like Gerald. Why is there so much yelling right now?

A jagged crack spiderwebs across the pane. "Man, my truck," I groan.

"Your truck? You hit and probably killed an owl! A live animal! You're more upset about your windshield? You know, I heard rumors that you had a screw loose, the ones that said you were messed up and you were the reason why Jessica Hamil moved away, but you know what? I ignored them. Like a jerk."

She squishes back against the passenger door and gives a *humph* when I start driving again. I can feel her eyes boring into my head like a dentist's drill.

"You don't even care, do you?"

I don't answer.

"You're, like, not even remotely bothered by it. You don't care about the bird. About me. That's why you don't talk to me in homeroom or anywhere else in public. You wouldn't even let me tell my mom you took me to the movies tonight. You're not all there, Sam. Your mother was messed up too."

My headlights glint off something moving about a hundred yards up. Water. The river. Not too wide, but plenty fast in its current; a few kids last summer drowned in it. A few more this year'll probably join their ranks. I speed up.

"I mean, wow, I cannot wait to tell everyone at school tomorrow what an unfortunate piece of work you—"

Turning hard into the shoulder, I hear Debbie Dawson scream. I reach across her lap and yank the handle, letting the door fling open with the momentum, then watch as her eyes snap wide and her body slides from the cab onto the dusty incline below. I pause my truck. Hear a thump in the darkness, the sound of her rolling and yelping through star thistles down the bank into the water, where a splash announces she made it. A second goes by. Two. Three. Then more screaming.

"Samson! Sam! Help me!"

I close the passenger door so the cab light dims but leave the window rolled down. The frenzy of her splashing dies away as the current grabs her by the ankles and begins to pull.

I resume the drive home, then glance up, past the giant crack in the windshield.

I thought there were no witnesses to this evening's shenanigans—like other times I've had fun with the farmworkers—but I was wrong.

Stopping my truck in the middle of the road, I turn off my headlights and let the engine idle. I lean forward to the glass like a baby calf to its mother. And let the white orb of a full moon above bathe my face.

Three

IVY

When I get home, Onyx is yowling at the window, pawing at a pigeon resting on an electrical line. I check the clock; it's dinnertime, and borderline negligent to feed a pet so late.

"Come here, little lion." I scoop her up, then dish out wet food into a bowl. She delicately eats her gourmet mush, then switches to aggressively licking her plate until it thuds against the cabinet again and again, per usual. Once finished, she joins me on the couch in my small living room, where I sit staring at my phone.

My finger hesitates over the center of the genetics-testing website, cutely named DNAcorn. The word on the button, *Results*, seems to pulse from the screen, as if it knows the damning information it contains.

I got the notification that my report was ready while I was still in the café and half paying attention to the document I was copyediting; of course, the FBI would have known I'd receive it today. Instead of clicking on the link, I packed up and started home. My flare-ups can be triggered by stress, and I didn't want to be caught in public if this one was about to get worse.

Agent Ballo's dropped bomb—that I could be related to a serial killer—is enough to motivate anyone to submit their saliva sample. But I elected to send mine weeks ago, when it became clear that the tests my doctor kept ordering wouldn't provide answers about my condition—the reason behind the headaches, body aches, the sudden fevers, rashes, and sporadic taste of metal. I figured that more information is a win.

At least, I woke up thinking as much this morning—before my café visitor.

My father—adoptive father—knew he was going to die. We all did. Aggressive prostate cancer gives that clarity. In the months leading up to his death, he tried to tell me everything he thought I would need to know—his secret marinade for prime rib, when to arrive at the best dim sum restaurant in the Bay for freshly made dumplings. Knowing that he was dying liberated him in a way. He traveled where he wanted, ate his favorite foods, and had long conversations with loved ones.

Three years later, my mother unexpectedly passed from complications due to early-onset Alzheimer's. Losing both parents while in my twenties left me with a greater appreciation for making the most of what time we have.

But is the confirmation of approaching death a gift? Or a curse?

A car alarm erupts a few blocks away, and the sound reverberates in the narrow street beside my apartment. A framed photo of my parents; my brother, Carson; and me posing outside Ghirardelli's sits askew on my entertainment center, their faces angled toward the window, away from me. I don't bother righting the frame. Although I've never felt ashamed of being adopted, reviewing my results seems like something I should do on my own.

Screw it.

I tap the button. A page titled "Health Predispositions" populates with brightly colored bars displaying various genetic traits and conditions. The first, ALLERGIES, confirms it's unlikely that I'm allergic to cats.

"Got that, Onyx? You can stay." I rub my favorite roommate with my foot, and her purr vibrates through my ankle.

Scrolling down, I locate the reports that really matter.

A neon-green bar reads "BRCA Variants," which determines whether I have genetic markers for breast cancer, ovarian cancer, or prostate cancer. I suck in a breath.

Variants not detected.

I swipe backward, then tap the *Alzheimer's Disease* report, hearing my mother's last rambling words from her hospital bed after she slipped on a curb and cracked her head on the concrete. *Ball. Milk. Ivy.* My heart had jumped hearing my name on her lips while she was going in and out of consciousness—*Ivy*—before I realized it would be the last I'd hear from her.

The same phrase as for the BRCA test appears on the screen. *Variants not detected.*

Air floods my lungs and tears prick my eyes. My money was on cancer, as devastating as that would have been as a thirty-year-old. It's the only thing, I thought, that would explain the symptoms that keep presenting all over my body. The rest of the reports are negative: I'm a perfectly normal spit sample.

So what is it, then? What is this sickness that's causing me to sometimes feel like an eighty-year-old on the inside, complete with the occasional arthritis?

I was always grateful that my birth mother gave me up so that I could be placed with a family that wanted me, that guided me, that argued with me when I was wrong and forgave me when I asked. I had thought that was the end of this woman's generosity, but now it seems she and my birth father also gave me good genes.

Whoever they are. Whoever they're related to.

I open another web page and type the words "Full Moon Killer."

The search engine returns dozens of results. Headlines like MURDER IN THE PNW, DEAD WOMAN FOUND FLOATING IN RIVER, and FULL MOON

KILLER ACTIVE AGAIN splash the first page. A shudder courses down my back as I read the horrifying quotes, internalizing that a blood relative of mine could have done those things.

Do I have another brother? Sisters?

I return to the DNAcorn website. At the top of the genetics report, there's a button that reads "DNA Relatives." I filter the results by closest relation.

A name floats to the head of the list: Lottie Montagne. My first cousin on my mother's side.

Excitement and fear pummel my lungs, leaving me breathless. A biological relative. The only name I've learned in thirty years.

Does Ballo know about her?

"Lottie, Lottie, Lottie," I mutter, already sifting through the internet, doing some light cyberstalking.

In a way that's both scary and gratifying, the results are thorough. Lottie Montagne, the only one in this part of the world, lives in Rock Island, Washington; is twenty-eight years old; owns a business; and has a publicly listed phone number but social media accounts that are private and inaccessible to my prying eyes.

"Found you," I breathe.

As I write out a message to Lottie via DNAcorn's platform, I'm struck that she is my closest relation on this website. No indication of my birth parents or possible siblings.

In my message, I aim for brief: I'm adopted, it seems we're first cousins, and I'd love to learn more about her. Since she submitted her own test results to the website and allowed them to be searchable, I hope she's open to chatting.

The faces of my family, framed and perched on the entertainment center I got secondhand, seem to eyeball me, tilted as they are toward the window. As if scrutinizing or judging my actions—one face in particular.

Ballo was especially interested in items from my past. And while my mother was the historian of our family, I wonder if my brother recalls anything significant.

Heaving a sigh, I navigate to the last message I sent him a month ago. Though I'm reluctant to break the silence between us, I start a video call.

A note trills; then the screen widens to reveal Carson's thick black hair, gelled to the side. He's in his law office. He frowns.

"Hey. Everything okay?"

"Yeah, I, uh, just wanted to say hey and ask you about something. Is now a good time?"

"Ivy, just tell me."

"Yeah, I guess I was just wondering—"

"Oh God. Do you need to borrow money?"

"No. What? I don't."

"No? Because the last time we talked, you hinted at money troubles. You know how I feel about your . . . financial choices. How Mom and Dad would feel."

I fight the urge to hang up right then and there. Ever since I spent the last of my share of our inheritance, Carson's been insufferable. He hasn't touched his part of the pot—apparently, he's letting it accrue interest in some aggressive growth account his financial adviser suggested—and has taken every opportunity to rub my nose in my failure to retain our "last living gift from Mom and Dad" since we sold off their house.

Never mind that each amount I withdrew was an investment in my future—something they always emphasized I should focus on.

Carson doesn't need to know that every effort ended before it really began—in tears, no less, and a promise to myself to not get my hopes up again: the time I applied to graduate school but couldn't pass the GRE; the year I paid for monthly public speaking seminars that I got bored of after two months; when I enrolled in a marathon training class to prove to myself I could finish something and made it to only the first practice. Ever since my mom died, the lack of direction I've wrestled with since childhood—and in the shadow of Carson declaring at the age of ten that he would become a lawyer—has taken the wheel.

Carson doesn't care about any of those details, though. The only thing that matters to him is the money, and that I don't have it anymore.

"What the hell, Carson? That's the way you greet me? Just because you disagree with my choices doesn't mean that Mom and Dad would have." Heat flushes my cheeks, my temper snapping like a cheap coffee stirrer.

Carson lifts a single eyebrow. Yeah, I'm not sure I believe me either.

"Anyway, this is not about money," I continue, my irritation ebbing. "It's about me. Did Mom or Dad ever mention my birth family contacting them? Or anything specific to my adoption?"

Carson pauses typing something on his computer. He leans into his phone, and I can make out the shades of gold in his eyes. Sharp cheekbones he inherited from our mother give him a reprimanding air that I'm sure works to his benefit in court.

He scrunches his face. "Did you check in that filing box Mom made for you? Mine only had old T-ball trophies, but maybe yours has something more."

"I haven't. I think it's buried somewhere in my room."

"Can't keep track of that either, huh?"

He sucks in a breath, as if immediately regretting his words. The terse expression slides away, leaving wide eyes and an open face—the bighearted Carson who taught me wrestling moves because I begged him to, and who as a ten-year-old bottle-fed a kitten we found in our driveway.

"Shit, I'm sorry, Iv. I'm . . . I'm working late on a Friday and stressed. I wish I could help you more. If I think of anything, I'll . . ."

I wait for him to say he'll call or text me with any epiphanies. Instead, when he purses his lips, I know his voice has trailed off because he doesn't want to commit to contacting me again.

"No worries, Carson. I'll let you go."

"Hey, Ivy—"

"Yeah?"

"Is there something else going on? You don't seem . . . yourself."

We make eye contact through the screen. Everything I've been weighing the last few hours—my coffee-shop conversation with the FBI, the genetics test results, the continued lack of clarity around my health, and discovering my cousin Lottie—rushes forward and forms a lump in my throat. My chin wobbles before I adopt a smile.

"Just working with a lot of clients. Thanks for asking."

"Sure thing." He leans back in his chair, the moment severed.

We hang up.

I beeline to my bedroom and the shallow closet. Onyx stretches a paw toward me from the bed, but she stays put, as if sensing the tornado of emotions swirling within me.

Hidden beneath long summer dresses is a filing carton with my name on it. Once my mother had accepted that her increasingly poor memory was Alzheimer's, she went to work organizing. Most of the items from our childhood had been scanned and digitized years prior, but certain hard copies she boxed up for us. My carton holds medical records, dinged-up diaries, journals where I scribbled stories, and my adoption paperwork.

I open the manila folder. Everything is the same as when I turned eighteen and poked around for fun, and before that when I was twelve and concerned I might be related to a boy in my class who I thought was cute; he was also half-Chinese and half-white—the only ethnic information about me that my parents knew. Notes written in my mother's perfect hand cover three pages of now-discolored paper: a document signed by "T. C." that released my medical care to "Harold and Vivian Hon"; and loose, lined journal pages with phrases describing my birth parents' origins—"Maternal: Irish and English" and "Paternal: Chinese." I was born at Wenatchee Valley Hospital, in Washington.

No official legal documents. Nothing remotely suggestive of a violent relative among my birth family. But nothing that isn't, either.

Sliding the folder back into the cube, I notice that one edge is rippled. Water damage browns several inches of the folder, as if it had been submerged at one point. Memories of a flash flood return—my mom opening the garage and water spilling onto our driveway.

I pull the entire box out of my closet. A light-brown stain covers the base of the carton, along with each item that I remove and place to the side until the only thing left is one off-white corner poking out at an angle. A piece of paper, trapped between the cardboard flaps.

I pluck it out. An envelope, stiff and crinkly as if it too had been underwater. It's addressed to me at our house in Oakland, the handwriting unfamiliar. The postmark is too faded to glean anything except the year—'94.

Tucked inside is a folded sheet of paper. Gingerly, not wanting to tear the delicate page, I open it and read the first sentence:

> *Dear Ivy—*
> *You must know first and foremost*

The writing is too faded to complete the phrase.

I scan the rest of the letter, but the words still legible are fragmented and void of coherent sense.

> *coming for you*
> *watching you*
> *I needed to tell you*
> *wouldn't let myself. Especially if there was any chance*
> *physical health*
> *you deserve to know. I will find you*
> *hurt you.*
> *You should never have been born*

Chills spike along my arms. I search for a name, the identity of the letter's sender. But if it was ever there, it's gone now. I snatch the envelope from the floor and hold it up to the light from my window until I'm certain the ghostly postmark shows 1994 and the abbreviation for Washington State—where I was born, and one of the locations where the Full Moon Killer stalked and executed his victims. My address and name are written in boxy lettering on the envelope, while the note is written in slanted cursive. Totally different styles.

Minutes pass while I remain plunked on the floor, questions zipping through my mind. This box likely survived several moves and the home-renovation phases that my parents cycled through. Did they receive it in 1994, when I was five years old, or did it catch up with them sometime after and they hid it from me?

The letter's final legible phrase burns into my vision: *You should never have been born.*

Shadows stretch across the hardwood floor. People call to one another on the sidewalk below, and car doors slam as rideshares arrive to ferry diners throughout the city. Friday evening rolls forward, but I remain frozen—locked in place, imagining what I could have done as a five-year-old to deserve such a letter.

And, more important, who would send it.

I squint again at the faded writing. The FBI could probably decipher it—leverage some writing-analytics team to fill in the blanks.

Returning to my phone on the couch, I see that Lottie replied to my message on the genetics-testing website. She suggested a video call. Tonight.

Sharp pain stabs my ankle. Onyx stretches her paws forward, having followed me from the bedroom, and one of her claws snags my skin. A small spot of red blooms above my heel. She releases me, then rolls onto her back. Round, innocent eyes stare up at me—as if she just offered a warning that what I'm about to do may hurt.

I type out my phone number in the reply box anyway. Then hit "Send."

Agent Ballo's words have been with me all afternoon, but what I think about now is his countdown: thirteen days until the next full moon. Until, he implied, the Full Moon Killer strikes again. He would probably be eager to read the letter I just found, but I can't turn it over to him without knowing more about where it came from. The idea that I could be related to a murderer is disturbing, but I also don't want to cast undue suspicion on someone I don't even know. Maybe this Lottie Montagne can offer the information I need to decide.

My phone dings, and before I can talk myself out of it, I accept the call.

A woman with pale skin, bright-blue eyes, and blonde hair leans into the screen. She realizes that the connection has gone through and jerks backward, startled. A broad grin reveals crooked bottom teeth.

"Ivy? Hi, I'm Lottie."

"Hi. Thanks so much for agreeing to this," I say. We each lift a hand in an awkward wave, adding to the surreal feeling.

"Oh my gosh. Thank you for reaching out! I had no idea you existed, which is still so nuts. Well, I guess that's not true."

I raise both eyebrows and she hurries to explain.

"I just mean, growing up, I kind of always believed I would have a sibling or cousin, or some kind of playmate. I felt it was destiny on some level. So, in a way, I'm happy to know my older sister—or cousin—is alive."

She smiles again, her warmth infectious. I can feel myself sliding waist-deep into this reunion pool, and I'm not sure I want to get out. "This is all so crazy," I say.

"Completely. You must have a million questions. I have a few to start, if you don't mind?"

"Up to you."

We exchange basic information, and I learn that Lottie runs her own hardware store in the city of Wenatchee; our grandfather taught her mother—who taught Lottie—everything she knows. She's an avid reader, with no significant other, and she took the genetics test for kicks; there are no known health issues on either side of her family.

When I ask what she does in her free time, she grins, then angles the phone to capture a wall of bowls, mugs, sculpted animals, and oblong shapes.

"Pottery. I love ceramics. There's a kiln out back."

"Wow. That's impressive. Did you make all of those?"

"Not all of them. Most of our family—the Caines—has lived in this house or somewhere on the property at some point. Almost every-one has taken a turn with it. Here's one I made." She points at the edge of the screen to a deep bowl with a delicate rounded foot. "Our family owns thirty acres now, but we had a few thousand in the past. Each generation has sold off a bit more."

Her words *our family* send a ripple along my shoulders, and I'm not sure if that's good or bad. "I guess you know my birth mother, then?"

She nods, her smile fading. "My aunt Tatum, yeah. Everyone says she was a wonderful woman."

My chest tightens. "Was?"

Blue eyes pinch at the corners. "She died shortly after giving birth to you. It was a swimming accident in 1989. She drowned."

Confusion and disappointment sweep over me—the loss of a woman I have no recollection of, but which still stings.

"Oh," I finally reply. "That's terrible. Do you know my father?"

Lottie's pointed nose crinkles. "I don't. I'm sorry. I asked my mom, Tristen, when you messaged me, but if she knows, she wouldn't tell. She says she had no idea about you."

"Is my father alive?"

Lottie shakes her head. "No clue."

Though crestfallen, I try to muster a smile. I didn't know anything before this call, and now I can at least confirm a few more details about my origins.

"Hey!" Her eyes widen and so does her grin. "Why don't you come up here? Come for a visit and learn more about our family in person. You can meet some of our other relatives and ask my mom directly about your parents. What do you think?"

I scan her face—open, hopeful, and eager for my response. We are strangers to each other, yet she's willing to embrace me as if we were . . . family. I don't know what to say.

Agent Ballo's words, though, nudge me forward: *Tell me, Ivy. What do you know about your birth family?*

Then the waterlogged letter in the filing box makes me hesitate. Its author mentioned my "physical health"—could that be a coincidence? Or could the details of my medical history and the answers to my condition lie up north?

Past my phone screen, the photo of my parents and brother seems to be watching me, their faces frozen, unsure of which way I'm leaning—in which direction I am preparing to fall.

I flick my eyes back to Lottie's excited gaze. "I'd love to."

Four

TATUM

August 17, 1989

Pots and pans clang downstairs like Marmie's auditioning for the Fourth of July parade. I pause before my door, hesitating to step into the hallway, knowing each board will creak to alert my mother I'm awake. Scents of bacon grease and sweet buttermilk mingle together to tickle my nose and set my stomach to churning. I didn't eat dinner last night and really only picked at my lunch prior to that. Marmie must have noticed.

I turn and survey my bedroom's pink, frilly color scheme, a vestige of my eighth birthday. I should have updated it by now, bought some fabric from Mrs. Loomis down the road—maybe chosen a more mature lavender color to match the dried sprigs I keep in a vase on the windowsill above my bed—at least, changed the mauve curtains. Nine years later, the color reminds me only of the child I was. Of the child I gave up a short time ago.

My hands find my newly flat belly and rub the top part below my ribs. It's been almost four months since she was born—three months, two weeks, and two days since I gave her away.

I didn't want to; I loved her from the moment I knew I was pregnant. But I had to.

Rather, I was forced to.

Marmie's voice carries up the stairs and down the hall to reach my ears, calling my name.

"Coming!" I holler back. Smoothing the high-waist, flowy top down at my hips, I add to my wrist a bangle that Marmie gifted me earlier this year. She thought I needed cheering up from a broken heart.

She was right—I did have a broken heart, and in the most traditional sense: my boyfriend and I broke up back in February. Reason being he said he would never forgive me—couldn't—if I gave up our baby. But I knew better; if I kept her, she was as good as dead.

I head down the stairs, beneath the framed photos of relatives who grew up in this house, taking care not to slip on the worn section of the carpet runner, and pass the grandfather clock that's been a fixture here since Marmie was a kid. Built in the 1800s, the Victorian has a front door that's all stained glass and traditional archways. My mother's grandparents were given a plot of land from the government and helped to build Rock Island, our little town, from a few lean-tos into a bustling center of commerce in Central Washington. Politics and agricultural developments grew—then reduced—Rock Island's size over the years, but we're still here. The Caines never let go once something is in their grasp.

"There you are," Marmie chirps. She lays a plate of crispy bacon on the country oak table in the breakfast nook. Morning rays backlight her against a deep-set window that overlooks our yard and the valley beneath. Her light-blonde hair glows like a halo. "You seem tired. Did you not sleep well again?"

I shake my head. "Not really. Coffee?" I point to the carafe on the table.

"A fresh pot." She smiles, the skin pleating at her temples and around her mouth—a reminder I'm not the only one growing older.

Three months, two weeks, and two days older.

"Want me to pour you a mug, or a thermos? You're going to be late to work," she adds.

The after-school job I held all year allowed me to take a month off to recover from giving birth—not that Hector knew that. My boss thought my mother sent me to a fat camp, as did anyone who asked after me.

Marmie, of course, didn't know why either. She just knew I disappeared for four days and refused to discuss my whereabouts; she had no clue I was pregnant then, and I've been intercepting medical bills for months. Tasked with a deliberately mute daughter, she was able to convince the school board to provide makeup exams so I could graduate with my class, although not technically walk with them. I was too lethargic. Depressed. It had been only a few weeks at that point.

As one of Rock Island's nursing professionals, Marmie gave me all the over-the-counter prescriptions she thought I needed to regain my strength. Considering I refused to see a doctor or have anyone examine me, she did the best she could.

I'm sure she had her suspicions. After I gave birth, I started wearing my shoulder-length hair loose to better conceal my round, full cheeks. One might think they're typical of a seventeen-year-old about to enter college, but actually they're among the parts of my body that didn't return to normal postpartum.

I accept a warm mug of coffee made with two sugar lumps, the way I like it. "I'll take the bus. Faster that way. Shouldn't you already be at work too?"

The grandfather clock in the foyer chimed ten times while I was upstairs. Marmie is usually long gone by the time I get up for the midday shift. The hospital has been inundated with patients lately, making her role as a floor nurse that much more in demand—typical for summer, given the influx of tourists that come our way from larger cities like Seattle or Wenatchee, eager to commune with the great outdoors.

Marmie waves a hand. "They can wait."

She watches as I pick apart a piece of bacon. I lift a fork for the eggs and, in the corner of my eye, catch her sigh of relief. She says something about nutrition, but my mind wanders back to the last time I ate bacon. Months ago. Last year?

Knock. Tap tap. Knock knock knock. Marmie raps her fist against the table, breaking up my thoughts—the pattern she's employed since I was a kid to secretly ask if everything is okay.

"I'm fine. Really," I add, when she doesn't blink. "Did I hear Tristen earlier?"

"She went to the post office for me. Terry requested my famous chocolate chip cookies. You know how your brother loves them."

"Mm-hmm."

As the baby of the family and with Terry being older than I am by nine years, I don't really know his sweets preference, but I nod anyway, scraping my plate. A beam of sunlight hits the bare skin of my arm, and for the first time in months, I feel . . . better. More energized. Or something close to it.

"Thanks for breakfast, Marmie. You didn't have to be late for work on my account."

She scoffs but reaches for me as I stand. "Hey, do me a favor?"

Her fingers wrap around my wrist, and a gnarly urge to draw back and hide in my room rises from my belly. But I can't keep shying away from human interactions, no matter how badly I want to stay in bed.

"Be careful out there today. Okay? There's something going on over in Malaga, something spilling over from Wenatchee. Teenagers are being approached by other young people, and then their families never hear from them again."

"You mean that cult everyone is talking about? Do you think it has something to do with those poor girls last summer?"

"I don't know. I just know they . . . or someone . . . is targeting young women. That means you." She rubs my wrist with her thumb.

"Be careful, okay? You're just getting over . . . just getting better, and I don't want anything to happen to you. Maybe take Papa's whistle in case someone surprises you."

I reach for my mug and toss back the dregs. Caffeine is the chief reason I've survived the last few months, and I've developed a taste for even the grody parts. "Sure thing, Marmie."

She smiles, relieved. I mirror her expression until I turn my back. As I pass my father's whistle, left as a memorial to him on a hook by the front door, I know I won't need it.

The thing is, I already know the person targeting young women. They've been watching me for weeks now and made their position crystal clear.

They're angry with me. And if I don't do exactly what they want, they'll come after me again. This time, they'll force me to give up more than my baby girl.

Five

SAMSON

The Past

The final slice of cake sits in the fridge, loosely covered by that sticky plastic-wrap stuff. Only a few letters of the original *Happy Grad, Grad!* are left, making the last slice read "rad." Given I'm about to start my rad road trip, I take it as a sign.

Grabbing one of the good forks, the shiny kind with special indents along the edges, I treat myself to a fancy breakfast. Although graduation was only four days ago, my foster brother and sister prefer whole-grain cereals, toast, and healthy stuff blah-blah-blah early in the morning. Fine by me—I'll gladly oblige the house. Mrs. Rayvin might have shared a slice with me, but she's already left for the bogus early shift at Gorman's Dairy.

I slide the note I wrote her—a quick goodbye—beneath a fridge magnet that says FAMILY IS EVERYTHING. I think she actually believes it. My foster siblings do; neither of them ever ratted me out for hitting them. Then again, they're only in middle school. Might not know what to believe yet.

Anyway, I'll miss Mrs. Rayvin. She always treated me good. When I first got to this Podunk town four years ago, after seven years with Gerald—a living nightmare—I thought she looked like the old witch who eats kids in "Hansel and Gretel." White hair piled in a bun, fat haunches in the blue jean coveralls she wears to the dairy. But she gave me hot food, a hug every now and then, and let me do my own thing at night. She never turned me in, even when the sheriff came calling, nosing around after Debbie Dawson's body was found stuck in a sewage pipe upriver.

God, the moaning and groaning over that girl has been relentless. I don't see the pull, honestly. She was a young woman with a lot of life ahead of her, sure, but she was a pain in the ass to many people, not just myself. Zero fun, that one, and rude. If it wasn't me, someone else would have done a lot worse to her. I'm glad I can put this place and those limp-dick bundles of flowers I keep seeing on corners everywhere, signs of mourning for *our sweet Debbie*, behind me. Good riddance.

I wash my plate and the fancy fork, then place them to dry on a towel beside the tidy kitchen sink. Grabbing the duffel bag I packed last night, grabbing my jacket—though the weather is hot as a devil's armpit—I head straight to the front door, past the doilies Mrs. Rayvin lovingly placed on her old-as-dust couch, and don't pause until I step past the threshold.

After I turn the key in my truck's ignition—the deceased Mr. Rayvin's pride and joy, and a gift from Mama Rayvin since she says I remind her of him—I slam my foot on the gas and rev the engine, a goodbye purr. From what I can tell from photos, Mr. Rayvin and I didn't look that much alike; his bald head and black eyes seem the polar opposite to my sandy-brown hair and hazel eyes. But I never corrected her. I didn't see the point, if it meant some extra coddling and a set of wheels for me.

Once I'm on the highway, I stop myself from taking in any last views of this town or the main-street strip of commerce—a gas station, grocery mart, pizza shop, diner, and the Mexican restaurant that gives out free chips and salsa. I set my gaze ahead. Count the dairies until I reach Ferguson Farms on the edge of town, then inhale a final breath of cow-manure stench and hold it. Hold my breath as long as I can until yellow fields stretch out on either side and the fencing fades away behind.

Bye-bye, cow country. I am never coming back to you, and I'm putting as many miles as possible between me and all the assholes who never wanted me. Sayonara, Gerald, you molesting piece of shit. I'm on my own, finally.

A flash of white darts out from the gravel shoulder. My truck pops off the ground before it lands back with a thud. I pull to a stop on the side of the road. Mama Rayvin just fixed the windshield after that damn barn owl cracked it, so nothing else better be busted.

Mine is the only vehicle I've seen on this backwoods part of the highway the last five minutes. I get out, leaving the door open.

The carcass lies in the middle of the lane. A rabbit. I jog the hundred yards back to it and see it's good and dead. Guts spilled onto the asphalt and a pool of red already forming around it. Grody. I'm about to turn away, satisfied there's nothing left to see, when a thought stops me: *What if this is an omen?* Or something. Like what Mrs. Rayvin used to say sometimes gets delivered straight from heaven. A sign of what's to come.

I check to make sure I'm alone. This early in the morning, there aren't even any hawks or vultures yet to swoop in and take my prize.

I whip out my pocketknife from my jeans. Bending down, careful to touch only the hind leg, I lift it away from the torso.

Back at my truck, I find a towel in the bed and clean up my souvenir as best I can. Then I climb into the driver's seat and start the engine.

As my lucky rabbit's foot sways, dangling from a shoelace wrapped around my rearview mirror, I think I finally know what Mrs. Rayvin meant. Things happen for a reason. And all that I've already experienced has only been preparing me for this moment—to get out into the world, and to finally enjoy myself a little.

Six

Ivy

Waxing Crescent

The following Wednesday, the wind is calm on the flight up to Spokane, and I make a game out of finding patterns in the puffy clouds below. When we rise too high to see anything but solid white, I break out a crossword book that I grabbed in the airport terminal. Number eight down's clue, *A meeting; sometimes bittersweet and always with u*, teases a smile from me when I realize the answer: a reunion.

Lottie offered to pick me up from the airport, but I insisted on getting a rental for the two-and-a-half-hour drive to Rock Island. Having my own transportation will give me the independence I need to search out info about my medical history.

Plus, the idea of meeting my cousin, then sitting in a car with her for hours, seemed too risky a commitment. What if we don't get along? What if she drives like a maniac? Or is a smoker who likes the windows rolled up? No, better to have an intermediate-size, four-door life raft at my disposal.

Waiting for the keys to my new ride, I take a seat along the glass wall of the cramped rental-agency lobby and set my suitcase at my feet. Behind the counter, a woman with stringy brown hair and deep cigarette lines around her lips fusses with a banner. Instead of rolling up evenly, one side continues to poke out farther than the other. Now on her third attempt, she unfurls the banner behind the counter, then catches me watching.

"Largest squash expo on the West Coast, canceled after that girl died the end of last month," she says, huffing the hair from her eyes. "Losing that business stung pretty bad. I had a group of grandmothers from Omaha that rented a whole fleet of cars for the event. Now I got this reminder of it, an advertisement I had out front for months."

She lifts the banner high above her head to lay it flat on the counter. Its cursive letters are stark in extra-large print: *Spokane Squash Festaval. 15% Off Discount. July 26–28.*

I grimace at the typo.

"It's a great banner," I reply, but she's already bent down and disappeared from view.

"Hon?" A man steps into the lobby, dangling a set of keys. A blue car is parked at the curb in front of the office. "Ivy Hon?"

I grab the handle of my rolling suitcase. "Here."

The man does a full visual sweep of my frame, then snickers—taking in the jean jacket I tie-dyed purple and the letters I ironed onto my cotton shirt that read DON'T SAY FRISCO.

"Welcome to Spokane."

Getting out of the parking lot and onto the main freeway takes twenty minutes, but once the car reaches sixty miles per hour, I zone out. I don't think about where I'm going or what ulterior motive I mentally brought in my carry-on—instead, I enjoy the open countryside and the exit signs that become fewer and farther between as Spokane recedes in my rearview.

Although my conversation with Agent Ballo has been hovering in the back of my mind—the wide-eyed fear of venturing closer to a serial killer's territory—I'm going to be in Rock Island for less than a week. After I leave, the full moon won't occur for another three days.

When my phone's GPS announces my exit, I check to ensure it matches what Lottie told me. The ramp spits me out onto a road that curves east, and I pass a signpost announcing Rock Island is only three miles ahead. Douglas firs flank the highway. A knot forms in my belly as the road dips down a hill and the rooftops of houses and buildings become visible.

Street signs appear closer together. A church steeple looms past shops lining either side of the main road. Instead of stopping at any of them, I turn right to climb a steep hill, toward the tip of a picturesque Victorian turret. Leafy trees hang overhead, and dense greenery fills my rearview mirror, as though I'm being drawn into a waiting mouth.

Paved asphalt turns to gravel. Brick replaces the walls of foliage on either side; then a neatly trimmed hedge twice the height of my car replaces the brick. I emerge from the winding drive before a breathtaking three-story home. Built around the turn of the twentieth century or earlier, it has windows wrapping each level. I crane my neck to see the highest point—a turret bearing a rooster weather vane that lists to the right.

I park facing the house. A modest white staircase leads to stained-glass french doors and a wraparound porch partially obscured by more trees and bushes.

In Northern California, where I had access to the beach, hikes, and national parks all around me, I always felt lucky to live near such natural beauty. But standing in this forest with a house plunked down in the middle, I feel like a trespasser imposing on a fairy tale.

The front door opens and a woman walks out. The hem of her red floral dress twitches in the breeze. She waves, her broad smile dimpling both cheeks.

"Lottie?" I say, stepping from the car.

She crosses to me, and I extend a hand before she sweeps me into a hug. "Ivy," she says slightly above my shoulder. "It's good to meet you."

I freeze for a moment, feeling the boundless awe of holding a blood relative close. For some reason I didn't imagine this part—this strange, electric sort of magic.

We pull back to take each other in. Although her coloring is lighter than mine in every way—light-blonde hair loose at her rounded shoulders, freckles dotting her cheeks and high forehead—I recognize the bump on the bridge of her nose as my own. Our nervous smiles match.

"How was your flight?" she asks as I pop the trunk and remove my suitcase.

"Good. So was the drive. This area is so lush. Your home is gorgeous."

When she suggested I stay with her instead of a hotel, I initially balked. Part of me worried that Lottie might not be as welcoming as she seemed on the video call, but I reasoned that she was offering a once-in-a-lifetime chance to learn more about my birth mother's family up close. Plus, Lottie hadn't been born in 1988. It's not possible that she could have anything to do with the series of murders that began that year.

"You're going to like it here," Lottie says. She takes my suitcase, then loops an arm through mine. She leads me up the creaking porch stairs, the click-clack of her sandals marking each step. Inside the foyer, the smell of cookies reaches my nose and instantly makes my mouth water. Opposite the double doors, a grandfather clock stands at the base of a staircase to the right, and hardwood floors lead past two open rooms to the left. Thick, beige wallpaper with a curling-leaf pattern lines the hallway. The vibe is somber but warm, as if the bones of this house have already loved and buried countless kin.

Lottie lowers my bag to the floor. "You must be tired after the long trip. Do you feel like a coffee or tea? Are you hungry?" She clasps her hands as though she hopes I'm starved, eyes bright and round with excitement. This is my cousin, the woman whose face I first peered into five days ago. Lottie takes my shrug as a yes and beckons me into the kitchen.

We pass a formal sitting room steeped in brass, velvet cushions, and satin pillows, then an open pantry with enough plastic containers to feed a family of eight.

At the end of the hall, light streams into the kitchen through a deep-set window nook with a view of the valley below. A rustic table is tucked into the wall beside the window and opposite a long kitchen island that ends in a glass-front fridge. Although the entryway of the house felt dark, a little stifled, and buttoned-up, this setting feels like a spread in *Town & Country*.

I watch Lottie spin about the room, grabbing coffee mugs, pulling from a whitewashed cupboard one with the text F*CK OFF, GOOD MORNING on the side. A tattoo of three hearts trails the inside of her wrist. She seems normal. I wonder, given that I reached out to her on a genetics-testing website, then agreed to travel eight hundred miles, whether I seem normal to her.

"The foundation of this house was built in 1885, which explains just about everything." Lottie leans against the Keurig sputtering coffee on the tile counter. "It's old, but each generation has added on its version of modernity over the years. My grandmother—" She laughs, shakes her head. "Sorry, *our* grandmother, Agatha, added the greenhouse at the bottom of the hill. A Caine family member has lived here ever since the walls were raised."

"That's incredible," I say, meaning it. My mother's parents died when I was five, and my dad was raised by his elderly aunt and uncle. To have such a visceral connection to one's forebears feels exotic and a little scary.

A pinch of fear returns. "How many Caines are still in town? Do you see them often?"

Are any of them fond of handwritten letters?

Lottie starts a second cup of coffee. "Oh, some. A few have gone as far as Seattle in recent years, but most of us have stayed local. Other relatives are scattered around the country. I moved in here a few years ago when Grandma Aggie relocated to her own home on the property."

"She lives in the backyard?"

Lottie smiles. "You could say that. She and Great-Uncle Phillip each have their own homes a few miles away."

"A few miles is still in your yard?"

Both cheeks dimple. "The mighty Caines owned most of Rock Island for a long time, but each generation sold off more land. Nobody has wanted to really alter or risk the childhood home, though. Except our grandfather. The house needed a few structural improvements when he and Grandma Aggie moved in, and he added in a secret compartment to hide his cigars from his in-laws' disapproving eyes."

"Wow. Can I see it?"

Lottie leads me to the formal sitting room, over to a corner beside the window framed by brocade curtains. She takes a seat in a deep-red, velvet-upholstered chair, then reaches behind the curtain to reveal a square shape cut into the wall. She nudges it with her elbow, and the door pops open with a creak. A single cigar still wrapped in cellophane lies within.

"Pretty fun, huh?" she asks. "It's amazing to me how many memories were made here, the dreams and heartaches felt in this house. This place has been loved by so many."

I take in the scuffed wooden floorboards, the worn carpet runners, and recall the pencil marks on the kitchen doorframe—writing that reaches almost the full height of the doorway—recording names and growth of the Caine family. Writing that's too small and cramped to compare to that of the waterlogged letter.

"You mean, everyone lived here growing up?" I ask.

Lottie hesitates. "Not quite. I lived a few miles away as a kid."

I raise my eyes to hers, hearing the subtext that matters, and she purses her mouth.

"Did I not mention that over the phone? Most of the older generation grew up here," she says. "Our great-grandparents, then our grandmother and great-uncle. Then our mothers and our uncle Terry. Your mother, Tatum, was living here the day that she died."

Cold air glides beneath my hair. I stare at Lottie. This woman, my cousin. Who, in this moment, I remember I don't really know at all. Suddenly, each surface I've brushed in this house seems to vibrate, as if confirming the places my mother's hands also touched.

"No," I begin. "I don't remember that."

"There's a kiln out back—I think I talked about it—that apparently she used to love. Grandma Aggie has a throwing wheel, now somewhere in the basement, that was a fixture in the garage."

We're silent then. A bird chirps outside while I try to gather my thoughts. It's not damning that my birth mother grew up in this house—only unsettling.

"Would you like a tour, Ivy?" Lottie smiles at me, but she's less reassuring than before.

We walk through the first floor, with Lottie pointing out a door in the pantry that leads to the basement and former "servants' quarters"; then she brings my suitcase up to the guest room on the second floor. She points out special memories of her own from when she visited her grandmother here as a kid. We pause in the hallway to admire a photo of two dozen people crowded together before a long ranch house. A family reunion with cousins on our grandfather's side in Arkansas.

"Does Grandma Aggie look like you?" I ask, standing in front of a faded photo collage of children. "Who resembles her?"

Lottie breaks into a grin. "I'll be right back."

She turns on her heel, then at the end of the hallway climbs a second set of stairs leading into the attic.

"Meet you at the breakfast table," she calls down.

After some noise overhead while I sit in the kitchen, Lottie marches triumphantly toward me, her arms full of photo albums. We settle in. Late afternoon slides into evening. Each photo and anecdote Lottie shares elicits another question from me, then more wine from Lottie over a dinner of spaghetti carbonara.

I pull out a photo of Tatum at a nearby national park, where she's standing in a field of wildflowers. *My birth mother.* Cursive, looping handwriting covers the back of the Polaroid—Aggie's, Lottie tells me; it looks nothing like the writing on my dried-out letter.

When Lottie stands to grab a second bottle of wine, I hold up a hand. "You know, I'm not sure I should keep going here. Okay if I grab a shower, then go to bed?"

She smiles, her lips slightly purple from the pinot noir. "Suit yourself."

"Do you mind if I video some of these photos on my phone?"

"Not at all. That's why you're here, right? To learn all about the past?"

Her words land on so many levels for me. "Thanks."

Having already shown me where extra towels and blankets are, she slides back into the breakfast nook, then turns on the flat-screen television in the kitchen.

The grandfather clock chimes nine times when I reach the staircase, but I don't hesitate to continue climbing. Although I've enjoyed every minute with Lottie so far, I need to think. To process everything I've learned and experienced in such a short span. On top of Lottie's revelation that my mother lived in this house, the image of the water-soaked letter hasn't left my mind since I landed in Washington State. Did its author live here too? Is the person who wrote me a menacing note when I was five years old also the Full Moon Killer?

Uncle Terry and Lottie's mother—Tristen—were capable adults in 1994, unlike Lottie.

I take a quick shower, then return to the guest room next door. Mauve curtains with a polka-dot pattern look plucked from a prior decade, but the room is spacious and the bed doesn't squeak. I'm grateful for a comfortable place to regroup.

I pull up the nanny-cam app on my phone. The small screen pauses long enough for me to worry; then a sleeping Onyx appears beneath the illuminated television in my living room, where two political pundits are debating something in earnest. "Miss you, little girl," I say.

I hear a sharp noise, but it's not coming from the camera feed. It's a scratching sound, out in the hall. An insistent, repeating grating at my bedroom door. The doorknob, which I locked out of habit before getting into bed, twitches up and down.

Someone is trying to enter the guest room.

I don't breathe. Every muscle in my body tenses, waiting for the ancient lock to break and the door to swing inward.

The noise stops. Footsteps creak downstairs. Then a loud thud reverberates through the house.

Muffled voices carry to the second floor. Lottie's strained whisper and another, deeper voice. A man's? The words *shouldn't have come* are audible, then *It wasn't your place.*

Images from the water-damaged letter flicker behind my eyes, along with the phrase *You should never have been born.*

More angry words fly between them. Then the front door slams.

I count my heartbeats. One. Two. Three. All the way up to forty-two. Wait for furious footsteps to barrel their way up the staircase.

Instead, quiet, measured steps climb the stairs and stop at Lottie's bedroom down the hall. The door shuts.

Another thirty heartbeats elapse; then the grandfather clock begins to chime.

Seven

TATUM

August 17, 1989

Bells jingle the entrance of another customer to Chic Threads, tearing me from my thoughts. I look up from behind the laminate counter and brush back a hair that fell from my new powder-blue scrunchie. A young woman enters, probably a few years older than me. A coed, judging from the Greek letters on her sweatshirt. She seems familiar, but Wenatchee is a real city compared to Rock Island—tons of people shop here, both men and women.

"Welcome in," I say. She continues pushing clothing on hangers around a circular rack. She lifts a size-Small blouse, then replaces it in the Large section. I swallow a sigh, guessing I'll have to reorganize dozens of items after she leaves.

Through the glass behind her, past the neon painted letters promoting the store's latest sale, two boys wearing swim shorts and dragging rafts amble down the riverbank. I'm surprised that kids are still rafting after what happens every summer—someone drowns. The river's currents can be intense, and people should really know better by this point.

One of the boys is smaller than the other—maybe five years old—and he struggles to keep up with his older brother. My thoughts immediately switch to another baby—my own—and I wince.

Will she resemble me when she's older? Does she now? Brown hair and green eyes, a wrinkle in her nose when she sneezes, and hips she'll always think are too wide? Or will she take after her father?

"Can I help you?"

I startle at the question I should be asking and find the young woman staring at me, her words a mix of concern and annoyance. Instead of approaching her and offering assistance as I meant to, I paused to silently watch those boys over her shoulder. Like a weirdo.

Wake up, Tatum. You've still got medical bills to pay, even if there's no infant to feed.

"Oh, yes. Sorry, I . . . Do you need help finding anything? We have lots of items on consignment farther back too. Behind David Bowie." I point to the framed poster of the singer in full stage makeup, hanging beside our accessories bin.

The woman shakes her head, hoop earrings knocking against her sharp jawline. Teased bangs reach at least three inches high, and I have to wonder if the style at Washington State is more sophisticated than our rural standards. My scrunchie, matching blue off-the-shoulder ROCK ISLAND HIGH SCHOOL sweater, denim capris, and white sneakers seem the polar opposite of this girl's sweatshirt, pink shorts, and black leggings that hug her perfect curves, untouched by pregnancy. Although the weather is easily eighty degrees today, the air-conditioning indoors feels like it just dropped the temp to fifty.

I leave her alone and return to the counter. Hector's inventory accounting notebook remains open where I left it. I'll never understand why people pay so much for the ripped-jeans style that Madonna is sporting these days, but Hector is for sure pulling in the dough.

Glancing down at my own capris, I eyeball the well-sewn hem. I could probably create a good knockoff version of those jeans myself. And for free.

"Hey, can I ask you something?" The girl holds up a mesh top that George Michael would kill in. The kind of edgy trend that has never been my thing.

"Totally. You need another size?"

"Oh no," she says, shaking her head. "I just . . . Your sweatshirt says Rock Island. Did you know either of . . . those girls from last summer? The ones who died?"

I suck in a breath. Stop leaning over the counter in my helpful-salesgirl stance. "Geri Hauser, I didn't know; she was a few years older. But Stacey Perez, I did. Stacey and I had chemistry together. We were friends."

The girl nods, clutches the top closer to her chest. "Did they ever catch whoever did it? It's the same guy, right?"

I glance at the clock: two minutes until my fifteen-minute break and the arrival of my coworker Mal to take over the front. Thinking about the murders strings my nerves taut. I discovered I was pregnant right after Stacey was found a few miles upriver in Wenatchee, north of where Geri Hauser was found dead just a month later.

"No, I don't think so," I reply. "Everyone was really tense about it for a while, but it seems like the police have given up on finding him."

The girl steps toward me. "Is it true about the full moon too? I read all the papers when I was home from State last summer. I tried to keep up, but the news out in Pullman didn't cover the murders as much. Is it true?"

I check the clock again. One minute. "Is what true?"

"Did the guy kill each of them under a full moon? I don't think I could ever go out again at night in your town, if I were you. He's still out there."

Hearing an outsider talk about it with such intrigue—almost excitedly—makes my stomach knot. The impulse boils in me to yell at her to stop gossiping about people's lives—real girls who used to sit in homeroom and pass notes to me when Mr. Fitz wasn't looking, who deserve better than to be talked about between overpriced MC Hammer pants.

Instead, I release a deep breath as I spot Mal's waist-grazing braids approaching the storefront. She beams at me as she pulls open the glass door. "If you need anything else, Mal here will be happy to help you."

The girl shrinks backward, as though disappointed I'm not interested in rehashing the victims' details. Something shiny along the accessories carousel catches her eye, and then I'm forgotten.

Mal slides her purse beneath the cash register, where we store employee valuables. "Hey, gorgeous! What's new?"

"Hey. Just the usual around here. I haven't seen Hector since he popped in at the start of my shift. But it is break time. Cool if I step out?"

"You got it. Tatum—" She lifts a hand to my elbow and fixes me with a knowing gaze. Electric-blue eyeliner amplifies her concern. "You doing okay?"

Mal was my rock when I returned to work. I told her I had a baby, that I gave her up shortly after giving birth, and am still processing the loss. She's the only one who knows most of what happened . . . aside from him. He knows it all.

"Fine. Just need a smoke." I grab my Virginia Slims from beside the calculator, then stride to the door, stopping short of running outside.

"Be back in twenty or I'll come after you," she says, her voice a sugar-sweet threat.

On the sidewalk, I turn right and pass the used bookstore I usually browse on my break, and continue until I'm around the corner and hidden from customers' views.

Facing the road and the stretch of shops opposite, I light a cigarette and breathe deep the soothing nicotine. I know it's not great for me—the research shows that. But my fingers are crossed I can get my grief under control before any damage catches up to me.

I huff at my optimism—as if I'm not already damaged.

When I'm done with my cigarette and my fifteen minutes have elapsed, I head back toward Chic Threads. On the green stretch of grass leading to the riverbank where I saw the two boys, a man in a white T-shirt and jeans watches me. His hand shields his eyes from the sun, obscuring his face but flexing his thick arm.

The customer who kept asking about the murders returns to mind, and I hope she's already left by the time I get back. But here, in the open, without anyone around but this man staring at me, her words vibrate in my ears. *He's still out there.*

The man takes a step toward me. I look around for anyone else, someone who might be an island of safety in case he breaks into a run, but no one is shopping on this block midafternoon. I pick up my pace and am two doors down from the clothing store when the man's voice rings out, strong and deep. "Hey!"

Hungry footsteps match my jolted pulse. He leaps in front of me and grabs my forearm.

"Get the hell off me!" I scream, recognizing him up close.

"You can't keep avoiding me," he snarls. "We need to talk."

He drags me down the sidewalk and into the street. I twist from his grasp, then bolt for the shop. Yanking the steel handle, I slip past the glass door and run straight to the employee room in the back.

Mal asks me a question from the cash register. But I don't hear it. Not above the frantic heartbeat in my ears.

Eight

Ivy

From the hilltop, we have crisp views of town below and the more commercial Wenatchee ten miles west. Lottie points out her elementary school, the Columbia River that snakes alongside the town, then right, toward the clothing store my mother worked at the summer she died—the exact location is evident to Lottie's keen gaze, but not mine. I smile anyway, thinking of my birth mom as a seventeen-year-old working the register of some eighties fashion shop.

Lottie wanted to show me the view before any cloud coverage rolled in—*Washington summers can be overcast,* she explained—but I'm eager for caffeine and warmth; we head inside.

We enter the kitchen through the back door, and Lottie retakes her seat from last night in the breakfast nook. My gaze falls to an open photo album on the table.

Tatum was beautiful as a young woman. Short brown hair that hit just below narrow shoulders and a shit-eating grin in all the photos of her with her sister, Tristen, and older brother, Terrence. When I pointed this out to Lottie last night, she grew solemn and said, "Yeah. There don't seem to be any photos of her after she gave you up."

I didn't know how to reply to that. Instead, I added a Post-it note to mark the page, as I'd done whenever I found a photo of Tatum that struck me somehow. The photo of her creating a game of anagrams for someone's birthday seemed like a snapshot from my own life—playing word games and completing crossword puzzles whenever I'm waiting somewhere.

"Coffee?" I ask Lottie.

She points to the Keurig on the counter. "Already locked and loaded for you."

I make myself a cup with two sugars, then join her at the table. Lottie lifts her eyes to mine, and there's a shine to them.

"You okay?" I ask. "I thought I heard . . . well, someone arguing with you last night."

She crosses her arms. "Yeah, you did. I'm sorry about that."

Pause. "Can . . . I ask who that was? They sounded angry. I think they tried to come in my room."

Lottie sips coffee that she made before I came downstairs. "They weren't happy, that's for sure. It was Uncle Phillip. Great-Uncle Phillip, Aggie's brother. He gets confused sometimes, so maybe he thought he was going to wake me up."

"Is that why you seem upset this morning?"

Both hands curl around her mug. "Uncle Phillip doesn't bother me with his moods. We're all used to them at this point. But, yeah, he was . . . he was huffy about something."

"My being here?" The voice had said *shouldn't have come*.

Lottie pauses just long enough that I have my answer.

"Listen, I'm not here to disrupt anyone's lives or . . . anything. Really," I add. "I'm sorry my visit has already caused you difficulty."

"No, that's not it. Uncle Phillip was out of line. As the oldest between him and Grandma Aggie, he thinks this house still belongs to him or something. I don't know. Sometimes he just snaps. But that's not the reason I'm feeling bummy today." She pushes the breath out of her mouth with effort. "It's these memories. It's seeing my mom in these photos. She struggled to move on after Tatum died, so seeing her pre–Tatum's death—all playful and light and laughter—that's hard to see too. My mom blames herself."

"Really? Tatum died in a drowning accident, though, right? Was your mom there?" A sip of coffee burns my tongue—punishment for my lack of tact. "Sorry if that's a little forward. I don't mean to—"

Lottie tucks her head. A section of light-blonde hair falls to rest below her collarbone. "It's okay. They're your family too. No, my mom wasn't there. But she thinks something she did that day may have contributed to the accident. She refuses to talk about it."

We're each quiet a moment while—I can't help it—I wonder whether Tristen's guilt might be indicative of something more intentional. Malicious.

I choose a piece of buttered toast that Lottie set on the table before I came downstairs, then take a bite. Lottie shared during our video call that she's unaware of any medical condition on either side of her family. Still, I wonder if that's simply what she believes. Could Tristen know more than what she's shared with her daughter?

"So," Lottie says, perking up, "how would you feel about attending a party today?"

I shrink backward. It's been ages since I went to a party, let alone one where I don't know anyone. "What are we celebrating?"

"My cousin Yara—on my dad's side—is graduating high school. She had to finish summer school before it was official, so that's why it's a bit later than usual."

"Good for her," I say. "Will anyone from the Caine side be there?"

Lottie nods, her own mouth full for the moment. "Oh yeah. Extended family is invited. I think my mom said she'd try to join, but it depends on her workload."

"Gotcha." Posing questions to Tristen could yield info regarding my birth father. Even if the thought of meeting more people than I've encountered in years makes me anxious about another flare-up. "Yeah, that sounds good. I'm in."

Lottie clears her throat. "Uncle Phillip will be there too. But don't worry. I'm sure he'll be better in the light of day."

We finish our coffee while I wonder if Uncle Phillip is a werewolf, or what other reason Lottie might have for excusing a grown man's bad behavior.

I get dressed in the guest room, admiring how the framed photos of trees hung on each wall create an outside-but-inside vibe, then pop over to Lottie's room for her approval. She examines my green satin blouse, distressed jeans, and black heeled boots, and gives a thumbs-up. I check out her outfit—it's almost identical to mine but for her white top with green polka dots. We realize it at the same time and start giggling.

Suddenly, I'm looking forward to meeting more of the family.

———

We arrive at a single-story house with an expansive yard—it belongs to Lottie's aunt and uncle on her dad's side. I have no idea how many acres the yard behind the house comprises—*One? Ten?*—but at least thirty people crowd the mown grass, while another twenty stroll along the creek beyond.

We head around back, passing a banquet-style table of potato chips, pigs in a blanket, deviled eggs on ice, three vegetable trays, taquitos, guacamole, salsa, and other snacks, next to a Costco-worthy quantity of soda and seltzer water. Enough for fifty people and then some.

On the short drive here, my nerves coiled tighter in my gut with every signpost that marked us closer to our destination. The hosts of the party aren't technically related to me, by blood at least, but plenty of other relatives at this gathering will be. People I have seen photos of in Lottie's kitchen, people who have slept in the same house where I'm staying now. People who might know who my birth father was. Or who might have sent me that threatening note. Or one of whom might be a serial killer.

Ahead of us, clumps of people orbit a young woman wearing a graduation mortarboard. I twist the fabric of my sleeve between my thumb and forefinger. Take a deep breath. Keep carrying forward, following Lottie.

First things first: Meet people. Then begin digging up family secrets.

Above the table, suspended on twine and draped from the house's gutter, a banner reads YARA SANCHEZ, GRADUATE! Lottie immediately approaches the girl.

"Woman of the hour!" Lottie cries, sweeping her cousin in for a hug.

Yara throws her arms around Lottie, kicking up grass in her wedge heels and white, sleeveless summer dress. The mortarboard's gold tassel dances.

"You must be Ivy," an older woman to my left says, touching my elbow. "I'm Crystal Lynn Wilkes. Yara's math teacher. She just finished telling me you've come to visit from California."

"Nice to meet you."

Crystal Lynn's white hair is styled in waves; gray curls at her temples frame kind eyes.

Lottie waves me over. "Yara, there's someone I want you to meet. This is Ivy Hon, my cousin."

Instantly, I feel heads turn our way, and conversations lower to a dull murmur, but I step forward and shake the girl's hand. Yara beams, big and wide the way only a teenager can—effortlessly and without any idea of the credit-card debt ahead.

"Congratulations on your graduation," I say.

"Thank you! Lottie said you're half-Chinese. Fun to have someone else biracial in the family. For forever it's only been me and Ulysses, my brother. We're half-Mexican." She points to a tall, lanky boy standing along the back fence with two other much-shorter boys. As I follow her gaze, I take in the crowd and confirm most people in attendance are white. The only people of color seem to be myself, Yara and her brother, and their mother, Lottie's aunt Pita.

Heat rushes to my ears, the August sunshine suddenly bearing down in earnest. I'm not sure why Lottie felt the need to volunteer my ethnicity to Yara, and I'm annoyed I was "othered" before I even got here.

"Thanks for having me," I reply.

"Ivy, do you want a drink?" Lottie thumbs toward the banquet table, and I give her a tight smile, still discomfited but relieved for the quick exit. Yara waves goodbye to us as someone else approaches.

"Punch or spiked punch or soda?" Lottie holds up a blue plastic cup from beside two bowls. "I'm sure you know from the genetics results, but our family's fifty percent Irish, fifty percent English—unless there's booze involved before noon."

I take the cup. "Then one hundred percent Irish?"

She laughs. "Smart girl. We must be related." She winks, then reaches for a ladle.

We cheers and each take a sip. It's only noon, but I can see most people are holding a plastic cup. *When in Rome,* I think to myself. If ever there were a blank check for questionable drinking, it would be when meeting biological family for the first time.

I turn back to Lottie and aim for casual in my tone. "Do you see your mom anywhere? I'd love to meet her."

And pick her brain about my birth father and Tatum and what regrets she still carries about the last conversation she had with her little sister. Nothing major.

Lottie scans the crowd, then shakes her head. "No, she's not here yet. She better hurry up; there's going to be cake soon."

"Tristen Caine miss out on cake? Unlikely." An older man, probably in his seventies, approaches the banquet table with a limp and an impish grin. The thickness of his white hair contrasts deep lines that crisscross his face and the sunspots dotting the loose skin of his cheeks. Lean shoulders strain the pattern of the plaid shirt he wears beneath a pair of overalls, and I get the sense that this country mouse still mows his own lawn.

"Phillip Caine," he says, grabbing my open palm. His grip is strong, calloused, and dry—and too aggressive for my taste. "And you must be my grandniece, from what my other grandniece here is telling everyone."

This is the angry voice from last night? Ranting about how I shouldn't be here?

Lottie purses her lips. "I did share about your visit with a few family members, but Uncle Phillip is exaggerating."

"Only a little," Phillip says with a wink. "But it'll be obvious you're related to me since you're such a looker."

A high-pitched laugh tumbles from my throat, and I take a sip of punch to cover my unease. A quick glance at Phillip's cup shows he's at least one deep himself. Over the rim, I catch Lottie's eye.

"Okay, thanks for chatting," she says. "Good to see you, Uncle Phillip!"

She turns me by the elbow, then introduces me to her aunt Pita, who stands with Lottie's other cousins. We make small talk, and I'm relieved to speak with someone I'm not directly related to.

"How's your dad, Lottie?" Pita asks. "The university keeping him busy?"

"Oh yeah. He says Spokane is full of excitement these days, with the new school year starting in a few weeks."

As Lottie's aunt talks about Yara's college plans, I excuse myself and return to the banquet table in search of a water bottle. Heads turn as I pass, and I walk faster. Uncle Phillip ambles toward me, more than a little wobbly in his step. Before he can lock me into another awkward conversation, I spin around and ask Ulysses, Yara's brother, how high school is going. He seems surprised but pleased to be asked.

"Good. Only two more years to go."

"It'll fly by. But some days will drag," I add. "Do you know every-one here?" I nod to the crowd of people in the center of the grass, then the wanderers over by the creek, where I saw him earlier. A group of men and two women greet each other. Instead of shaking hands, they grasp forearms.

"Oh no. I mean, my mom's side couldn't come up from Mexico, and most of my dad's family is here, but a lot of people are my dad's friends. Members of some club they all belong to. A bunch of your family is here too." He gives me a tentative smile. "Your great-uncle Phillip, I think you met, and your grandma Aggie was here somewhere earlier. There's Terry, over there. I think he was your . . . your mom's older brother."

Ulysses points to the thick oak tree in the corner. A tall man is turned away in conversation with a redheaded woman. Terry turns par-tially, and I get a profile view of ruddy skin and a rounded chin. I scan the yard for Tristen, based on the photos Lottie shared, and spot two young women who could be twins grasping forearms before they release into a hug. They join a group of older men.

Two attractive guys in their twenties return from the creek bed, where a trio of older women giggle together. The taller one approaches Crystal Lynn, who first welcomed me.

"Do you know . . . much about my mom?" I ask, turning back to Ulysses. "About Tatum Caine?"

Ulysses downs his soda. "I don't. Sorry. Just that everyone gets really sad when she's mentioned."

I want to ask more questions, to probe further and learn if he's heard any health-related rumors about my family—histories of head-aches, cyclical muscle aches, general fatigue—but he steps back toward the party.

Cake is cut shortly afterward and served—chocolate with banana buttercream: delicious. Phillip stands off to a corner, talking to a man I haven't met. Two other men approach them, and the first man leaves.

He returns with a plate of cake that Phillip dismisses with only a shake of his head.

An hour later, Lottie begins rounding us toward the exit, and we say passing goodbyes, but everyone else seems to be heading toward the exit too. Terry has disappeared, though I don't recall seeing him leave.

"Is the party over?" I ask.

"Not over," Lottie says above my head, searching the crowd. "Just winding down. Everyone will want to get home well before dusk."

"Why's that?"

But she gets sucked into another goodbye, and the faces she speaks with begin to blur together thanks to the punch and the daze I feel being here. When Lottie elbows in to hug Yara, I excuse myself to find a bathroom.

I enter the house through the patio sliding-glass door. Bags of food, empty Tupperware containers, and stacks of cups line a long kitchen counter. A printed sign reads GOTTA GO? with an arrow pointing to the right.

Down the hall, I find two doors, both closed. Not knowing which to choose, I turn the first handle. A man and a woman are on the bed with their arms around each other, kissing deeply. His fingers are unbuttoning her dress.

"Oh, I'm sorry," I say. The toilet flushes next door, as if emphasizing how wrong I was.

With a squeak, the woman pulls away, and I see her face. Crystal Lynn. Yara's math teacher. I recognize the man as the young, attractive one I saw approach her earlier. He touches her elbow, unfazed—almost annoyed—by my interruption.

"So sorry," I say again, then beat a quick turn into the now-empty bathroom. I slam the door shut and lock it.

Chuckling, I take stock of what just happened. Crystal Lynn is an adult, and at least twice my age. She's perfectly capable of deciding whom to kiss, and so is that guy. Still, something feels off about the pairing—beyond the *Harold and Maude* story line. About this whole party.

On the drive back, Lottie cuts through town on a different route so she can show me one of her favorite spots growing up: the entrance to the riverbed where people launch motorboats and dinghies in the summer—and where, she says, the youth get trashed after dark.

In front of the water, a bench is covered with candles. Flowers in cellophane and several poster boards are visible from where we idle at the curb. Phrases like *Rest in Peace* and *You will be missed* are stark in black marker.

"What's that?" I ask.

"Oh," she says, sucking in a breath, "that's the memorial. A woman died here last month. She was killed."

Something clicks in my memory. Information that Agent Ballo shared in the coffee shop: after a hiatus of thirteen years, the Full Moon Killer took a new life.

I want to ask if this is where my mother drowned—if alcohol was involved, knowing she was only seventeen—but Lottie's knuckles suddenly appear white on the steering wheel. She pulls away, and we continue the rest of the drive in silence.

When we arrive back at the house, the Victorian pointed rooftop seems to stab into the orange-streaked sky.

Nine

The Past

Yes, sir! That's my baby. No, sir, don't mean maybe.

Singing the oldie that got stuck in my head around Manteca, I let the steam of the shower hug me like a warm blanket. Water spills onto the tiled floor. No bath mat, shower curtain, or extra towel in sight. My flashlight rests propped up in the sink, illuminating the mirror in a funky glow.

I rip open the soap bar I stole from the 7-Eleven in Sacramento and enjoy the scent of an Irish spring. Damn it feels good to take a shower after the last month of sleeping in my truck and camping along Pacific Coast Highway. Homeless showers at the free faucets on the beach get the job done, but there's nothing like hot running water in your nooks and crannies.

I grab the towel I took from Mrs. Rayvin. Part of me wonders if I should feel bad about taking it, like the school counselor said I should after I got caught stealing from the store on campus—*stealing* being liberally applied here, since the store and its candy cabinets were unlocked and free for the taking—but that's as far as it goes.

Whistling as I towel dry, I pause to admire the goods in the wide mirror above the double sinks. I'm no Arnie, but the muscles of my torso bulge where magazines tell me they should. My brown hair is almost blond thanks to the summer and really needs a comb nowadays, but I didn't find one when I went snooping through the house earlier.

Each room was empty except for the couch in the living room, the dining table by the kitchen, and the twin bed in the downstairs bedroom. Nothing in any of the drawers besides a stack of business cards for the Realtor who's showing this place.

Letting the towel drop to the floor, I turn and grab my jeans and a T-shirt I lifted from Penney's. Roll on some more deodorant from my backpack, then take my flashlight.

A quick scan of the master bedroom shows I didn't leave anything behind, but I do another sweep anyway. No sense in being careless just because I'm excited.

When I met the girl I'm going to see tonight—Cathy? Clara?—in the 7-Eleven parking lot, she was with a bunch of her friends. Probably around my age—maybe a little older—and with the confidence of a cow in heat. She approached me straightaway as I was getting out of my truck.

"Hey," she'd said, "do you go to CJC?" She was standing with her hand on a pointy hip in a short skirt and stringy tank top. Blonde hair was dyed pink, long and straight and covering small tits. If it wasn't ninety degrees and if she didn't smell so clean, I'd have thought she was a hooker. I vowed no more hookers after what happened in Tulare.

On the freeway, I'd seen a bumper sticker that read CHICO JUNIOR COLLEGE: FIND YOUR PATH. CJC.

"Yeah, I do. I'm in my last year there." I stood up a little taller, wondered if the stubble I'd finally started growing helped the cause.

She asked my name, what I was studying, and if I was interested in a party later tonight.

I licked my lips and said, "Only if you're going to be there."

Behind us, giggling erupted from her friends, who were watching the whole dance. She gave me the address, then said to come around ten, that she was already looking forward to seeing me again.

Outside the home for sale, I stroll slowly and casually with my duffel bag over my shoulder to where I left my pickup at a construction site around the corner; no one thinks anything of an empty truck beside a digging crane. I know I never do.

It's been around a month since I got on the road. Pretty tame, most of the way. My date with Debbie was the last time there was an opportunity to let loose. My fingers itch to wrap around a warm breast. A thigh. A fistful of hair. Just thinking of it strains my pants. I throw the book I've been reading in the back seat of the truck, all dog-eared and full of creepy stories to get me through the lonely nights.

I turn the ignition, and the engine roars to life. Once I'm out of the subdivision, I flick on my headlights, then pull hard onto the main road like I'm breaking a horse.

———

"Ronnie, you came!" The girl comes bounding toward me as I reach the gravel pathway to the house. We're in the sticks, on the outskirts of Chico, and I can see why the location was chosen. Music booms from the open front door, partiers inside jumping and dancing to a rock song.

She immediately grabs my hand, dragging me indoors to the group of friends I saw earlier at the convenience store. I focus on her green pleather skirt, the shine of it in the haze of a red light bulb that's been installed in a dining-room lamp. The kitchen glows with the same red hue.

"Stoplight party. Ever been to one?" she shouts above the music. "Wearing green means 'go' or single, red means that person's in a relationship, and yellow means . . . well, it can't hurt to try." She fingers the top of her green skirt, then winks at me. From the slurring of her words, I'd say she's already a few drinks deep. I slip an arm around her waist.

"I guess I'm dressed appropriately, then, huh?" I wave an open palm at my green camo shirt, lift both eyebrows, and make her laugh.

"I love your earring," the girl coos, drawing in close and fingering my earlobe. "A single stud is super hot."

"Candace, you want?" Her brunette friend lifts up a glass filled with amber liquid. Beer, from the smell of it. I don't know how anyone drinks that piss.

Candace steals another glance at me. "Sure," she says with a smile. The friend offers me some, but I shake my head. Don't want to spoil the fun ahead.

Two guys sprawled in the living room bicker about conspiracy theories. One of them swears that JFK was shot by his brother. They start hemming and hawing about Iran–Contra, and I think, *Now there's a conversation I could get into*, when Candace pushes me into the kitchen corner.

She peppers me with questions. I tell her I grew up in Central California—the truth—but that I moved up here this year to be with my ailing grandmother and finish my associate's degree at CJC—a complete lie. She tells me how she's studying to be a psychologist, and she plans to transfer to UC Davis. She starts sharing that she just had a bad breakup when I get bored and take her by the elbow. Draw her nearer.

"Hey, want to give me a tour of the house?"

She focuses on my lips, breathing heavily. The sour smell of beer punches my nose, but I keep a straight face. The two guys have moved on to serial killers, and they're naming who they think is scariest. Richard Ramirez. Some German guy. Some Japanese guy.

"Okay, okay," the kid with the buzz cut says. He sits up straight. "I got the answer. The scariest killers are the ones who are actually targeting *other* killers. Vigilantes who seem like they have a heart of gold, you know, given their victims, but are actually just as fucked up as the rest of them. Sociopaths in disguise. Like police officers."

"The fuck out," Other Guy says. "Cops are not vigilantes. Do you even know what a vigilante is?"

Candace grabs my jaw. She loops two fingers into the top of my jeans. "My friend Vanessa lives here," she pants. "Her parents are out of town at some pharmacy conference, so we can go up to the master."

Taking me by the arm, she ignores her friends calling her to take shots. We dodge a guy who scream-sings a Run-DMC song, and it's nice to see I'm not the only one into good music.

We get to a bedroom at the end of the hall, then slip inside and shut the door behind us. The girl doesn't bother turning on any lights, instead reaching for me, pressing me against the wall and gyrating against my groin. I'm hard, but not for the reason she thinks.

In the window opposite the door, the moon is bright and round and unfettered by drapes pushed to the sides.

"I wanted you as soon as I saw you," she says, purring in my ear. "You remind me of my ex-boyfriend. Tall, charming, handsome. Hazel eyes I could get lost in."

I push her onto the bed and notice hers for the first time. Brown, half-closed, relaxed. Blonde-pink hair fans out around her head like a wig that Gerald used to wear when he'd make me do things to him.

Stroke his fake hair. Hold his hand. Touch between his legs.

"You sure no one is going to come upstairs?" I whisper.

She nods. "Yeah, I'm sure. We're all alone, Ronnie."

"Say my name again."

"Ronnie," she moans, and I feel transformed over her. Rocking my hips onto hers, I lean my body weight across the shallow of her stomach. Using my elbows, I pin her arms to her sides, and she bucks, aroused by the restraint.

As though I'm a leader of the free world, a force to be reckoned with, a man and not some foster kid that no one, not even my mother, wanted. Even Gerald ignored me unless he was touching me. "Say it again."

"Ronnie."

Suddenly Candace's eyes widen, illuminated by the moonlight. They bulge from her small face, like a calf. Little gasping noises begin choking in her throat. I squeeze my hands tighter around her neck.

Yes, sir. That's my baby.

She gags, claws at my hands, coughs once, but she can't inhale any breath to do more. My arms shake against her sudden frenzy, but I tighten my grip, press my thumbs into the hollow of her throat. Moonlight stretches across the bedspread, a spotlight, as she thrashes right and left, heels kicking the bottom of the bed, and almost in time with the song blasting on the stereo downstairs.

I redouble my effort, knowing the moon is watching through the window. My only judge and coconspirator.

The bedroom door slams open, and a couple falls onto the carpet, laughing and shrieking. Plastic cups spill from their hands, and the liquid sloshes, slaps the wall beside them.

The girl laughs, then stands up, straightens her green dress, and notices my hands around her friend's neck. Her smile disappears. The guy glances up, still on the floor, and breaks into a stupid grin. "Oh shit. Sorry, didn't mean to interrupt you guys. There's condoms in the empty fishbowl downstairs—"

I break into a run, hearing the deep gasp for air that Candace makes and the alarmed voices that follow me to the ground level, then out the front door. I sprint down the street to where I left my pickup right by the main road, jam the key in the ignition, then take off before anyone follows.

As I pick up speed, my headlights flash on the reflective letters of a sign announcing I'm leaving Chico. Easing off the gas, I pull over to the dirt shoulder and cut the engine. My heart is beating wildly in my chest, but when I check the rearview mirror, I look as excited as I feel—eyes bright, cheeks flushed, a sheen of sweat across my forehead. Even though my favorite stud earring must have fallen out while I was running. Small price, I guess.

Thinking back on Candace's frightened expression, the sound of her choking—dying before we were interrupted—I stroke the left inseam of my pants, and unzip.

Ten

Ivy

First Quarter

Lottie parks the car, then looks in the rearview mirror to adjust the blonde curls she spent an hour on this morning. She catches me watching her. "Aggie was a beauty queen before she became a nurse, and she never let anyone forget it."

I smile. "Thanks for setting this up."

"Hey, you got it. We're all so excited to learn more about you!" Her eyes land on my phone screen in my lap. "Is that Onyx?"

I raise both eyebrows, embarrassed that she saw me watching my cat via the nanny-cam app. "Yeah, it is."

"Why are you spying on your cat?"

"Aw, I just miss her, I guess."

Lottie tilts her head to the side for a better view. "She seems like a sweetheart, all curled up beneath the window."

"She is."

I've been gone for two days now, and Onyx seems perfectly content alone—almost as if she's been waiting for me to leave, get out and get my own life, for the last two years. She seems to sleep most of the day, then plays with dirty socks she finds under my bed. I spoke to her once through the camera's microphone, but she jumped and ran skittering back into my bedroom, terrified by my phantom voice. So now I just watch while she zooms around my home *Risky Business*–style.

Lottie's cell rings. She steps out of her Honda Civic and answers. "Hey, Darla. What's up?"

A muffled voice says, "Hey! So I know you're on vacation, but Mrs. Ainsworth is here. She said she spoke to you about a special order, and I can't find it anywhere."

Tucking my phone into my pocket, I join her outside. Lottie mouths "Sorry" over the roof. She steps a few feet away, while I stand and take in a square, two-story Colonial painted white and the grassy hillside it occupies. The river that flows through town sparkles below in the morning sunshine.

Here there's less of an arbor vibe than over at Lottie's, but plenty of trees. The only other neighbor we passed is a good quarter mile down the road. The closest thing to a high-rise in sight? A pig silo on that property. I am a long way from home.

Lottie ends her call, then reaches into the back seat. "Ready?" she asks, withdrawing a sealed carafe of lemonade.

We follow along the side of the house, passing a wooden trellis with climbing vines that reach halfway up the wall and escort us into the back. A considerable vegetable garden spreads across the yard, soaking in the rays.

"Did you say Aggie was a retired nurse or farmer?" I ask, stepping wide of a leafy squash plant.

Lottie smirks over her shoulder. "I can't imagine Aggie ever really retiring. She says that's when you die."

Three rows of planter boxes line up four deep to form a grid of fresh vegetables and flowers. A woman in a wide-brimmed hat pokes her head up from over the springy leaves of a tomato plant, clutching a trowel. Aggie.

Ash-blonde hair escapes her gardening hat, while a denim button-up shirt protects her lean frame from the sun. As she straightens and blocks out a vegetable stalk behind her, I realize where I get my height from—a feature that always made me awkward growing up, stooping to better accommodate family photos with my parents and brother. This woman, my grandmother, beams at Lottie, then fixes her eyes on me.

"That's exactly true, my dear. The moment you stop producing is the moment of death. At least internally." She dusts off her gardening gloves and comes over. Her steps are slow, but her expression is bright and alert.

"You must be Ivy. I'm Agatha. But everyone calls me Aggie," she adds, and draws me in for a hug. Still in a daze at coming face-to-face with my biological grandmother, who doesn't resemble in the slightest the family I grew up around, I allow the hug from this stranger. I breathe deep, try to calm my sudden nerves, and get a lungful of the fragrant scent of rosemary. A meal of chicken and potatoes flashes to mind, making my mouth water.

I pull back. Up close, deep lines embrace her eyes, matching those around her mouth, and I try to find the younger version I saw in photos on Lottie's kitchen table. Aggie is unchanged but for a general weathering of her skin due to time and, probably, grief at losing her youngest daughter.

"And your favorite people call you Grandma Aggie." Lottie plants a kiss on Aggie's cheek. They have the same blue eyes, the same pointed nose and square jaw. Lottie was effusive in meeting me, but she seems to glow as the only grandchild on this side of the family—or, rather, the only one until recently.

I smile, definitely not ready to call anyone "Grandma."

"Too true, my dear," Aggie says with a twinkle. "Welcome to my home, Ivy. Shall we have some tea on the back porch? It's such a beautiful day."

"Yes, I'd love that. Thank you."

Behind her, another hundred yards off and down the hill, a roof is visible through a thin grove of trees separate from the rest of the property.

Aggie catches me staring. "That's Phillip's home. He's not very sociable during the workweek, so you'll have to excuse his not joining us."

"Great-Uncle Phillip?" I turn to Lottie, who nods.

"That's the one. He does consulting for sustainable irrigation in the area and usually has some new client to tend to. Shall we?" Aggie removes her gardening hat.

She directs us to a cement patio with cushioned garden chairs and a large opaque glass table. Lottie sets her carafe beside another pitcher and several plates of crackers, cookies, cucumber sandwiches, and little cakes on porcelain dishes with pink flowers. I raise an eyebrow at Lottie, who returns a knowing glance. Grandma Aggie's beauty-queen days must have involved classes on decorum and homemaking.

We spend the next hour discussing my upbringing and how my life has been all these years. I explain that I'm currently doing freelance copyediting in the Bay.

"How was life here? What was . . . what was Tatum's like?" I hesitate to speak her name because so far no one has—no one has mentioned the woman who links us together.

Aggie's bright expression falls. "She grew up in the house that I did—the one that Lottie now lives in. Between my income as a nurse and her late father's life insurance, we didn't want for anything. I like to think she was happy. Granted, I never bought her or her siblings fancy things until later, when my career started to take off, but our family was stable, thanks to the land. The Caine properties have provided through the generations—the same reason why we always pass the main house to the next generation for when they're ready to start a family. Usually, at least."

It's Lottie's turn to blush a deep pink, but she doesn't say anything. She shared with me the intense pressure she feels being a single twenty-eight-year-old in a town where people her age already have kids and have been divorced once, sometimes twice; apparently, men find it intimidating that she can build a birdhouse, a doghouse, and a she shed, if needed. The familial obligation to carry on the mantle likely amplifies that pressure, especially as her mother declined to move into the Caine house with her own family. Too many ghosts.

Aggie takes another sip of her tea, wistful. "Tatum was planning on going to college at Washington State to study nursing, like me."

I stare out over Aggie's planters, lush and thriving with curling tendrils and summer flowers in bloom. "Do you know . . . why she gave me up? Do you have any of the context for adopting me out? Sorry if that's abrupt."

The prim shape of Aggie's mouth falls open, and she glances at Lottie as if I've asked to harvest her prized zucchini. She peers behind me a moment. Long enough to make me wonder whether someone has joined us.

As I watch the way Aggie tries to gather her thoughts, or her strength, a nagging sense of guilt makes me question whether I should have asked. Yet there's no one else to bother about this—except for maybe Tristen, Lottie's mother, to whom Lottie hasn't introduced me yet.

"I'm sorry to pry. I know this must be hard for you—"

Aggie presses both hands together in her lap, shakes her head. "This is your story, Ivy. And you deserve to know what I can share with you. But I don't have the answers you're looking for."

"Well, did you ever meet my father? He was Chinese American," I add.

Aggie frowns. A strand of blonde hair escapes from her low bun, but she makes no move to tuck it back. "I didn't. And Tatum never spoke of her pregnancy to me."

Lottie sucks in a sharp breath. I try to speak, but my throat clamps shut, hearing this inadvertent confirmation that my mother was ashamed of me. Maybe she didn't want me, and regretted my existence—at least that's how it feels. Somewhere past my ribs, a sharp pain stabs my insides, like a tiny fork from Aggie's perfect place setting. Tears prick my eyes, and I blink them back.

"I wish she had," Aggie says. Her gaze drops to her lap, as if my show of emotion is too much for her. "She was certainly withdrawn that last year."

"It's not your fault. She was young. Seventeen, right?"

"Yes."

"So barely an adult. I'm sure she was scared."

Aggie hesitates before meeting my gaze. She hugs her toned forearms, and I wonder whether weeding is an aerobic activity. "Sounds like something Tatum might have said. She was always encouraging me to go deeper, to see the other side of things. I wasn't so great at that then."

"It seems like Tatum may have been depressed, and for good reason. Does . . . our family . . . have a history of depression? Or any kind of medical conditions?"

I'm reaching on this question; I know it. But the opportunity to confirm some health history that might clarify my symptoms is there.

Aggie smiles. "My husband's family was a bit of a wild bunch. And on my side there was likely some depression, but back then everyone just called it the doldrums."

"No cancers? No anemia? White blood-cell deficiencies?"

Both women give me their full attention now, and I grab a cracker to nibble on. "Sorry. You know, anything unusual, medically. Since Lottie and I both took DNA tests."

"You really shouldn't apologize so much, Ivy. It's a bad habit we women have." Aggie shakes her head. "Not that I'm aware."

I turn my head toward the leafy tomato plants in the nearest planter to me. Swallow back the cracker and my disappointment at the continual lack of answers. Lottie didn't have any either.

Aggie exhales, then reaches for her iced tea. "Well, Ivy. I know that I missed you at the graduation party. I had to leave early to run some errands. Did you enjoy yourself?"

"Yes, everyone was very nice." Reflecting back on the unique couple I walked in on—everyone was nice and hammered. "I was only surprised when the party ended so soon."

"That's pretty common these days." Lottie sighs.

"Because of the recent murder?" I try to keep my voice even, but just discussing the Full Moon Killer—being in his territory and speaking to our shared relatives—creeps me out.

Aggie cringes. "Probably. The police haven't shared anything, of course. It feels like déjà vu all over again, same as thirteen years ago with the last full-moon attack. No answers, just anxiety."

"Are people feeling more vulnerable now?"

"Oh yeah," Lottie says. "The victim was a day-care provider to a lot of families. A curfew was in effect for a week following the discovery of the body, but everyone has continued to observe their own curfews since. No one wants to be outside close to dark these days."

"Understandably," I murmur.

Both women focus on the drinks they hold in their hands, their faces scrunched.

"Well . . . Grandma Aggie . . . you've definitely got a talent for growing things," I say, nodding to the planters. "No need to leave your home with produce this good."

"More than that." Lottie perks up. "Grandma Aggie is a prizewinning gardener. She's won basically in every category across the fruits and vegetables."

The conversation moves to Aggie's green thumb—prolific, obviously—and I'm grateful for the mundane subject choice. Discussing a squash's flat, wide leaves holds no hidden barbs poised to kick me in the heart.

While Aggie suggests what plants might grow in my apartment, I let my mind wander back to her pained expression when I first asked about Tatum. Despite her ignorance of Tatum's pregnancy, I saw no hint of further secrets there.

We take a walking tour of Aggie's new sprouting radishes, and then I thank Aggie for the cookies and finger sandwiches. For agreeing to meet me in the first place.

"It was my pleasure, Ivy," she says.

Lottie gives her grandmother a kiss goodbye before we climb back into her Civic.

Back at the Caine house, as Lottie calls it, she removes her jacket and hangs it on the rack by the door. "Feel like wine time? It's five o'clock somewhere."

"Yes," I breathe out. "Whatever you want, but that would be nice."

She strolls into the kitchen. "Coming right up."

Upon seeing the coatrack designed for a restaurant or family of eight, the formal sitting room decorated in bronze and brocade, the grandfather clock that is easily three times my age, I feel so tired I could collapse right on the indoor welcome mat. My surroundings here are the polar opposite of my upbringing in so many ways. Exhaustion threatens to overwhelm me, and I head to the guest room first.

"Be there in a minute."

"Hey, Ivy? I brought up one of the photo albums to your room," she says, now out of sight. "The one with the most sticky tabs on it. Might be good to get a head start on recording your favorite photos before you leave."

"Good idea. Thanks."

As I lie down on the bed, the springs creak from my weight and probably tip off Lottie that I will not arrive in sixty seconds. My eyes close against the green wallpaper, the mauve curtains from 1979, and the vase of fake flowers that seems present in every room here.

I reach for the photo album that Lottie placed on my bed, and it slips to the floor. A triangle of yellowed paper, jarred loose, sticks out from one of the last pages. A newspaper article.

Sitting up, I lift the album onto my lap. Unfold the four-by-four-inch square, brittle with age and torn around the corners. Although I quickly scan the body of the article, my eyes catch on the headline:

FULL MOON KILLER'S LATEST VICTIM: TATUM CAINE

The paper flutters to my lap. Glasses clink in the kitchen, and I hear Lottie singing an old Willie Nelson song.

"Ivy? You want red or white?" she shouts up to me.

Suddenly, Lottie's discomfort at the riverside memorial and Aggie's loss for words read less like dismay over the latest victim and more like guilt that they were keeping a secret from me. Tatum isn't a presumed drowning victim. Tatum was murdered—and by a serial killer the FBI thinks is related to me. To her.

Tatum was a victim of the Full Moon Killer, and Lottie lied to me about it.

Adrenaline floods my limbs, and I grab my car keys and yank my cargo jacket from the foot of the bed. I'd convinced myself that, since I planned on leaving before the full moon and was focused only on learning my medical history, there was no danger here. But what if the killer decides that as the daughter of a previous victim, I'm too tempting a target—or a risk?

Heading down the stairs, I tuck the newspaper article away in my bag, then pause in the hallway.

"Actually, I'm going out for a bit. I'll come back before dinner, okay? Thanks for the wine offer."

As I let the door slam shut behind me, Lottie's confused question follows me down the porch steps: "Ivy? Where are you going?"

I jump in my rental, suddenly feeling as though I'm fleeing a prison, and drive on autopilot. Questions spiral in my head, and I wonder how stupid I may have been in coming here. *Here.* To the home of a murderer so efficient they've never been caught.

Barreling down the hill, I roll to a stop at the bottom to turn left. As I pull onto the main road, a car appears behind me, where I know there was none before. In my rearview, I watch as the blue—or green—sedan follows me into Rock Island's downtown. I drive all the way through, past the church, the bar, a feed store, and toward Yara's parents' house, but the boxy car tails from a mile behind.

When I circle along a side road that Lottie took me on, then loop back to the main road, the car is gone. I search for any vehicle that appears to be idling or taking an interest in me, but each one I pass continues without slowing down.

On my left is the bar I saw—Lainey's Office—when I first arrived at the Caine house. I park in the lot, look around me for anyone watching, then walk to the bar, clutching my cell phone in my hand like a weapon. I pass a pinball machine and approach the sleek counter, anxiety rippling through me. In the relaxed ambience, now I'm unsure if a car was hiding beneath the trees, waiting for me to leave Lottie's, or if I've simply graduated to "paranoid."

I take a seat at the copper counter. A woman with a lightning bolt tattooed across her cheek cleans a knife with a towel. "What'll it be, sugar?"

"I don't know. I'm not . . . What do you serve here?"

"Uh . . . liquor?"

"Right. Yeah, I don't know. I need a minute." I palm my cheek, feeling so overwhelmed I could cry. What am I doing here? Why did I think I could make sense of anything relating to my mystery illness, let alone my adoption? How naive was I to assume people would just welcome me with open arms and that the facts would be exactly as they summarized them?

"Sweetie, do you want something to drink?" The bartender's eyebrows are pressed together. "Can I call someone for you?"

"No, I'm . . . I'm just kind of out of it. I'll have—"

"A whiskey. Neat," the guy next to me says.

The bartender continues peering at me. "Sound good, doll? Or can I get you a cab?"

Glancing at the man beside me, at his short glass of golden liquid, I say, "No, that's great. I'll have that."

Pop country music spools through speakers from each corner, the bass vibrating in the chilled countertop. A pair of men cheers somewhere behind me, and someone else is bragging about how he took his date last night to the river and, *Well, you know how things go, heh heh.*

The bartender sets my glass before me. A large square ice cube occupies most of it, jostling the amber liquid.

Sweat breaks across my temples as I pull out the article and read the headline again: Full Moon Killer's Latest Victim: Tatum Caine. The byline says Liam Weathers.

Why did no one tell me? Why didn't Agent Ballo?

Sharp pain stabs behind my eyes, and I know a roiling headache is building. This same thing happened a few months ago when I found an old voice mail from my mom. Hearing her voice triggered an afternoon of crying and bingeing ice cream—then a migraine that lasted three days.

I reach into my bag, still slung across my chest, to grasp the bottle of painkillers I packed. I pop off the childproof lid and pour three pills into my palm. Tossing them back and feeling their reassuring weight against my tongue—tasting the relief that's coming—I swallow them down with a swig of my drink.

The man beside me stares at me; I can see it in my peripheral vision. Reluctantly, I turn until we make eye contact. He smiles. I glance down at the bar, the pulsing in my skull insistent.

"What's your name?" he asks.

I just want to be left alone, to focus all my energy on surviving the first signs of a flare-up. Then the pain eases a fraction. I'm able to look up again. He's tugging on his beard—watching me as if memorizing my features.

"Ivy. Yours? Are you from here?"

"Poe," he says. "Just passing through. What's that paper you have?"

"It's . . . uh . . . a newspaper article. Have you heard of the Full Moon Killer?"

This stranger—a beautiful one at that: piercing eyes, strong nose, and hands that dwarf his whiskey glass—grins. He licks full lips, then leans toward me.

"Yes, Ivy. I have."

Eleven

TATUM

August 17, 1989

My heart bucks in my chest. Sweat continues to moisten my palms, my underarms, the top of my forehead. I clutch the scuffed linoleum tile, searching for an anchor to keep me from sliding off the world and into a void. Maisie Appleby once had heart palpitations during gym. Am I having those? What did Coach say then?

Breathe. Calm down. You're safe.

Footsteps shuffle into the employee room. Tan sandals that were on sale last week stop five feet from where I sit, crouched beneath a rack of fall coats that we haven't put on display yet.

"I'm fine, Mal," I say.

"Really? You didn't seem fine, coming blazing into the shop and running back here like a madwoman. What happened?" She parts the fur and fleece above me. Blue eyeliner pinches at the corners of her eyes as she takes me in.

I straighten my sweater, then adjust the strap of my tank top beneath. "This guy . . . he was . . . he was watching me on my break from by the riverbank. Then he chased me back to the store."

Mal raises both eyebrows. "That's weird. Why would anyone run *toward* Hector's clothing and consignment shop?"

She smirks, brilliant in fuchsia lipstick.

"I'm serious, Mal. He was staring at me while I was smoking on the corner, and—"

"Tatum, sweetie. Calm down. I saw you enter the store, and there was no one behind you. How are you sleeping lately?" She pauses. "You know, postpartum depression can be really hard. Make you feel things you wouldn't normally feel. Postpartum psychosis is something else too, that can make you see things."

"What?" I shake my head, getting to my feet.

"Your energy could be completely skewed after giving birth. I read about it last year, how psychology and acupuncture can treat emotional disorders—"

"Wow, Mal. Just because you're working on a psych degree does not give you free rein to psychoanalyze me. So kindly leave me the hell alone."

I go back to the front of the shop, with Mal trailing behind me. She's probably miffed at me now, but I don't care. Considering I'm officially being harassed at all chief locations of my life, I don't have the energy to deal with Mal coming at me too.

As I watch her refresh the outfits on the mannequins in the window of the store, my mom's warning rings in my ears: *Be careful out there today.* Maybe I should have grabbed my father's whistle after all.

The bells chime, signaling a customer has entered the shop, and I stop counting inventory at the desk. A man—a young man—saunters to a set of graphic tees printed with lyrics to a Clash song. He lifts up a white shirt on a hanger. "Excuse me. Do you guys have this in a large?"

He makes eye contact with me. "Oh, hey. Tatum? Tatum Caine?"

Mal passes me on the way back to the employee room. "He's cute. Is he the guy who was checking you out?"

I ignore her and plaster on a tight smile for the guy. Sharing with Mal the specifics of what just happened outside would probably only cause her to look at me with more suspicion, since apparently I'm capable of totally imagining things.

Line right up, ladies—Dr. Mal is in, and she's dishing out unwarranted diagnoses.

No, I know exactly who wrapped his palm around my elbow and squeezed like I was a fresh orange. And this guy standing beside the ripped jeans is unknown to me. His green tank top shows off muscled deltoids I would recognize from a block away.

"Yes, that's me," I say. "Can I help you?"

"Ah, hey. It's been a while." He ducks his head. "I'm Dermot. I was a few grades ahead of you, but we went to Rock Island together. Did you just graduate?"

Tan skin seems to glow in the store's fluorescent bulbs the closer he approaches. Green eyes with yellow rimming the edge of his irises make him resemble a cat. Whichever breed is the hypnotic kind.

"Yeah, I did. I think I remember you. Are you visiting home?"

He nods. "Yup. Just here for the summer from USC."

"In California?"

He nods, then slides his hands into deep pockets. "Totally. It's a fun spot. You work here long? What have you been up to?"

The true answer to that question—*Oh, got pregnant, adopted out the baby, broke up with the father, struggled with grief and depression since then, and graduated by the skin of my teeth*—doesn't seem as sexy as I suddenly desire to be. Dermot takes another step toward me so that he's leaning against the checkout counter now. Heat seems to radiate from his built-like-a-brick-house frame.

"How is a girl so beautiful still hanging around Rock Island?" His grin reveals a flash of white between full lips. "When do you get off?"

I tuck a strand of hair back in my scrunchie, buying time for a reply. I can't recall if what he's saying is true. Did we go to the same high school?

Does it matter? As I stare into those gorgeous eyes, butterflies of excitement stir in my stomach for the first time in ages—probably since I found out I was pregnant and shared the news with Bowen.

Bowen. The only guy I've ever loved and who turned out to be so very different from who he said he was: a man who would never leave me, never hurt me.

"Feel like hanging after work?" Dermot asks, planting both hands on the counter.

I spy Mal by the window display but turned halfway toward us, listening. A grin curves her mouth, visible from here. "Where at?"

"The river." His eyes narrow as though he knows something I don't, drinking me in.

Given everything swirling around me, in my life and this town, my answer should be an automatic no. But he bites his lip and leans closer. "What do you say? We can catch up. Watch a few kids float by."

The normalcy of the invite—the polar opposite of the entire last year—wakes some old version of myself, buried beneath the disappointment, loss, and fear that stacked up like a geology assignment. Too alluring, too unique, to let this moment pass me by.

Then I suck in a sharp breath. "No, I can't. I'm sorry. I just have—"

"—to do inventory. She's such a hard worker," Mal says to Dermot, as she steps between us. "I'll cover for you today, Tatum. You should enjoy the sunshine. Go."

"But—"

"Her answer is yes, handsome stranger. She'll be off at five."

Before I can protest further, Dermot breaks into a grin. "See you then."

Twelve

IVY

Poe rests his chin against the palm of his hand. He's listened to me drone on about my family, the strangeness of being raised elsewhere yet recognizing myself here, about the little I know of the Full Moon Killer's victims, and he has interrupted only a few times to ask clarifying questions. At first I was reticent to dive into details about my visit here, but when he shared he just arrived in town today for a conference over in Wenatchee, and that he lives in Seattle, I loosened up a bit. He's an outsider too.

He runs a hand through dark hair that reaches his chin. The color of his eyes is hard to tell in the bar lighting. Brown, maybe.

"I think if it's this important to you," he begins, "or whatever, to figure out why this serial killer targeted your mom, you should do it. Maybe your cousin would be interested too. Lucy?"

"Lottie. Yeah, maybe."

"You could start with researching the basics about the killer. His first victims. See whether any of the families are still local—although, never mind, you wouldn't want to bother them. Not unless you couldn't help it. But their friends or coworkers could be kicking around."

Poe drinks the club soda he switched to an hour ago. He said he had an early day tomorrow and needed to stay sharp, that he doesn't like feeling out of control—same as me.

"In my experience," he continues, "if you don't take the opportunity when it presents itself, the shadow of it will follow you around."

I eye him over my gin and tonic. Check out the beard up close. He's probably my age or thereabouts—twenty-eight or so. His confidence and the way he speaks would peg him as older, and there's a quiet about him, a magnetic kind of brooding, that makes me want to learn more. Besides, lately I feel as though I'm twenty-two, fresh out of college, without a clue about what I should be doing next.

The bartender taps the counter with a lacquered fingernail. "Another round, you two?"

I shake my head, then admire the three empty glasses, the basket and grease-stained wax paper before me. I've been here way longer than expected, and I'll probably pay for this whole evening tomorrow morning. For now, no regrets.

Poe cracks his neck to one side.

"I'm good," he says to the bartender. He throws down enough cash to cover his round, mine, and my food. I reach for my wallet, but he places a hand on my elbow.

"My treat. You saved me from the usual boring evenings during work trips." He cocks an eyebrow, and I believe him. "Plus, it's my apology for leaving early. Conference starts at eight tomorrow, and I need to get to bed. You know how salespeople are—always high energy and in your face. A convention center of them is bound to be intense."

I dip my head, suddenly aware that we've spent the last three hours talking about me. Aside from his occupation and that he's from Seattle, I don't know a lot about Poe.

"Wow. I didn't realize it was so late. I should be getting back too. Hope the conference goes well."

"I'm sure it will." He turns to me with bright eyes. "Hey, if you want info on this serial killer, you should really check out the mecca of small-town information."

"What would that be?"

He smirks, and a happy twist hits my ribs. "The library. Go check out the library for leads."

I watch as he stands to leave. "Thanks. I'll do that."

When I return to the Caine house, Lottie is reading at the kitchen table, wearing a baggy sweatshirt and her hair in a high ponytail. The last of the sunset gleams orange and red behind her in the deep-set window of the nook. The loose family photos and photo albums that lined the gingham tablecloth earlier have been cleared away. She looks up. Concern creases her face.

"Hey," she says. "Cookie?" She pushes forward a plate piled with chocolate chip cookies and Oreos.

I shake my head. "Sorry I ran out earlier."

"Don't worry about it. I'm sure this is completely overwhelming. It's okay if you just needed to get away."

I nod, once again impressed by the extent of this woman's understanding.

With ginger movements, I reach into my bag, unfold the newspaper clipping, and place it on the table. Lottie scans the headline, her eyes growing wide.

"Holy shit. Where did you find this? Is this real?" She lifts the article to read it. "It says Tatum was a victim of the Full Moon Killer. How is that possible? She drowned."

I lean against the doorway. "I found it in the photo album you brought up to my room."

"Oh my God. I had no idea. I'm so sorry."

"Who created all of these photo albums? Are there more?"

"Aggie. She's a big scrapbooker, or was. The attic might have some stored away."

I remain standing, not sure what to make of Lottie's reaction to the article. "You really didn't know?"

"No, Ivy. I swear. Is that why you ran out?"

"Yeah. I was pretty shaken up. I'm sorry I left like that." I pull out a chair and take a seat beside her.

"Don't apologize. I get it." She nudges the plate of cookies toward me.

"Why would someone tell you that she drowned and let you believe it all this time?"

Lottie scrunches her forehead. "Maybe it was a lie that made sense when I was a kid, and it served double duty of making me wary of going near the river. Every year someone drowns in it, kayaking or rafting."

She checks the time on her watch. "I'll call my mom tomorrow and find out. Find a time that we can go over to her place. You can ask her about your birth father too."

The fear that's been growing in me since I found the article makes me grip the edge of the table to keep from bolting again. "Do you think . . . my father might have had something to do with her murder? Do you think the Full Moon Killer could be my father?"

It's too convenient that Tatum adopted out her child, then died several months later. What if the . . . *my* . . . father didn't want to give up the baby? What if he was resentful, angry, and hell-bent on punishing Tatum? Thinking back on the memorial that Lottie and I drove past—the wilted flowers, the teddy bears, and posters written in magic marker—my father could be in his late forties or early fifties. A viable age for a serial killer.

Does Agent Ballo suspect the same thing? I brought the card he gave me with his number written on the back.

Lottie's mouth drops open. "Whoa—I don't . . . I mean, that's . . ." She pauses to gather herself. "Do you?"

"I don't know. I don't know anything about him except that he's Chinese American. Do you have a lot of Asians in Rock Island? Or the surrounding area?"

Lottie's mouth forms a straight line. "Did you see Yara's graduation party? Rock Island has mostly been white my whole life, and I'm sure whiter during our parents' lives. It's only recently that the Latino community has started growing here. But the Seattle Asian community has been huge for a long time."

"What do you know about"—I recall the names Agent Ballo gave me—"Stacey Perez and Geri Hauser? The first victims of the murderer."

Lottie slumps back against her chair. "Nothing. It all happened so long ago. The Full Moon Killer is like the boogeyman that parents tell their teenagers about to dissuade them from partying once a month. Or it was."

While I was sitting outside the bar for a few minutes before driving home, I looked up the most recent victim. Katrina Oates was a beloved childcare provider at a Rock Island day care. She was found at three in the morning along the riverbank by teenagers, with lethal amounts of morphine in her system. Not the poison that Ballo said was the Full Moon Killer's MO, but a fatal substance nonetheless. Twenty-seven, she'd worked for her aunt, the owner of the day care, watching dozens of families' kids alongside other staff members. She was remembered for her bubbly laugh and her dreams of one day opening her own childcare business.

"What was that like?" I ask. "What was the sentiment in town after the body was found?"

Lottie exhales. "Lots of fear. You saw a snapshot of it at Yara's party. No one wants to be caught out after dark these days, but least of all young women. I can't believe this guy hasn't been found after all this time. It's so nuts that I'm still living with the same monster as my mother."

"Why do you think Katrina Oates was targeted? Why this woman now, and not another one five years ago? Why did the Killer come out of hiding after thirteen years?"

Lottie shakes her head, blonde hair glinting in the overhead kitchen light fixture. "No one ever really pinpointed his reasons. Only that he seemed to like young women, and preferred poisoning or overdosing his victims. Very creepy to be a girl around here. We grew up feeling way more vulnerable than the boys."

"Was it ever confirmed that the killer was a man?"

"No. But I can't think of how a woman could be offing victims over the years and across towns in the area. One or two kills, I could understand—but eight bodies and during three decades? I don't think so." She offers a wry smile to show she's partly joking. A chill dances along my back anyway, sitting beside my cousin, a stranger I just met via video call a week ago.

Was that last Friday? Reflecting on the past few days, I don't think I could have predicted the range of emotions I'd experience in such a short span of time.

"But what if the female killer was extremely good at multitasking, and she had some kind of special talent for getting stuff done?" I ask. "She never forgot to pick up the kids from soccer practice *and* she kept a full tank of gas for abductions."

Lottie chokes on her wine, narrowly avoiding spitting onto the tablecloth.

———

No cars are on the road the next morning, and the only traffic I encounter is pedestrian. I'm grateful for the easy drive because I leave the house much later than I want, thanks to a new flare-up of symptoms that kept me in bed too long. The raging headache I woke to dimmed only after another round of painkillers and an eye mask that shut out the sunlight streaming through the pink curtains. Two days are all I have left to ask my relatives the right questions before I fly home. To find out what's happening to my health.

When I could look at my phone without wincing, I read up on lunar phases in bed. Funny that I'd never thought about them before now, even as my family and I celebrated the Mid-Autumn Festival every year growing up. We'd head to the neighborhood park after sunset, break out the moon cakes that my mom would spend the afternoon making, and enjoy tea that my dad brought along in a thermos. All of us kids would run around with lanterns, skipping over other families' celebratory picnic baskets, then return to our own blanket with our parents and snuggle in together. Ironic to realize that, as I was enjoying a cup of tea under a full moon and fighting with Carson over the last moon-cake slice, in that same moment some relative of mine may have been stalking their latest victim.

At the Rock Island Library, a bronze plaque shines beside the entrance to the one-story brick building: A GIFT TO THE ROCK ISLAND COMMUNITY BY JEDIDIAH CAINE, FEBRUARY 2, 1949.

Is that my ancestor? Lottie wasn't kidding when she said the mighty Caines built this place.

"Hi there. Need help finding something?" a cheery voice rings out when I step inside. Behind a low wooden counter nearly covered in stacks of books, an older woman presses her hands together. Thick, curly brown hair pinned back by two barrettes gives her the appearance of a young girl. I was bummed when Lottie said she had work to do and wouldn't come with me to the library, but the librarian is exactly as Lottie described her.

"Yes, I'm interested in newspaper archives. From around the late 1980s through the late aughts."

"Local, regional, or national?" The woman beams, as though she loves a challenge.

"Local. To start."

"Everything is available in both digital and print back to 1980. Head down to the end of that aisle. For digital, you can access the library server on one of the computers right along the wall." She nods to a section behind a shelf of travel books where desktop monitors are set up on a few tables.

"Thanks."

In the rear corner of the library, I take a seat at a flat computer monitor displaying an intranet browser. Searching for "Full Moon Killer" produces scores of results. I skip to the oldest.

The first several articles, all from the *Wenatchee Gazette*—apparently, Rock Island wasn't big enough to have its own newspaper—report the bare minimum. As Agent Ballo summarized, the first victim, Stacey Perez, was strangled and poisoned. Her body was found caught in the weeds of an island in the middle of the Columbia River in neighboring Wenatchee. The journalist who wrote the article, Liam Weathers, also wrote the article about Tatum.

According to the reporter, Stacey was in her junior year of high school in 1988. She'd been a well-liked cheerleader, and she'd hoped to move to California for college after graduation. Her family said she was loved by all, and they could not think of a single person who would want to harm her—contrary to the bruises found around her neck.

Almost a month later, twenty-year-old Geri Hauser was killed while home for the summer from Washington State. Geri had been working part-time as a video-store clerk on Rock Island's Main Street. She was majoring in film at college and was considered popular among her friends; she'd even joined a sorority. She too was found on the riverbank, in the town south of here, Trinidad, and her cause of death was the same poison found in Stacey's system: paraquat, an herbicide used to control weeds in agricultural settings. The same journalist mentioned that paraquat was used so commonly that any number of local farmers could be suspected.

"So, Liam Weathers," I mumble to myself, "what else do you know?"

I skim through a few more articles, jotting down dates and facts in a notebook I brought with me, but they're largely recaps. The police didn't have any solid leads. A year of full moons came and went without any additional victims.

My thoughts drift back to the guy from the bar last night: Poe. The teasing grin he wore, while also taking my whiskey-fueled confession seriously by providing me next steps. *The library. Go check out the library for leads.*

"You finding everything okay?"

I meet the librarian's curious stare overhead. "Uh, yes. I am. Thank you."

"If you're doing an assignment for school, you should also probably use the bigger publications, like the *Seattle Times*. Less of those archives in print, but a lot are available in our database."

I purse my lips, hide the smile that creeps forward whenever anyone suggests I might be in college. It happens less frequently nowadays, but I still get a kick out of it.

"I think I found all the relevant newspaper articles. Do you have any books about the Full Moon Killer?"

The woman's face lights up as if I've just asked about the Dewey Decimal System. "Follow me."

We head back across the library, past more computer stations, and down an aisle with a laminated sign hanging from a hook that reads TRUE CRIME in curlicue Sharpie. At the end, where the aisle meets brick, she sweeps a hand at a shelf. It's full of biographies of murderers, unsolved crimes, pop-culture mysteries, and serial killers. Instead of being organized by author surname, they're grouped by subject matter—the criminal's name.

"Thanks," I say. "This is impressive."

The woman shrugs. "That's a word for it. People have cultivated an interest in this stuff over the years. The library just tries to keep up with demand."

Under *F*, between Satarō Fukiage and William Patrick Fyfe, are four books about the Full Moon Killer. Greedily, I take the first one and sit on the floor of the library, desiring to stay close to this gold mine.

Just as I've finished skimming a chapter describing a victim's decay in the nineties, my phone vibrates across my lap. A text from Lottie.

Meetup with Uncle Terry?

Terry's profile flashes to mind, the bump in his nose visible from where I stood by the snack table at Yara's party.

When? I text back.

Three dots blink in quick succession while Lottie types a reply. As she does, I gather all four books, then bring them to the front desk for checkout. Understanding the basic facts of the Full Moon Killer's case, I hope, will be helpful.

I'm completing a library-card application when my phone buzzes again.

This afternoon. Head out at 1pm?

"Come back soon," the librarian says. Clutching the reusable bag she gave me, I leave the building and beeline toward my car, eager to get to Lottie's and figure out a plan.

Terry is nine years Tatum's senior, and speaking to him could offer up details that Aggie's memory might have glossed over in our earlier conversation. Some indicator of health problems on his dad's side. Part of me was—is—disappointed that Terry didn't bother to introduce himself to me—his newly discovered niece—at Yara's party. Then again, I'm sure not everyone is as delighted as Lottie to learn I'm alive. Uncle Phillip isn't.

I pause ten feet from my rental, terror suddenly rooting me to the ground. Glass shards cover the black pavement beneath the driver's-side door, where the window was smashed in. Jagged edges line the frame. Electrical wires hang from the body of the car where the sideview mirror should be, and a quick glance to the other side confirms its twin is missing too.

Heart racing, I step around the half moon of shards to peer inside. Glass covers the fabric seat, the center console, and both footwells. More red-and-blue wiring extends from where the rearview mirror once was.

Someone vandalized my rental car while I was inside the library. Sometime during the last two hours, as I was imagining what it might be like to be the victim of a crime. Metallic fear slides to the back of my throat, and I whirl around to see whether anyone is watching me.

Only one other car, a two-door hatchback, occupies the lot, and it appears untouched.

A legion of ants seems to crawl along my arms. I fumble in my purse, searching for the Swiss Army knife I've carried for years.

Only then does it strike me that all three of the mirrors—both sideview mirrors and the rearview—are missing; all the tools I need to search behind me, to check for anyone following me.

Thirteen

SAMSON

The Past

A month and some change later of dicking around in California, I remembered—oh, right, I can leave the state; there's nothing keeping me here. No job. No responsibilities. No school and no one babysitting me, like another green social worker doing the semimonthly rounds. I'm nineteen years old. It's time to see the world.

Once I crossed state lines, the first car I passed on the freeway had a bumper sticker that read ORY-GUN with a picture of a rifle next to it. I felt like it was a sign that heading north was a good move. That hunting or violence or a little more aggression—all things I'm not averse to—would be welcome. Here were my people!

Birds call to each other as the sun sets over the clearing I chose. Laying out my sleeping bag in the middle of an Oregon forest feels like the perfect way to start my post-California leg.

I pitch the thick roll forward and let it fall beside the fire I built with tinder and super-dry wood from nearby. Official campsites are about a quarter mile up, but there aren't any markers where I chose, so I think I'm good. No nosy campground managers coming my way.

Orange and red streak the sky above. It's beautiful. Stars are beginning to appear, and a few planets are already twinkling brighter than the rest. Strange that I can find them magical after so many years of being forced to do things under a starry sky, as a child forced to survive some way, somehow.

Anyway. The nomad lifestyle has been rad—except for the other animals also living it. Raccoons are the worst, big-ass rats with larger claws and less fear. And fuck mosquitoes. I've been wanting a tent for weeks, but I can't see a good way to steal one.

My sleeping bag will do for now. It's been great to have one on the road when motels are too expensive and I'm running low on funds, or when the police are combing the beaches at night and I end up having to sleep in my truck bed. Pretty soon, though, I'm going to need a Laundromat.

I survey the small clearing I picked clean, then head right, away from the road. My initial confidence at the choice of site begins to waver. No stick of firewood in view.

"Greedy summer tourists."

But I don't hike too much farther before a flash of yellow catches my eye. A plastic wrapper, several of them—from brightly colored candy—form a trail to where I'm pretty sure the official campgrounds lie.

No one from Chico would be all the way up here. No one cares four weeks later that I had an experience with that girl from the convenience store; she's alive. But I pull my hoodie down over my head, just in case. The last thing I need is someone to remember my shaggy hair, which needs a haircut in a totally bad way.

Voices carry along the sparse foliage. A man's and a woman's, laughing together. Then the woman shrieks. More laughter. Surprising that they're out here with me, given that Crater Lake is another seven miles west. A pamphlet I found at a rest stop said it was some famous national park.

I wince as another shriek rips through the night air. There's light shining amid the trees, stronger with each step I take. With the acoustics of this space, I hope they finish their bottle of whatever they're drinking and pass out.

Reaching down for a branch, I pause. Not a branch—a dead animal. Perfect. Of course.

Flies buzz in a cloud, laying eggs on its body. Disgusting.

It's been a long flipping day.

Without the flashlight I left back in my truck, I do my best to forage the ground. Most of what's here are the charred remains of large tree trunks. Saplings rise among them as if part of a rebirth in the area. The sun is disappeared from the sky now, leaving only cool-blue moonlight to guide my path.

The couple has gone quiet. Curiosity leads me forward, toward the burning flames behind a few trees ahead. Instinct makes me crouch low, to choose my route around fallen brush and logs carefully to avoid alerting them that I'm near. As I creep closer, a single silhouette separates into two bodies. The woman straddles the man atop a log beside their firepit. Hands grip hair, and mouths hungrily search for a deeper kiss. He pulls her tank top off her shoulder to kiss her neck, then, rocking her bony hips forward, he slides a hand between her legs, and she moans.

My jeans strain against my growing chub, and I'm enjoying the foreplay free of charge when my eyes catch on the Ferrari parked twenty feet from their campsite. The car all by itself would be worth a fortune, but I'm not so dumb as to try and steal it with no idea where to cash it in. Its contents, however. This couple must be loaded to be so careless about driving their sports car out to the dust and dirt of the mountains.

A twig snaps beneath me, and I freeze.

The man continues his handiwork, but the woman pauses. Checks in my direction, over the twirling flames. I know she can't see me beyond the fire. Can she?

"Adam," she whispers. "Adam, someone's watching us."

The guy stops. "What? No one's out there, baby. We chose the most secluded campsite they had."

"No, I swear. I heard something."

"Baby, if there is someone out there, it's no one we care about." He sits up straight, then takes a swig of red liquid from a water bottle beside them. "Hear that? It's some fucking *loser* who can't get a girl and probably jacks off to National Geographic videos!"

"Adam, shh! Lower your voice!" the girl says, but she's laughing through her hand.

His shouting reverberates against the tree trunks, the branches, the animal carcasses I passed, and deeply in my chest. *Some fucking loser.* Anger rises in me, though I know it shouldn't. This guy is just a drunk asshole, and this woman a dumb Valley girl who can't do better.

But as I take in their setup, see the fancy car, the two-room tent pitched across, the wide barbecue probably still sizzling with steaks they bought on the drive over, I feel certain that I'll never have any of that. I'll always just be the foster kid who wet the bed, who's only good enough for fondling in the dark, bad enough for my mother to abandon after caring for me for two years, and too repulsive to make even a hooker touch me.

Satisfied that no one is out here, the man resumes kissing her. She casts another long glance my way, and I close my eyes, suddenly scared we'll make eye contact and she'll see me. No one speaks.

When I look again, they've moved to the ground. She's shed her shirt, the muscles in her back flexing as she climbs on top of him and he pulls a blanket over them both.

By the time I return to my campsite, the night animals have resumed purring, chirping, and scrabbling through the underbrush. I continue to the left, about a hundred yards toward the road, where I find a whole stack of wood discarded.

It takes several trips, but I manage to pile all the extra wood by the firepit I dug with a rock. When I fall asleep, the flames are still lively. Shame, anger, or whatever—heat from the wood—continues to burn my cheeks.

Birds trill the next morning before the sun rises. I stay huddled in my sleeping bag as long as I can before their melodies are too much, too loud and demanding. My fire fizzled out long ago, but a few embers glow. I add more tinder to a pyramid of sticks and blow low and long at the tiny sparks. I'm tempted to rip up one of the books I stole from my English class, when the fire catches. I carefully position fresh wood until the burning tendrils swell into a solid flame.

The moon recedes into the sky overhead, as if leaving me to my plan.

Returning to the couple is easier in the growing daylight but painful while carrying my torch. At first the heat was welcome in the cool, brisk morning air. Now the flaming branch I hold is almost too sweltering. Beads of sweat form in my inner elbow. Tiny, burning splinters slough off into the brush as I pass.

When I arrive at their campsite, I scan the space, noting that it's much smaller than I thought. Nothing personal has been left out—no backpack or wallet discarded on a stump in a drunken daze. *Damn.* Only the doused campfire and empty bottles remain as evidence of the couple's date night. They must have relocated to their mansion-tent sometime after I left. I watch the polyester material for signs of movement and see none.

Even the birds that were calling to one another are silent, holding their breath for what they sense is about to happen next.

I step over a log beside the firepit to grab a small can of kerosene. Quietly, slowly, I unscrew the cap with one hand. Lifting the can to shoulder level, I douse the tent, then extend the burning torch. Polyester strips curl upward in flame, and the acrid smell of nylon singes my nostrils.

When I'm certain the flame is too large to be extinguished by morning dew or otherwise, I toss the torch to the ground. The dry brush of July ignites, spreading first around the campsite, then dancing to the car—far faster than the fires I used to set around Gerald's property.

The screaming begins when I'm fifty yards away. I don't bother verifying the man and woman are leaping from bed in pajamas or crawling stark naked from their den. I don't care.

As I reach my campsite, the screams jump up an octave.

"Fucking losers," I say, toeing damp earth onto my fire. Then I shake the pine needles from my sleeping bag and begin rolling it into a tube.

Fourteen

IVY

"Oh my God, Ivy." Lottie leaps from her car toward me. The four-door Honda idles at an angle in the library's lot, opposite the broken glass of my rental. "What the hell happened?"

I stare at seventeen across in the crossword book I grabbed from the airport: *Put your best foot forward; the importance of.* The clue stumped me while I was waiting on hold with the police department, but after I ended my next call with the rental-car company, I think I got it. I count out the open squares and allow myself a weak smile. *First impressions.*

"Are you doing a crossword?" Lottie asks, her voice still high.

"Yeah, sorry." I shake my head and tuck the puzzles in with the library books. "Just something calming to focus on."

My cousin steps forward, then sweeps me into a hug. "Jesus, I'm so glad you're all right. How scary."

We pull apart as blue-and-red lights flash. A patrol car enters the parking lot, adding to the sense that I'm in a dream.

When the officer steps from the car, she does a brisk walk around my rental, radioing police jargon to someone on her walkie-talkie. She lists the damages on an official form, then takes photos on a tablet from several angles. As she finishes, the tow truck joins us in the parking lot.

According to the rental company, my car needs to be towed to Wenatchee, to an auto-repair chain they have a relationship with; the repairs will take a few days. Since the police confirm it was a break-in, my plans to leave in two days shouldn't be affected. I won't be held responsible for getting the car back to the airport.

While relieved that any legal blowback won't land on me, I'm crushed this happened when I'm finally gaining my footing—learning more about my history and uncovering secrets I would never have known without flying here. And questions continue to swirl in my head as I wonder who would destroy my rearview mirrors. Someone I offended—angered—by being here?

"Well," Lottie says, after the officer leaves and my busted car has been towed away. "Still feel like a trip to Terry's? I can promise you there will be booze, at least."

I nod, knowing that going back to the Caine house to twiddle my thumbs is even less of an option now.

———

Looming over the rest of rural Rock Island, the tall building Terry lives in projects power, sterility, and superiority from the other side of the Columbia River. A few miles out from the main stretch of town and before hitting Wenatchee city limits, Lottie and I had to cross a two-lane bridge that looked (and creaked) as though it was built before Grandma Aggie was born. Once we landed on the other riverbank, the area was transformed. The South Side, as Lottie called it, resembled a page out of Telegraph Hill—glass walls and concrete prevailing with little to no brick in sight.

We file into a sleek lobby with a mosaic of a river teeming with fish. The elevator spirits us up seven floors, with no music or advertisements to stare at on the way. Only our aluminum reflections in the panels—Lottie's thick eyebrows stitched tightly together, her jean jacket rolled up to her elbows as if she anticipates a fight; and my blank expression, having no idea what lies ahead.

I'll admit I was relieved we'd be meeting Terry on our own, with no onlookers to remark on how little I resemble my blood relations—or to chafe the mild agoraphobia I've cultivated the last two years.

When I sent my neighbor a message yesterday, asking her to visit Onyx using the spare key I gave her ages ago, the usual angst about imposing on someone—the worry that I would ask too much of them and cause them to retreat from me—reared its head. She agreed within minutes, then sent me a photo of Onyx happily curled up on her lap. I was reminded then that I should cut myself some slack.

The elevator pings. Lottie and I exchange a glance.

"Here we go," she says with a wince I don't understand.

The doors slide open to reveal an older man with thinning hair and ruddy cheeks who's wearing a bathrobe and house slippers. Small hands tuck into terry-cloth pockets, adjusting their grip on God knows what. This is Uncle Terry, my birth mother's oldest sibling?

"Hello, family," he says. "You must be Ivy. When Lottie asked to meet with me, I thought her mother was finally going to pay me back the loan that started her business, but hey—that's life. Or rather, life if you're a Caine. Everyone always expecting something from you."

He steps back, allowing us to exit. "Feel like a beer?"

I search for a normal reply to this welcome, but he begins trooping down the hall.

Lottie stares straight ahead until we arrive at the last apartment on the left. A window at the end of the hall presents a view of the river and Rock Island's downtown. Based on what little I know of Terry, I wonder if he enjoys literally looking down on the place he came from.

We enter a spacious penthouse decorated in creams and beiges. Artistic baskets are placed on minimalist shelves of wire, while the only book visible from the doorway seems to be a coffee-table book on houseplants. A window covers the entire wall to our left and provides a view of the valley. I glance at Terry's bathrobe and slippers, total eyesores in his pristine home; there's most likely a well-paid interior designer nearby. Probably a housekeeper too.

Armchairs with no arms are angled to face a long white sectional couch. Terry sits in one with his back to the door while Lottie and I take a seat opposite. His bathrobe falls open, and I suck in a breath, afraid he's shirtless underneath, but the plush fabric only reveals a Seahawks shirt. Thank God.

On the drive over, Lottie shared that Terry is on Wenatchee PD's forensics team, and I recalled him at the graduation party, standing off to the side—withdrawn, though speaking to a woman. I'm not sure what idea I had of him, but it wasn't this.

"First off," Terry says, twisting the cap from his beer, "even though she never told me, I *knew* Tatum had a baby, I knew it. Marmie—your grandmother—insisted she was just putting on weight from the stress or whatever from the year, and that was it. Glad to meet you."

"Thanks for agreeing to talk. Lottie has been super generous with showing me around, and I was hoping to meet more family members while I'm here."

Terry points a finger at my chest. "Are you here to cash in on the family inheritance? Because Mom's not going anywhere for a while, at least. Way too spry."

"What? No—no, definitely not trying to. I'm sorry if I gave that—"

Sharp laughter interrupts my stuttering.

"Ah, just funning with you. Lottie showed me the genetics write-up. I know you're family, and you're here for the right reasons." He drags a sip from the bottle. "You can ask me anything."

I take a breath. Try to regroup. "I really appreciate that. So, you weren't told Tatum had a baby. When did you first suspect she was pregnant?"

He pours golden liquid into a pint glass he brought from the kitchen. Smacks pale, pink lips. "I was working for the Seattle PD at the time, but I came home for Mom's birthday late March, and Tatum had put on significant weight. Like, a lot. She was probably—well, your size, Ivy, normally; that March she was huge. She tried to hide beneath baggy clothing, but that belly was hard to miss. When I teased her about it, she blamed stress for the weight gain. She was trying to keep you a secret, and I have no clue why."

I nod, doing the math. "My birthday is in May, so yeah, she would have been close to nine months pregnant then. What did Aggie attribute the weight to, exactly? What kind of stress were they both suggesting Tatum experienced that year?"

Terry takes another drink. "The Full Moon Killer. It was the summer before that the first two victims died. Everyone is pretty stressed about him these days too. Given the . . . you know, new, unfortunate event."

Lottie maintains her indifference from the corner of the couch. Something about him seems to unnerve her.

"Uncle Terry," she says, "what does that have to do with our family?"

He leans forward, sets the beer down on the oak coffee table—no coaster. "Wasn't saying that. All I can tell you is Tatum was friends with one of the victims. Stacey something. And our mom thought Tatum was stressed out because of that girl's death. Then nine months later, Tatum had Ivy."

"Perez. Stacey Perez," I add.

He snaps his fingers. "That's it."

"Did you know her?"

He shakes his head. Thin, red hair flops in the back. "No, not from Eve."

I nod, feeling like this is my in. When I arrived days ago, I thought I wanted only the answers behind my flare-ups. Then I found the newspaper clipping declaring my birth mother was a serial-killer victim, and my rental car was attacked. Now I'm learning Tatum was friends with the first victim. What did I walk into, exactly?

"Do you remember the police investigation?" I ask. "Did they have any suspects at the time?"

Terry pushes out his upper lip. "Not that I recall."

"What did Geri Hauser and Stacey Perez have in common?"

"How's that?"

"I mean, why them?"

Terry pauses to consider my question, deep lines visible around his mouth. "I heard Geri was in some kind of networking organization. All in the Family, or something."

"The eighties TV show?"

He shakes his head, frowning. "No. Family something. I don't remember. But maybe that got her in touch with the wrong people, or person. I started my forensics internship in Seattle that summer, so I remember the timing of the murders. I had my ear to the ground for those details."

"Are you doing forensics for the latest Full Moon Killer death here?"

"Nah, they won't let me. Say it's a conflict of interest on account of Tatum."

"You mean because she was a victim of the killer's?" Lottie pipes up. "Not a drowning victim." Her normally airy voice has a hard edge to it. I steal a glance at her. Both arms are crossed, matching her legs and ankles.

Terry exhales a deep breath. "Yeah, that's right. I wondered when you'd find out. I always felt bad that you didn't know, but you were too young when you first started asking about her."

Lottie bites the inside of her cheek. "I've believed she drowned my entire life. That her body was swept out to sea, and that's why there's no grave."

"Your mom didn't want anyone to tell you. No one was allowed to—not even your grandma Aggie. But then that wasn't a problem. She didn't want to talk about it."

There's a silent moment of understanding that passes between Terry and Lottie. As uncle and niece, they appear loosely related. But it's their grief and sadness at the years taken from them that serve as the connection now.

They both lift their eyes to me.

"Sorry, Ivy." Terry clears his throat. "Tatum was your mother. Or your birth mother, I mean. That's your loss too."

I smile automatically. "It's different, though. That's okay."

Terry asks me about my family, my childhood in California, and the outskirts of the Bay Area where I grew up.

He volunteers that he chose money over proximity to family early on, and spent the better part of the last thirty years in Seattle. He moved back home only a few years ago, after he got a job doing forensics for the Wenatchee PD. The family still hasn't forgiven him for leaving—despite several loans he's made to *certain* family members, he adds, while casting a side-eye at Lottie that's probably meant for her mother.

"You sure neither of you want a beer? I hate drinking alone," Terry says, downing the rest of his glass and making me question the truth of that statement.

Both Lottie and I shake our heads. "But I do have another question for you," I say. "Did anyone ever try finding me, that you're aware of? If you suspected Tatum was pregnant, I wonder who else did. Was there someone who could have been invested in revealing this secret about the Caines?"

Terry wipes his mouth with his knuckles. I cast another glance around his apartment, this time searching for any example of his handwriting. Does it match the pointed lettering of the anonymous note?

"We used to be hot shit around here, Ivy. The Caine name carried a lot of weight, and I could see someone wanting to make your birth into a scandal. The Sanchez family used to hate us, but then Lottie's uncle fell in love with their daughter, Pita, and the feud kind of fizzled."

I make eye contact with Lottie, but if she knew about this, she doesn't let on. "Did anyone from the Sanchez family ever show a dislike for Tatum?"

Terry shakes his head, pushes out his top lip again. "No. No one that I knew about. The only person I ever knew gave Tatum a hard time was her boss at the clothing store, Hector Hermann. Making her work late, talking down to her, docking her pay when she chatted too long on the job. I met him a few times, and he always seemed like the type to harass young girls. Big pomp, small—well, you know."

"Did the police question him?"

"Oh yeah. But for the life of me, I never knew why they stopped."

———

Sunday early-morning sunshine streams through the parted mauve curtains. The aroma of coffee seeps up from the kitchen, where Lottie is speaking to the manager of her hardware store over the phone.

Splayed on the bed, I gaze at the books I borrowed from the library. All four of them lie open, with sticky notes jutting from various pages. I should feel proud of myself that I pored through them so quickly—within a day. Instead, I slouch back on the pillow propped against the wall and recall the memory of discovering the newspaper article poking from the photo album—the bold type proclaiming that Tatum was a victim of the Full Moon Killer. Tatum was barely a footnote in any of the books, but I've learned a little more—namely, that her body was never found, confirming what Lottie said, and that she was last seen leaving a party. The reporter who seemed to follow the murders the closest reasoned that just because there was no body to prove poison and strangulation didn't mean they should ignore the commonalities with the other victims: she was a young woman, a Rock Island native, and a student at Rock Island High School, who disappeared under a full moon beside a river.

I pick up *True Crime of Washington*; sticky notes form a rainbow of colors along its edges, with my writing covering the visible tabs. I flip to the middle to a chapter that has nothing to do with the Full Moon Killer, but it's the one that's held my attention since last night: "Women and Cults." The first sentence details how a cult took the Pacific Northwest by storm in the 1980s and manipulated men and women alike into luring in their families. The crimes the group committed—some allegedly leading to murder—stopped my speed-reading in its tracks.

The cult's name is One Family. Not All in the Family, like Terry remembered. The networking organization that Geri Hauser was involved in.

According to this book, it's only after years have passed that One Family survivors are willing to share their experiences, to offer perspective on the crimes committed in the name of the organization and the trauma each of them endured as part of their membership, and to explain the significance of their special handshake—grasping the forearm of another One Family member as a symbol that, once you join the Family, the strength of your bond extends beyond your fingertips.

As I reread these paragraphs, the smell of freshly mown grass hits me like I'm standing in Yara's parents' yard again. Groups of people performed that exact same, distinct greeting. Are Yara's parents members? Did I attend a One Family gathering without knowing it?

Geri Hauser was involved in One Family. Maybe Stacey Perez was a member too. Maybe Tatum.

I step out of the guest room, then slip down to the front door. Lottie is still in the kitchen on the phone with her manager, discussing a sander that's "worth its weight in gold."

Standing on the porch, I roll my head onto my chest. I leave tomorrow, and I'm not sure what I hoped to stumble upon this last week. What I expected to learn about my medical history when the Caines profess to be of hardy stock and no one among them knows anything about my birth father.

The thick green fir trees that form the border of the gravel drive-way sway with the breeze, and I let the visual take me away from my thoughts, the sudden anxiety that rose in me at the idea that maybe I attended a cult party without knowing it. Did Lottie know?

"Everything okay? You look upset." Lottie joins me from the door-way. Her eyes narrow, examining me, as if she already doesn't believe the lie I'm trying to muster.

I'm sure if I answer, my voice will break and reveal that I'm not remotely prepared. For any of what I've learned—and not learned—so far. Classic Ivy Hon, to lack the direction and foresight to plan ahead.

I am making progress, though. Inch by inch, I am. Growing up, my parents encouraged me to lead with my brain instead of my heart, but I can't help *feeling* as if there's more to unearth in Rock Island. Even if I end up leaving without discovering an exact diagnosis or my birth father's identity—or if it means digging into the history of a serial killer, whose overlaps with my birth mother are becoming too great to ignore.

Adopting an easy grin, I lean against the white wooden column of the porch. Slide my hands into my jeans, while Lottie peers at me.

"No, I'm fine. Really."

"You sure? Because I need to head into the shop today. There's a problem with a custom shipment that needs taking care of in person, but I can stay if you need to talk." Her tone rises at the end.

"You should go."

"Right. I should." She pauses. "I just feel bad leaving you on your last day here. Your visit has flown by."

"Yeah, about that," I begin, drawing the words out. Thinking on the fly, and imagining the sigh of disapproval my parents would share. "Would it be okay if I stayed awhile longer? We could get in some more quality time during the evenings this week."

Lottie's face relaxes into a smile. "Nothing would make me happier."

Fifteen

IVY

Once Lottie agreed to let me stay, I grabbed my laptop and got to work at the kitchen table. I pushed my flight out another week, then confirmed I could pick up a replacement rental car in Wenatchee. Overall, changing my plans midtrip cost a month's worth of rent, but any regret was stifled by the excitement—of, for once, seeing a project through and not abandoning it half-finished.

Until I considered poor Onyx. I pictured my sweet, inky kitty all curled up, no doubt, beside her automatic feeder on the kitchen tile. Even with my neighbor coming over every other day, that's no way to leave an animal for two weeks. So I called my brother.

Outside on the wicker love seat of the wraparound porch, I stared off at the hanging tree branches above where I used to park, then grew more anxious with each hollow ring of the phone.

When Carson answered, in the same frustrated tone he had last time, I felt the familiar defensive wave of anger rise in me. I bit my tongue and tried to keep my ask brief: I'm out of town and would he be willing to sleep over in my apartment with Onyx for a few days? Thankfully, he's always been a cat person; he agreed to stay through the coming weekend, adding that it was a shorter commute to his office. How selfless.

Explaining where I was, on the other hand, and what I was doing, was less straightforward. I could hear the hesitation—the hurt—when he replied, "Well, I hope you're enjoying time with your family."

I didn't know what to say to that, because *he* was my family, the only kind I had left after our parents passed. But sleeping in Lottie's house, the home that's been in the Caine family for generations, that didn't feel completely true anymore.

Instead of taking the bait, I simply said, "Thanks." We hung up, with me omitting that I had a nanny-cam app on my phone and would be watching if he wore shoes in my home. Or did anything to piss off my neighbors. Even The Rock would be mad if Carson practiced wrestling moves in a fifth-floor apartment.

I glance over to the garage, now vacant of Lottie's Civic. A gust of wind cuts through the heat of the day, swishing tree branches and brushing the skin of my thighs.

Lottie's offer to stay with me today was touching. But it's been almost a week that her store manager has been running the business, and I could see Lottie itching to handle matters herself. Honestly? I'm grateful for the alone time. Knowing that none of these relationships will be permanent anyway, no matter how warm or welcoming most people here seem, I can't let myself get too invested.

Plus, I have a new agenda. I know the Full Moon Killer is related to me—and that my mother was one of his victims. She'd been hell-bent on concealing her pregnancy, and she'd given the baby—me—up for adoption. The two events have to be related, don't they? Which makes it likely—more than likely—that the Full Moon Killer is my father.

This is about more than just finding out my medical history. This is about learning where I came from.

A stronger breeze funnels beneath the overhang of the porch, ruffling my shirt.

I head indoors. Sitting at the kitchen table, I open a new browser tab on my laptop. Liam Weathers, the journalist who wrote most often about the Full Moon Killer, hasn't had a byline in the *Wenatchee Gazette* in almost a decade. The internet reveals that he was living in Seattle as of five years ago.

A link to a *Seattle Times* article written in 1994 reveals that Liam won a journalism prize for his coverage of the Full Moon Killer. An image across the top shows a man with a lanky build and clean-shaven face beaming for the camera. According to the author, Liam's work in promoting the killer as a significant threat once victims began turning up first in Washington, then Oregon, was a public service. *We all have Liam Weathers to thank for encouraging public safety.*

Raising an eyebrow at the reverent tone of the article's author, I click back to the search results. Most of the photos that come up are of a young Liam, probably taken in the nineties, but toward the bottom I find a more recent one. Formerly short brown hair is now pulled back in a ponytail.

I click on the photo, and the home page for the *Wenatchee Gazette* appears. It's an announcement congratulating Liam for being hired as the new editor in chief at the same newspaper that launched him to stardom. The date on the announcement is three years ago.

Liam moved away from the region almost the entire time the Full Moon Killer was inactive. I wonder what his take is on last month's death.

I'm staring into space, considering my next steps, when I notice that Lottie left the television on low in the kitchen. The news anchors gaze seriously into the camera. A banner beneath them reads **Possible New Victim of Full Moon Killer.**

I grab the remote and turn up the volume. The male anchor's voice swells. ". . . found along the Columbia River in Malaga. The only information that police have released is that the male victim was found early this morning, with signs of battery and strangulation evident. Whitney, can you tell us what you see on the ground there in Malaga?"

The camera cuts to a woman with sleek black hair wearing muted red lipstick. She reports that investigators are still trying to determine the time and cause of death.

Cold air dances across my forearms. There was another murder, possibly by the Full Moon Killer. This time while I was asleep and in the same county.

My hands begin to shake, and I press them firmly between my knees. I wasn't supposed to be here this long. I was planning to leave before the next full moon, and there are still four days remaining. I've learned from my reading that what Agent Ballo told me wasn't strictly accurate—forensics couldn't always prove that the victims were killed exactly on the night of the full moon. But would the killer really strike this early?

Behind the reporter, a man stands in tall grass at the water's edge and shouts at another man wearing a suit jacket—in eighty-degree heat. I can't grasp everything he's saying, but the phrase "Do you know who I am?" is as clear as the chime of the grandfather clock by Lottie's front door. He turns his back to the camera, and his ponytail flickers in the wind. Liam Weathers.

My dad's voice comes to mind with the gentle reprimand he'd offer whenever I would freeze from indecision, fearing that I'd screw up a choice I made. *Intuition is fine if you're going on a Sunday drive, Sweet Ivy. But if you want to get to your destination, you need a map.*

I stand and confirm that my Swiss Army knife is in my bag, then sling the shoulder strap across my chest.

———

Malaga's main commercial area is barely three miles long, and the road and clean sidewalks are empty on a Sunday at lunchtime. Official signposts direct me to the riverfront at the north part of town, but I don't need them to find my way.

Scores of people clump in groups, trying to get a look at the area police have cordoned off with yellow tape. Officers in dark-blue uniforms spread out along the riverbank, looking for something. I park my new rental car, a scratched sedan painted pea-soup green—the only available car during tourist season—but instead of joining the crowd and trying to get an eyeful of the scene, I search for a long brown ponytail.

A news truck belonging to the cable channel I was watching back at the Caine house is parked in the corner of the lot beside several other logo-painted vehicles. I walk toward them, hoping to see Whitney Cruz, the reporter I saw on television earlier. Maybe she'll be able to point me toward Liam Weathers.

"No further questions."

"But, Mr. Weathers! Do you believe the Full Moon Killer is behind this latest death?"

I turn to a cluster of reporters. Liam Weathers stands with his back to me, his signature ponytail swaying with his energized movements. This is the journalist who first linked Tatum to the Full Moon Killer, before the police had even made that assessment public.

"Unlikely. It would be the first time the killer has gone after a man. It would mean the killer has changed his MO from exclusively women, from the use of some form of poison or drug, and from murdering under a full moon—and that would be a surprise to everyone, including me. The only thing this new victim has in common with *some* of the others is there are signs of strangulation. There's no evidence of poison or excessive morphine, this didn't happen under the full moon, and this victim is the wrong gender. Sadly, this death could be the work of anyone."

More questions follow as cell phones are thrust into Liam's face to record his words.

"No further questions," he says. "Let's let the police do their job."

He turns and strides over to a younger man who wears sleeves pushed up to his elbows. He offers Liam bottled water.

"Excuse me," I say, walking right up to them. The younger man facing me frowns.

Liam sighs. "Can I help you?"

Svelte and about my height, Liam Weathers gives me only half a shoulder.

"I—yes. I'm sorry to bother you. I'm Ivy Hon. I was hoping to speak to you about something. Is there a good place to talk, maybe a little more private?" I keep both hands on my purse strap, feeling on edge among so many people.

"What is this about?"

"Tatum Caine's death. You wrote an article about her, claiming she was a victim of the Full Moon Killer. She's my birth mother."

Thick eyebrows rise higher with each sentence I speak. He nods, throwing a glance to the younger man. "Yes, yes. Uh, yes. Let's go . . . this way."

He leads me to a park across the street. The noise of traffic carries from the road, but we are, for the purposes of a private conversation, alone—out of sight of anyone at the crime scene.

Suddenly, I wonder if I've made a mistake. I don't know this Liam Weathers apart from his name—and the fact that his absence from this area matches the Full Moon Killer's period of inactivity. The memory of my vandalized car returns to mind, along with slithering fear.

I do the only thing I can think of. I send my brother a ping with my location. Granted, he's in the Bay Area watching Onyx, but if something happens to me, at least he can offer the police a starting point. A dog begins barking down the street, pricking my nerves, before it abruptly stops.

Liam Weathers faces me. "So, Ivy Hon. What can I do for you?"

I shut my eyes a moment. Try to organize my jumbled questions.

"Okay. So you were awarded some journalism prize for your reporting on the Full Moon Killer in the nineties. And you were the first person to suggest my mother was a victim of the killer. You're the authority on him, and everything that's happened since, right?"

"All true."

"I imagine that expertise extends to the victims too, then?"

He nods.

"Okay, great. What happened just before Tatum's death? Who did she see, and where did she go?"

Liam frowns. He steps closer, and I shuffle back out of instinct. "Look, Ivy. I'm not sure you're going to find what you're searching for here. Your mom is gone. Isn't it better to leave the grisly details in the past? Where they belong?"

"I'm sorry, but no. I'm only beginning to learn about her. I need to know."

He nods. "It's been a long time since I've thought about this stuff. I was as glad as anyone when the killer stopped."

Was he? Those articles were the main source of his fame.

He looks down at a yellow patch of grass, seems to collect his thoughts, then meets my gaze. "On her last day, after Tatum left her house, where she was living with her mother, she went straight to work at a clothing store. She saw and spoke with Hector Hermann, her boss; Mal Ngo, her coworker; and her sister, Tristen. Tristen and Tatum later went to a party together, where Tatum stepped outside and was never seen again. Witnesses saw someone following Tatum to the river, but they never confirmed who it was."

My pulse races. One of the library books mentioned a party, but not that her sister was there. "Well, where was Tristen? If Tatum and Tristen went to this party together, what does Tristen think happened?"

Recalling Lottie's admission that Tristen blames herself for Tatum's demise—and Lottie's misunderstanding that Tatum drowned—I wonder if there's more that she doesn't know about her mother.

Liam pouts. "You'd have to ask her, because she never went on record about what happened that night. About what drove Tatum to separate herself from her sister and go outside alone."

I jot details in my notebook. "Okay, so Tatum is presumed dead—"

"Ivy," Liam interrupts, his voice gentle, "trust me when I say your mother is gone. Technically, her case is unsolved. But 'presumed' is the same as 'dead' when someone's been missing for this long. I'm sorry."

I pause my note-taking. "I get it. But how did you make the connection that Tatum was a victim of the Full Moon Killer if there was no body?"

Liam gives a pitying sigh. "I know this must be hard for you. You just came looking for your birth mother and find out that not only is she gone, but she was likely murdered. That's a lot for anyone to take in."

I square my jaw. Feel my temper spark at this guy's patronizing tone. "Right. It is. But that still doesn't explain how you link Tatum and the killer."

"It's not obvious? She disappears from a house party under a full moon. She's a young woman. She's a student at Rock Island High, just like his previous kills, and this happened a year after Geri Hauser was killed."

"Right. But . . ." I pause my reply. Take in Liam's scowl.

Each reason he cited was mentioned in the library books I read; I guess I was hoping for some concrete detail that would indicate whether my birth father was involved—if he could be the killer.

"Was Tatum dating anyone then?"

Liam doesn't blink. "No."

I watch for some kind of tell, some giveaway that he's hiding something. "Okay. Well, what about today's victim? The rest of the press seems to think this death is the Full Moon Killer's work. But you don't?"

Liam narrows his eyes. "Like I told the police, we're still four days out from the end of this lunar cycle, Ivy. It would be strange to me if the killer struck outside of their normal cadence. And if the killer took a male life, since they've only ever targeted female victims."

He slides his hands into the pockets of his khakis. "I'm sorry I can't tell you anything more about your mother. Her murder fits the pattern, but there often aren't any easy answers in cases like this until the killer is caught." He looks me up and down. "I'll give you the same advice I'd give any young woman in this area before the full moon. Watch yourself."

He steps past me, crosses the street, then blends back into the crowd of crime-scene gawkers. For a moment, my breathing is the only sound in the park. Then the dog resumes barking from somewhere down the road.

———

A neon sign glows in the slanting afternoon sunshine, the word BAR blinking like a cut-and-paste image from Vegas. As I push through the kitschy saloon doors of Lainey's Office, excitement tightens my chest. I'm hoping to see a familiar mop of chin-length hair seated at the bar.

The bartender perks up from where she's slumped against the slick copper counter. "Welcome in. What are you drinking?"

"A beer, please. Something light."

On a Sunday afternoon, we're the only ones present. I take an empty booth behind the pinball machine. A twinge of embarrassment squeaks within me at how much I was hoping to see Poe again, the guy from the other night. For the distraction, the tips, and some of the lighthearted conversation that's been missing from my life since my mother died.

With a full pint and a comfortable seat, I pull out the library book on true crime and its chapter on local cults. There's an index, which doesn't mention Rock Island but does include Wenatchee. I flip back and forth between the index and each reference, and learn that the original headquarters of One Family was in the northern part of the city. The index cross-references photo captions too, and I find a section on One Family membership rituals in Spokane; demographic changes in the cult in Portland, Oregon; and images of protests held by cult members in Seattle in the 1980s.

A photo above a section about forced participation in protests stops me from turning another page. A young man, midstride, slings his arm around a woman with dark hair that tumbles down thin shoulders— Geri Hauser. Neither is looking at the camera. Behind them, a banner draped across the side of a barn reads ONE FAMILY.

The man is lean, his thick beard neatly trimmed along his jaw. He could be a much younger version of Uncle Terry. I unlock my phone to swipe through the videos I took of the Caine family photo albums. Halfway through the second recording, I find an image of Terry at the kiln in the backyard of Lottie's house. His hair is longer than in the photo of the protest, but it's unmistakably him.

Condensation slides down my beer glass and pools in a ring.

Why did Terry omit the fact that he knew Geri Hauser, a victim of the killer?

Flipping to the index, I search for "Caine." There's a single entry, but instead of more images of Terry, as I expect, I find a photo of a young woman on a page about One Family's adoption of social move-ments in the early nineties. She wears a loose-fitting dress and stands before a dozen people sitting cross-legged on the pavement behind her. Beneath the image, the caption reads:

Tristen Caine leads a One Family demonstration against big-city corruption.

A shiver courses between my shoulder blades. Tristen was a member of the same networking club—cult—as Geri Hauser. The killer's second victim.

I push the air from my mouth and let my shoulders drop. Take a sip of my beer. Feel the cool liquid travel down my throat and coat my insides, and process what I just learned.

What else are the Caines keeping secret?

I find Lottie's number in my phone.

"Ivy?" she answers. "How's it going? Everything okay at home? I should be back by six."

"Yeah, I'm just . . . on the porch." I wince, internally noting I am a good several miles from the house—wondering how many times that lie has been said in this bar over the years.

"Oh, good. What's up?"

"Listen, would it be okay if I met with your mom tomorrow? There are some things I'd like to ask her, and I think you said she finished work for that client today."

Lottie is silent on the other end. A man in the background asks about pliers. "Sure, Ivy. I'll give her a call and see about timing."

We hang up. Anxiety swirls in my stomach. Dread. Plus a bite of fear and the sense that I'm about to disturb a still pool of water—to transform its placid surface into a sea of rippling consequences.

"Hey there," a warm voice calls from the counter. "Ivy."

Poe locks eyes with mine, and he takes a tentative step toward me. He tucks a fringe of hair behind one ear. "Didn't think I'd see you again."

"Hey. Yeah, I thought you left town." My stomach knots in a new way.

He rolls his shoulders back in a short-sleeve collared shirt, as if working to release some ache.

"I had planned on it. Then a big farming corporation asked for a sales consult at that conference yesterday, so I'm staying awhile longer. Mind if I join you?"

I take in his self-assured, all-American-boy appearance and for a moment wonder what life must have been like for him up until now. Easygoing? Uneventful?

For once, and especially in this increasingly bizarre environment surrounded by ghosts and veiled secrets, I wouldn't mind the proximity to someone. In the past, I've been reticent to make new connections—stressed, from the moment I exchange names with a potential love interest or friend, that I'll say the wrong thing and someone else will leave me. But that was in California. Here in the Pacific Northwest, anything feels possible.

I wave him in, motioning to the seat opposite mine. "C'mon in. The water's fine."

Sixteen

TATUM

August 17, 1989

"Tatum, missy. I don't pay you to daydream, now do I?"

Hector peers at me from behind his Coke-bottle glasses, wrinkling the graying mustache I so despise. He pays me enough to sell clothing on consignment, but not enough to quit daydreaming myself away from this place. Away from my life.

"Sorry, Hector. I was just reviewing inventory in my head." I offer a sheepish smile, but he only frowns.

"Ever since you returned from that weight-loss camp, you've been distant. Although, at the very least, it seemed effective." He sweeps a glance down my chest, and I pretend not to notice. "Where's the music?" he asks.

"Oh. Sorry." I fumble for the power button on the new boom box he bought earlier this summer, then position it on the register counter. Paula Abdul's "Straight Up" begins thumping out its chorus on the local radio station.

"That's better," Hector says, raising his voice. "Have you seen Mal?"

I nod toward the back room. "She's pricing jeans."

"That's good. Can't have both of you slacking off at the same—" The door chimes to announce the entrance of a customer. He whirls to the front, exchanging his scowl for a beaming grin. "Welcome to Chic Threads! Tatum here can help you with anything you need."

He steps past me—to go police Mal's algebra, no doubt—and reveals a young woman in a flowing white robe. Blonde braids frame a round face, while her generous silhouette seems magnified in the transparent fabric illuminated by the afternoon sunshine. I wave to my sister.

"Hey, babe!" Tristen chirps. "The man isn't getting you down, is he?" She glances back at the EMPLOYEES ONLY door as it clicks shut. A sequin top catches her eye, and she begins pushing clothing around the nearest circular rack.

"No more than usual." I absorb my older sister's grin but can't muster her enthusiasm—I haven't been able to for months. "Marmie said you sent off Terry's care package. How many cookies actually made it to the post office?"

Tristen palms a romper, clutching the polyester material before moving on to a cotton shift. "Half. Or thereabouts. I just stopped by to check in and see how my favorite sister was doing."

She speaks while examining a decorative button, but I can hear the disguised concern. Tristen and everyone else walking on eggshells around me, per usual. Well, everyone except Hector.

"What are you up to tonight?" Tristen presses a red leather jacket to her chest, like she's auditioning for Michael Jackson's "Thriller" video. "Let's go to a party."

"For that club you were telling me about? The other family you think is your family?"

"It's called One Family, Tater. If you're lucky, I may explain it to you when you're older." She throws me a teasing eyebrow waggle, then slides the jacket off the hanger. I watch her pull it on, then zip the two panels closed. She lowers the zipper to cleavage level.

"Just enough to keep them interested," she says with a wink. Finding the price tag under the arm, she whistles, then takes off the jacket and tucks it back on the hanger. "Seriously, though. There's another get-together at the old Santorini house. You should come tonight. Get your mind off of . . . stuff. One Family is always interested in more people to join and further the cause."

"And what cause is that?"

"To share the message of peace and harmony. Duh."

Tristen continues to shop as she speaks to me, but I see right through the forced nonchalance. She was an absolute mess after breaking up with her boyfriend last year. She dropped out of college, got into drugs, fell into a deep depression—and Marmie was at her wit's end with her; she kicked Tristen out. It was then that Tristen joined up with One Family and seemed close to her old self again.

Our father was always the religious leader in our family. After he died, Marmie was uninterested in attending mass anymore. We were more than Chreasters—Christians who attend church on Christmas and Easter—but stopped short of getting confirmed. Interesting that Tristen now seems revived by religion, or whatever this Family claims it's about. I just know when I was going to Sunday school, the acts of engaging in recreational sex and drugs, like I've heard One Family does as a matter of policy, were a no-no.

The fact that this cult has also been rumored to be behind the disappearance of girls my age in the area makes me pretty doubtful about joining. But, despite all that, my sister seems happy again. I have One Family to thank for that. And I'd rather die than tell Marmie and take that happiness away from Tristen.

I step out from behind the register and cross to my sister, who's straining to reach a dress on her tiptoes. "Let me help you there, little lady."

Tristen wrinkles her button nose at me, the smattering of freckles along the bridge making her appear younger than twenty-one. "At least you use your height for good."

I smile, and something in her expression softens. She takes my hand. "So you'll come tonight? I have clothing you can borrow."

She grabs the fabric of her own shapeless robe and swishes it side to side.

"Do I have to dress all earth mother like you? Or can I just go in shorts and my Cyndi Lauper T-shirt?"

"Cyndi Lauper is fine. She'd probably be into One Family too, if we could only get close enough to tell her about it. God, sex, and communing with nature seem right up her alley."

A sideways smile from my big sister.

"I'll be at the house by eight o'clock. Be ready." Tristen sweeps me into a hug and breathes deep in my hair. "Mmm. Smells like fresh meat."

I laugh, pushing her away. "This does not mean that I'm joining, Tris. I'm just going to check it out since you keep harassing me about it."

She grins. "There's my favorite human. I missed that fire."

After a last longing look at the red leather jacket, she leaves, the bells above the door jangling her exit as if they're heralding some new chapter ahead. Despite my reservations, I wonder whether One Family could be the key to some balance in my life too, the way it has been for Tristen.

"Tatum! We need you," Mal's voice rings out from the back. "Hector got stuck between the rolling shelves again!"

Grunts and swear words bellow from behind the EMPLOYEES ONLY door, and I go to lock the front the way Hector insists we do whenever we leave the store unattended.

As I pass the clothing racks my sister was circling, I think of the way she used to stick up for me in elementary school, cajole our mom and dad into taking us to the aquarium on weekends because she knew I loved the stingrays, and never let me out of the house with my pants unzipped or a button undone.

Knowing my sister the way I do, I'm sure she would never steer me wrong.

Seventeen

Ivy

A mile past the library, I idle at a weather-beaten signpost marking a paved road.

The sign was once eye-catching, I'm sure, with its blue aluminum and crisp white lettering. Now the sheet metal is slapped with dirt streaks, bird poop, and several uneven ripples where it was likely bent or run over in the past. Despite the wear and tear, the sign's words remain clear: TRISTEN'S TAXIDERMY.

When Lottie told me the landmark to look for, I was glad she couldn't see my jaw drop over the phone. Taxidermy, while perhaps a beloved practice by some to preserve memories of hunting trips or long-deceased pets, has always struck me as creepy.

I lean over the steering wheel and take in the yellow one-story house to the left. Fields of tall grass flank both sides of a dirt driveway. Behind the house, twin doors of a matching yellow barn are wide open, the glint of something metal visible from the road.

Two wooden pikes hammered into the ground resemble parking spots, so I pull into the closest one. A quick glance in my rearview confirms the light mascara I applied this morning hasn't smudged. I swipe on some lip balm with a shaking hand.

The reality that I'm about to meet my dead mother's sister—to come face-to-face with someone who knew Tatum intimately and in ways that I'll never experience—has me anxious; I want my aunt to like me, even as I'll be watching her every twitch for a sign that she's hiding something.

I exit the car, then lean against the driver's-side door. The entrance to the barn is fifty yards away, empty fields beside it and behind. Tristen's property is seven miles outside of Rock Island's downtown, which itself is already considered remote by my standards; peering past the barn to a rocky outcrop from a hillside and a flock of sheep grazing on land fenced in by barbed wire, it's clear that we are alone.

As I approach the barn doors, the smell of iron and something chemical stings the air. I lean in through the wide-open entrance—keeping one foot outside.

"Hello?" I wince.

Humming vibrates across the air from an industrial freezer in the corner. On a workbench in the center of the shop, a plastic case lies open, revealing steel blades in varying sizes and the biggest pair of pliers I've ever seen. A set of shears, smaller than the giant-size pair I see on the wall, is open beside them, as if interrupted midcut. Dark red stains the tan table. Gallon jugs of liquid line aluminum shelves; two of the handwritten labels read "Alcohol" and "Borax." I remember to take a second look at them to mentally compare them to the writing on the letter I received when I was five. This writing is also pointed, but it may slant too far to the side.

"Ivy?" a woman calls from behind, and I jump.

She's early fifties or older, with honey-blonde hair wrapped in a gray bandanna. Her apron is covered in black-and-brown stains.

"Yes, hi." I clutch the strap of my shoulder bag, still on edge.

"I'm Tristen." She wipes her hands on a (very small) clean section of her apron. "Let's head inside, and I'll take this damn thing off." She turns and starts walking.

I swallow the surge of fear that clamps my throat. "Sounds good," I say to her back.

Tristen crosses to a concrete walkway leading to the front door of the house. As I follow her, an image of Lottie enters my head, of her gliding down the porch steps of the Caine house to greet me. Beaming, round face. Open arms. A one-woman welcoming committee to rival any Hallmark card. This is her mother?

"How was the drive?" Tristen throws over her shoulder.

"Scenic." I catch up to her at the front door, but she only purses her mouth in response.

As we step indoors, a stuffed elk head greets me from the wall with glassy eyes—a twin to the one perched beside the grandfather clock at the Caine house. I take in the open living room and the windows lining the north and south sides of the house. From here, I can see the road and the flock of sheep grazing the hillside. A shiver crawls across my neck, wondering how long Tristen was watching me before she came outside.

"Thought I could finish an old coonhound before you arrived." Tristen grimaces, then slides her hands into the apron's deep pouch. "Make yourself at home."

She directs me to a worn couch covered by a knit blanket, and I sit. Then she steps around the corner into the kitchen, passing a breakfast table stacked with plastic jugs filled halfway with clear and pink liquids.

Alone, I look around. A hawk, frozen in midflight, stretches above the fireplace mantel, as if reaching toward the fox head on the opposite wall. In the corner, next to a glass hutch, an otter's gullet hangs agape, while a border collie stares at me from beside an armchair. The guard elk is in good company.

A knife strikes a dull plate or cutting board in the kitchen. Images of Tristen standing over an animal carcass—then a body—enter my head. The strong hands I just saw wiping the hem of her apron could easily wrap around a neck.

I take a deep breath, try to get ahold of myself—ignore my rattling confidence in coming here alone. Lottie would have known if her mother was somehow involved in Tatum's death—wouldn't she? Don't children observe all their parents' good and bad traits? She would know if her mother were capable of harming someone.

"Have you lived here long?" I ask, finally finding my voice. "Lottie tells me you raised her near the Caine house."

Tristen returns without the bandanna, leaving her hair loose and curling. She carries a tray of crackers and salami, and two glasses of iced tea. She sets the tray on a scratched, dark wooden table, then takes a seat on a rocking chair beside the couch.

"It's been about—oh—two years? I moved out here when Lottie got her business going. Didn't need me as much anymore."

Dutifully, I take a sip of iced tea. Its bitter taste puckers my mouth.

"It's been great spending time with Lottie," I say. "And I'm glad to learn more about your family while I'm here."

She hasn't touched anything on the tray yet. "I can't seem to take my eyes off of you. You look a lot like Tatum."

My lips part, but any words get caught in the sudden tide pool of emotions in my chest—disbelief, since I've seen photos of Tatum and know that she had nothing like my coloring, and a quiet wavelength of pleasure that I might resemble her.

Growing up, people complimented me in grocery stores as I stood next to my mother; they'd say that I had her beautiful bone structure—high cheekbones, small chin, wide temples. Mom would always accept the well-intentioned comment, but I would blush, knowing I couldn't possibly share her features genetically. To learn now that I take after a parent, to objectively resemble someone, would be wildly exotic. My eight-year-old self might skip down the pasta aisle.

"What makes you say that?" I ask, wanting and not wanting the answer.

Tristen leans onto her knees, hugging her elbows. "Your forehead, I think. Or your nose. I don't know, it just feels like I'm talking to some alternate universe version of my sister again."

A soft chuckle gets muffled behind her hand. "Wow, this is weird."

"It is."

Another moment passes—awkward, though not uncomfortable—and Tristen relaxes into her chair. "Well, Ivy. I have about a million questions for you, but Lottie gave me a brief rundown over the phone. You traveled two states to meet us and learn more about your roots. So what questions do you have for me?"

Big blue eyes, Lottie's eyes, peer at me. They narrow, as if bracing for what are sure to be difficult questions I've come to lob her way; I wonder if Lottie already confronted her mother about the lie of Tatum's drowning. Although the last thing I want to do is offend Tristen or alienate a potential source of information, the next full moon is only a few days out.

"Well, I thought I learned a lot after completing DNA testing—"

"Which is how you and Lottie found each other."

"Right. There were so many genetic reports, but then I came here and am discovering so much more. Like, Tatum was a victim of the Full Moon Killer."

Tristen's warmth evaporates. She goes as still as one of her taxidermied animals. Slowly, she nods, then peers out the window behind me. "I'll bet that came as a shock to you. It certainly did to me thirty years ago."

"Were there ever any leads on her attacker?" I ask in a small voice, trying to match Tristen's dimmed energy. A stab of regret pokes my ribs, but I don't give any indication of it; this woman—my aunt—could be hiding something back in her barn or know of some connection between her cult and the serial killer. "Why did the police think Tatum was one of the Full Moon victims if they never found a body?"

"It was a reporter, actually, who put two and two together. Something to do with clouds or sun . . . his name was . . ."

I grab a slice of salami from the plain white ceramic plate. The letters *LM* are painted on the lip. Maybe for Lottie Montagne. Did she make this? "The journalist. Liam Weathers."

Tristen nods. "That guy. Yeah, he realized that Tatum disappeared directly under a full moon. I was pretty horrified at first. Actually tried to get him fired from the *Wenatchee Gazette* because I couldn't stomach the idea of my baby sister being murdered by a serial killer."

"I'll bet that was hard."

"Yeah. As time went by, more people were killed or disappeared under a full moon, and I guess the idea stuck."

"Have there been any theories as to why the killer chooses that specific day?"

Tristen shrugs. "I've thought about that. Anecdotal evidence and ancient religions suggest that the moon affects the brain the same way it affects the waves in the ocean—since our brains are composed of so much water. The theory is that the moon then pulls on us, makes people act batty once a month. Maybe that's the case for the killer."

"And how did your time with One Family play into Tatum's death?"

Tristen turns her attention from the window to lock on my gaze. My breath hitches, and I wonder if I've gone too far. A sneer tenses her face.

"You know about that, do you?" she asks, her voice soft, almost dangerous. "Don't you want to ask me if I like peanut butter or brussels sprouts? Aren't those questions that people ask when reuniting with families?"

I don't speak, not daring to push any further for fear of getting kicked out before she answers.

Tristen swears under her breath. "You probably think it outlandish, foolish, and stupid to get involved from today's perspective. There's so much more information available now. Young people are on guard against organizations looking to take advantage of them."

"You didn't realize One Family was a cult?"

"I knew people thought it was. For me, it was a home. A church. A new religion."

Tristen shakes her head. Her hands clutch the wooden armrests as if on a roller-coaster ride she doesn't want to endure. "It was a time of fear in the late eighties. People out here were still wishing Reagan could have had a third term. There was talk of satanists, razor blades being hidden in Halloween candy, and Iran bombing us into oblivion. We were fearful that another draft would be instituted. We were all desperate for something to grab on to in the shitstorm of that era. One Family knew that."

"I don't understand," I begin. "You didn't join up willingly?"

"No, I did. Everyone did. But One Family knew how to identify the loneliest and most vulnerable out there. Everyone who joined was trying to fill a hole inside them. I had just come off a year of depression after someone I really loved left me; I had taken to burning items of his in the kiln behind the house. It turns out Tatum had just lost someone she really loved too."

"Oh?" My heart pitches. "Who was that?"

Tristen makes eye contact for the first time since venturing into the past. "You."

I pause, absorbing the words. Part of me wants to believe her—I can feel my internal child trembling with emotion at the idea that I was wanted, despite being given away—while a part of me rejects this whole conversation as a tactic to distract me from learning about Tatum's death and the Full Moon Killer's role in it.

"Was Tatum also a member of One Family?" I ask.

Tristen drags a fingernail across the wood. "No. She never got that far. She died before officially joining up."

"Do you think she would have?" When I read about the cult and its power over Washington State, I wondered whether I was born into it. If my birth father was part of it too.

"I was the only person trying to recruit her, thank God. We had certain . . . rules . . . that weren't really appropriate in hindsight."

"In what way?"

Tristen waves a hand. "Today, One Family is rebranded as a non-profit organization that assists the homeless. But back then, it was different. It was a cult. I was actually in charge of burning all paper copies of One Family's original code of ethics."

"Why would you have to burn them?"

Tatum hesitates. She holds up a finger, then crosses to the hutch and pulls open its bottom drawer. From it, she takes an extra-large plastic bag containing a flat blue folder. She hands it to me and sits.

"I saved one. For shits and giggles, I thought back then."

Inside the folder, I find a single piece of paper. Six rules are type-written in bold face.

Rule 1. One Family members and their kin are beholden to the laws of Nature and God. No disrespecting either.

Rule 2. One Family means one love. Within One Family, all members are married to one another and should not stray from each other.

Rule 3. All members are expected to raise the Family's children.

Rule 4. Members who are unmarried according to Washington State must recruit on a quarterly basis, using tactics up to and including romance.

Rule 5. Recruitment is the only exception to Rule 2.

Rule 6. Members must commit monthly confession in order to adhere to Rule 1.

"Wow, this is . . . intense," I say.

Tristen watches my face. "The more time passes, the more the rules look and sound crazy to me."

My eyes catch on Rule 6. "What was the monthly confession?"

She inhales a deep breath. "Blackmail. We'd have to confess the ways in which we broke Rule 1 that month, and the elders would hold that information over our heads. Make us do whatever they wanted and continue to for years on end. Usually steal money from our real family members to finance One Family activities."

"So you couldn't ever leave without all that coming out."

She nods. "Exactly. When I finally left One Family, it was because I didn't want Lottie to grow up in that kind of oppressive environment— I had just found out I was pregnant, and her father had been asking me to leave One Family for a while then. I worked odd jobs, so when the things I did or said over the years came out, I didn't lose any credibility in some career. Just relationships."

She crosses her arms. I hesitate to ask about Terry and his connection to Geri Hauser, despite my certainty there's something more there. Tristen's discomfort wading into these memories is obvious.

I lean forward, as much as the deep seat of the couch will allow. "Was the Full Moon Killer connected to other One Family members?"

"People died, if that's what you're asking. People disappeared frequently, but that was the nature of the time. Anyone could go off the grid and cut ties if they really wanted to, but I don't know of other deaths linked to One Family and the killer. None apart from Geri Hauser."

"Were you friends with her?"

Tristen shakes her head. "Her death was before I got involved with the Family."

I clench my jaw. My pulse rises, quickens in my limbs. "Was your brother, Terry, a member?"

The tired disappointment that drew Tristen's face disappears. Her eyes snap to mine. "What?"

"Was Terry a member of One Family too? Was he dating Geri Hauser when she died? I found a photo of them together around the time of her murder."

"What are you saying?" Tristen growls. She grips the rocking chair, nails digging into the armrests.

"I . . . I'm sorry. I was just wondering . . ."

Terry Caine was involved with a murder victim; then his little sister Tatum was killed by the same attacker. If that's not a clear link, I'm not the only Asian in Rock Island.

Pursing my lips, I ignore the urge in my belly telling me to stop, to maintain the new bonds I'm forming with my biological family. I return Tristen's steady eye contact as if I'm facing off with the taxidermied fox behind her.

"Look, if Terry was dating Geri Hauser close to her murder, then a year later Tatum dies—could Terry somehow have been . . . involved?"

Tristen rises from the rocking chair with the slow grace and menace of a safari animal, curls forming a wild mane around her furious expression. "No. Now it's time for you to go."

I get up and leave, and return to my car, cursing myself for pushing her. There were so many questions I didn't ask—about my birth father's identity, about a possible diagnosis. I should have asked if she knew where I was this whole time and if she sent me a letter in 1994. Instead, I've doused a potential bridge to more information in kerosene, then lit a careless match.

Sliding into the driver's seat, I lift my gaze to Tristen's porch. The front door is shut and the curtains are drawn.

———

Back at the Caine house, the ground floor is dark when I slip inside. Late-afternoon shadows creep through the window of the kitchen nook on the other side of the house. The eerie glow seems to reach for me.

My gut clenches. Alert. Certain that something is wrong.

I flick on the hall light and flinch beside the coatrack in the corner—a mound of dark coats that could hide a full-grown man—but none jumps out. The beady-eyed elk head guards the stairwell. I slide past it, averting my gaze, and bend to whatever instinct draws me upstairs.

When I reach my room, the bed is as I left it—made, with the pillow indented where I sat against the headboard and swiped on mascara. My suitcase remains unzipped, a white-and-gray shirt poking out.

Everything appears normal, except the drawers of the nightstand. I haven't touched them since the night I arrived and considered unpacking what few items of clothing I brought; I closed them tight then and definitely did not leave them inches ajar as they are now. I turn in a circle, positive that I'm missing something. Another detail. A reason to further justify the coiled tension in my core.

I inhale a breath—and nearly choke on the scent.

Eucalyptus. The smell of the Tiger Balm my mother used to apply on my tender skin whenever I got a bruise—only I didn't bring any. And I know I didn't leave the drawers open.

Peering into the nightstand, I see the sharp white corner of an envelope. I pull it out. My letter. Someone retrieved the envelope from my suitcase, then placed it in this drawer.

Fear creases my forehead as I recall that Lottie always leaves the front door unlocked, citing small-town trust and the fact that the Caine house doesn't exclusively belong to her.

Someone else was in my room. Did they have to hide the letter in a hurry when they heard me drive up?

My heart racing, I grab my Swiss Army knife and creep downstairs. With each step and creak of the stairwell, I hold my breath—listening—anticipating the sound of shuffling footsteps behind me.

Panting in the foyer before the stained glass of the entryway, I pause. Strain my ears. Only the soft ticking of the grandfather clock registers against the many hiding places of the cavernous Victorian.

Eighteen

Samson

The Past

Green mountainsides of Oregon and Washington blur together as Samson's Rad Road Trip continues, and everything feels surreal this far north. Like I'm the star of some documentary or sitcom in another world, and each move I make will be analyzed and promoted in some announcer's voice.

Will Samson win the heart of the girl? Unlikely.

But will that heart continue pulsing after he rips it from her chest? Stay tuned to find out, folks!

A pit stop in Portland, where I stole a bicycle from outside a brewery, then got chased for three blocks by two burly men and a woman, confirmed that city was too nice to stay at—Portland, the city of bridges, and sweet as pie. Any fun I got into would likely be noticed and reported too quickly for me to enjoy anything. So I kept going east, thinking I'd try my luck with more campers over in Mount Hood, then up near the Indian reservations. Neither location presented the right opportunity. I ended up siphoning some gas from a beat-up jalopy at night, then carried on.

It was overhearing someone in Yakima that sparked my interest, talking about how Seattle's crime rates have gone sky-high in recent years. As that barfly moaned about how city folk were pushing into the rural areas and bringing their vice with them, I realized that a metropolis like Seattle, under cover of rainy days and serious population density, would be rife with possibilities for this nomad. Seattle was only a little farther north and to the west, and judging from the map in my truck, I could even stop by the Hanford Reach, a stretch of the Columbia River that the same barfly was raving about as the most beautiful place in the Pacific Northwest.

Nature, I'd had enough of growing up in the sticks of Central California. But nature lovers—packing snacks, expensive gear, and maybe a gun or two—I was all for.

I breathe in and fill my lungs with the fresh air swirling along the banks of the Columbia. The area I've paused beside—around a fifteen-minute hike from the parking lot—stretches for miles into grassland. In the opposite direction, towering bluffs and delicate flowers. Not a trace of cow manure.

The river is the length of three big rigs stacked across. Waterfowl float on the current, a pair of them followed by a smaller bird—maybe their adolescent. I hold my breath as I take in the beautiful vista, the family of ducks, and taste the faint scent of something sweet nearby. Wildflowers.

A gunshot erupts from over the next bend, and a flock of birds launches into the sky. I bare my teeth.

Another tourist.

A grassy trail leads inland toward the sound, and I keep an eye on the location the birds came from. I tread carefully, not wanting to twist an ankle on the uneven terrain. The path slopes into a canyon. Whooping and singing carry from below; then another shotgun blast reaches my ears.

"What kind of idiot makes that much noise while hunting?" I ask aloud. It's been a few days since I've spoken to anyone.

A porcupine ambles out from the waist-high grass about ten feet ahead of me. I bite my lip, almost in disbelief. I've only ever seen one in storybooks. A sign back at the parking lot warned against taking wild animals by surprise—chiefly, foxes, coyotes, mule deer, and elk.

I grew up around cows. The most docile, dumbass animals that God created and put on this earth. The idea of coming face-to-face with any kind of beast with teeth and claws, any being willing to put up a fight, seems to me something to be avoided.

Adrenaline pulses in my fingertips as I continue forward. Geese circle overhead, not yet reassured that the danger has passed. I pause occasionally to listen for other signs of life—either from the idiot hunter or otherwise. Although I have no desire to pounce on an animal by mistake, something about surprising a human makes my mouth salivate, and I tense all over.

Then I hear it.

A low groaning sound. Inconsistent and gravelly. To conceal my approach, I hug the curving dirt wall created by some river tributary or earthquake or whatever creates canyons in a plains field. My stomach knots as anticipation and excitement fuse together. The low rumbling noise seems to bounce off the rock, amplifying its volume. I'm close.

Two feet splay out on the red dirt of the earth. Yellow shoelaces of hiking boots drape the ground in large loops. A shotgun stands propped against a tiered rock formation in the dirt wall.

The hunter. I steal a glance around the final bend, just in case he's still targeting a flock of birds and has his gun pointed at me, only to find him lying flat on his back, gazing up at the blue summer sky. Scratch that—not gazing. Sleeping. On a blanket laid out on a black tarp, camo hat shading his eyes. The bastard is napping.

I walk upright, at a normal pace, over to the dozing man. Packaged beef jerky peeks from each pocket of his camouflage vest, while a set of empty plastic beer rings is folded underneath this guy's husky frame.

Husky. Something Gerald called me until I hit my growth spurt at age fourteen.

With my sneakered toe, I nudge his heel. The snoring hitches, then continues, business as usual. An orange badge sits nearly hidden behind some of the jerky—a hunting pass.

This guy must have come out here alone, itching to use the new pass he probably had to enter a lottery for, and unwilling to let a day go by without a beer. Pathetic. And—thinking of the wild shot that set the flock of birds in a frenzy—dangerous.

Digging behind the jerky requires less dexterity and finesse than I initially fear. This guy is passed the hell out. I check the top two pockets and find empty gum wrappers, but the bottom two pockets of his vest offer the real Cracker Jack prizes: two credit cards, thirty twenty-dollar bills, and his car keys.

I tuck the keys back inside without blinking. I'm brazen in a lot of ways, both for my age and for the times, but I'm not stupid. Stealing a car when I have a perfectly good one would be a bonehead move. I check the duffel bag beside his camo trousers. Lots of good stuff in there—a first aid kit, rain gear, a headlamp, more snacks, a hunting knife, rubber gloves, and trash bags—but the standout win would be the handgun. A nine millimeter, if my brief gun education by Old Man Gilpin was accurate.

Why bring a handgun out here on a hunting trip to bag some waterfowl? The hunter might have a paranoid streak.

"For good reason," I say out loud. Grabbing the nine-millimeter and the hunting knife, I start pulling out trash bags and the first-aid kit to take with me, when I realize I could use everything stuffed inside the duffel—even the lousy nutrition of the convenience-store chips.

The man stirs. He snorts twice, then rolls his head to the side. Blurry vision, no doubt, makes him rub his eyes upon seeing me. He starts to sit up, but I release the safety of the handgun. The ominous click that reverberates from one rock wall against the other makes him freeze.

"Sorry, pal," I say. "Wrong place, wrong time for you."

The gunshot erupts in the canyon much the same as it did earlier, but this time the ducks are long gone. The hunter slumps back flat on the ground, the camo hat knocked clear from his head.

Standing over the body, I purse my lips. The bullet hole is slightly off-center above the eyebrows. Blood trickles from the circular wound. I wait for the guilt or rush of emotion that I've seen people exhibit in movies after killing someone—but nothing comes. Nothing ever does.

It's been a while since I've used a gun like this. I'm sure it will come in handy again.

Sliding the driver's license, credit cards, and cash into my back pocket, I hoist the duffel bag over my shoulder. I turn back the way I came and begin the hike up to ground level, to the tall grass and rushing sound of the river.

The coyotes, foxes, and maybe even the elk will appreciate the gift I left behind.

Maybe the porcupine will return for a quick nibble too.

As I reach my truck and throw the black bag in the cab, a pang of disappointment lingers. I turn and survey the vista behind me, part of me sad to be trading this in for big-city living. Yet totally relieved I'll be able to be myself in plain sight soon.

I retrieve the map from the glove box and unfold it to display Washington State and my route up the middle. Seattle is only a few hours away, and once there I'll want to keep a low profile as I learn the rhythm of the city.

After I land in Seattle, that's it. No more bumfuck countryside, no more backwater amenities and hillbilly gossip.

Wherever the road leads next on my way up north, I'll have to pause somewhere for gas again and to stretch my legs. Maybe I can poke around that location for a few days. Kick around with the locals for a bit. See the sights. Enjoy what they have to offer before settling into metropolitan life.

A hundred miles speed by while I daydream about life by the water. Cool air. Sea breeze. Salt on my tongue instead of eau de manure in my mouth.

Signs begin to appear more regularly and announce the city of Wenatchee is coming up in ten miles. Restaurants, bars, gas stations, and fast-food places too. All likely to be pretty expensive.

I take the next exit into a small town instead. This seems as good a stop as any and probably cheaper than the city.

Rolling into the downtown, I spot the perfect place to get my bearings. Get a drink. Maybe some fries. And ask around for camping sites. Maybe a motel if I decide to hang out awhile, thanks to the hunter's flush pockets.

The words LAINEY'S OFFICE blink in neon letters from the bar's window. Rustic saloon doors make me feel like I'm traveling back in time to the Wild West.

A bartender with a lightning bolt tattooed down her cheek throws me a flirty grin. "What'll it be, stranger?"

I slide onto a barstool, then tap my fist on the copper counter. "Whiskey. Neat."

She grabs a bottle, not even bothering to check my ID. No regrets about growing this beard the last couple of months. I watch as the dark honey liquid fills a snifter.

"Thanks," I say. "So what's there to do here in Rock Island?"

"Hot days like these, you'll want to head down by the river. Kayak rentals are available along the boardwalk."

I sip my drink, thirsty after the drive. "Rad. I'll check it out."

Nineteen

IVY

Waxing Gibbous

Cutting the engine of my rental, I park along a curb in Wenatchee's commercial district.

Poe is motionless on the sidewalk, looking up at the winery he told me he went to with clients last weekend. Longish hair that seemed brown in the bar's dim lighting appears sandy-blond outside beneath the summer sun. His beard is as I remember it, though: thick and full, and could probably chop its own stack of firewood. Seeing me, he breaks into a smile.

Although he promised he'd wait out front for me before heading to a meeting, I wasn't sure he would. He said his cell phone is busted, that he's waiting on a replacement from his work's IT department, so there was no way of knowing if his plans changed.

A spark of excitement lights up inside me as I cross to him. He's younger than I pegged him for.

"Sweet ride," he says.

"Beater cars are trending. Jealous?"

"Deeply. You ready for this?" He widens his stance.

"I think so."

Two days ago at the bar, I filled him in on the damage done to my first rental car. When he asked what my plans were for the rest of my extended visit, I said I wanted to learn more about the Full Moon Killer. Tristen's furious reaction to my questions about Terry's involvement with the murders stuck with me. Plus, one avenue after another for identifying my birth father keeps shutting down. If he killed my mother, I want to know. Don't I? It's not just the medical data; it's having a whole view of myself. Of where I come from.

"Nice. Don't forget—allow your uncle to talk. Oftentimes, people admit to all kinds of stuff when they're just trying to fill the silence." Hazel eyes narrow in earnest.

I nod, grateful for his tutoring. Poe says he's been watching people all his life, which is why he's so good at sales. He tells people what they want to hear, and observes them when they think no one is watching. It made sense to me, even if his words set off alarm bells in my chest—even if he's pulling those same tactics with me, it's exactly what I should be doing with my Rock Island family.

He tucks straight hair behind his ear. "You look great. I mean, it's fun seeing you in the daylight. I've been thinking about you."

Watching him stumble through a compliment, I step closer on the sidewalk beside him—bending to a desire to narrow the distance. Each time we meet, some current between us seems to amplify.

We lock eyes. A car honks from over at the neighboring stoplight, and I glance away.

"Yeah," I begin. "I've been thinking how nice it is, that we randomly met here."

"Couldn't agree more." He beams. "I gotta get going, though. My meeting started ten minutes ago."

"I'm sorry I kept you."

"Nah, don't worry about it. It's for that farming corporation I mentioned, and I could talk cow-country marketing in my sleep." He shrugs. "See you at Lainey's Office later?"

"If this goes badly, I might be there before five." I laugh.

He wraps me in a hug. Strong arms twine around my waist, pressing me to his canvas jacket. I breathe deep and his scent is sweet, like apples. Wildflowers.

"See you soon, Ivy."

I watch until he reaches the end of the block, then uses the crosswalk to turn left. Car traffic hums along the main road, in contrast to the untamed vines that snake up the walls of a building straight out of Tuscany. Noble Winery, notable for its good reviews and prime drinking location, according to Yelp.

The double doors of the courtyard are wide open this afternoon. After a quick glance back to the street, searching for prying eyes—anyone who might be watching, like the person who destroyed my rental car or crept into my room—I duck through, then step inside the tasting room.

Heads snap toward me at the entryway. At the counter, three stilettoed women whisper together, and the words "no suspects yet" reach my ears. At a bistro table in the center, a man wearing a jean biker jacket leans over a white wine, frowning at his phone's screen. A group of bachelorettes in tiaras occupies the entire wall to my left, but their mood is grim. Not at all normal for a celebratory outing.

The body found at Malaga's riverfront two days ago hasn't yet been identified, and the stress on the area's residents is beginning to show.

No Terry in sight.

I step out back to a table with chairs at the edge of a yellowing embankment above the river. Withdrawing the crossword book from my bag, I lay it open on the table and examine four across: *If you have it, you don't share it; if you do share it, you don't have it.*

Counting the available squares, I solve this riddle faster than any other so far. *Secret.*

"Ivy."

Blue-gray eyes peer at me. The most somber of all the Caine faces I've met. "Hey, Terry."

I tuck the crossword book away in my tan bag, beside the notebook I've been writing dates and facts in. Terry slides into the Adirondack chair opposite mine with a glass of red clutched in his hand.

"I worried you didn't show but then homed in on that bedazzled yellow dragonfly." He nods to my shoulder.

I blush, glancing at the embellished brooch on my shirt. "Sequins. But I'm happy you found me."

A server arrives at our table and offers me a tasting flight. I hesitate, craving the numbing relief, before opting for a single glass of chardonnay.

The server disappears indoors while Terry fixes me with a curious expression.

"Not sure if anyone told you this, Ivy, but addiction definitely runs in our family. Blame it on the Irish roots. No judgment—" He salutes me with his wine. "Just wanted to share what I can."

"Thanks. That's exactly what I was hoping for—more detail. You've been the most specific out of everyone, so I wanted to circle back to you."

"Sure thing. What are your questions?"

Terry takes another sip of wine. A slight paunch strains his polo shirt, but it's an upgrade from the bathrobe I last saw him in.

My meeting with Tristen was eye-opening, if disastrous. Seeing One Family's bizarre former code of ethics made me realize that the graduation party I attended with Lottie was more than some celebration—it was a One Family gathering, complete with romance-based recruitment tactics, despite Tristen's claim that the organization had changed. Their rebranding had been thorough, at least according to their public-facing website. Instead of any hint of the cult's crime-related history or its continued, disturbing sexual recruitment strategies, the home page characterized One Family as a "nonprofit dedicated to serving the Pacific Northwest" and featured an image of a young woman in a One Family T-shirt giving a bowl of food to a man wrapped in blankets on a sidewalk.

I peer at my uncle, at the pudgy shoulders and his obvious appreciation for the finer things. Is his soft appearance a cover-up for a more sinister personality? A predator hiding in high Egyptian thread counts?

"I haven't heard a lot about Richard, your father," I begin. "Did anyone on his side of the family have medical conditions? Beyond addiction."

Terry folds his arms across his belly. "My dad's older brother had prostate cancer. He passed before Dad did. But that's about it. Younger brother is alive and healthy, living in Oregon."

"What happened to your dad?"

"A heart attack. When he was about my age, actually."

I take a pull of my chardonnay. "What about my birth father? Did you ever hear anything about him? Either from Tatum or, maybe, the police investigation of her disappearance?"

Terry's eyes pinch at the corners. "Tatum didn't have a boyfriend at that time, and there's no mention of your birth father. I read the file after I got in good with the team from Wenatchee Archives, where all of Rock Island's affairs are stored. Tatum had a date the day of her disappearance, according to witnesses, but it was someone else. A white guy she met at the shop where she worked. Not your birth father."

Someone else? Reflecting back on Liam the reporter's account of her last day, I remember Tatum met with Aggie; Mal, her coworker; Hector, her boss; and Tristen, before going to a party. Did Liam omit the fact that Tatum had a date, or did he not know?

Crestfallen at yet another sign that I'm missing important information, I focus on a knot in the wooden table, nearly hidden by a laminated happy-hour menu. "Well, did that person check out, at least? Did he have an alibi for when she disappeared?"

Terry nods, threading his fingers together. "Dermot McCoy. He did. And he left town shortly after. Went back to college early, once the police gave him the okay."

"I'm sorry—there was nothing in the case file about my father? At all?"

The factual air softens. "No, Ivy. He wasn't relevant."

The wine spools in my belly. Emboldened by the alcohol, I lean forward. "What about Geri Hauser? You dated her."

Terry snorts, then stops short. "I'll be damned. You're not letting this go, are you?"

I don't reply. I'm unsure how to reply to that.

He taps his lips with his finger. "So you didn't come up here for any inheritance—just the truth about all of us, huh?"

"Did you date her?"

"We went out a few times."

"How long before she was killed? Why didn't you share that earlier?"

He splays both hands flat on the table. "Call me crazy, Ivy, but that's not something I like to lead with."

"Why not?"

Terry turns his head toward the river. "It wasn't serious. Everyone dates everyone in a small town; it's gross." He laughs, looking to me for a smile, but I don't appease him.

"Look, Ivy, I was questioned by the police for days. I had nothing to do with Geri's death, and it was heartbreaking to see someone so young and beautiful be ripped away from her family and community."

I raise an eyebrow at the slick reply. "What about One Family? I found a photo of you and Geri at some One Family event. Were you a member?"

"No," he scoffs.

"But this club or cult—or whatever it was—plays into the Full Moon Killer investigation."

Terry purses his lips. "Ivy, I gotta say this is starting to feel like a deposition. I get that you want to learn what happened to Tatum, but—"

"You don't have the answers, I know. It's just that One Family and the killer were both active in this region for about a decade or so. Geri Hauser, the second victim, was in One Family, and tried to get you to join, right? And Tristen was in One Family too."

"That's right," he says, frowning. "Tristen didn't tell me and our mom about her membership until years later—said that building her world around it was her way of coping with her depression after a breakup, then dealing with Tatum's presumed death. She said Stacey Perez's cousin, Yolanda Underwood, was a member too. Yolanda helped Tristen to process Tatum's loss."

"That wasn't noteworthy to the police? That a cousin of a different victim was a member of One Family?"

He shakes his head. "That's as far as the connection went. The police asked everyone about a possible link between One Family and the Full Moon murders, but no one would talk. Cult members were instructed to keep their mouths shut or face punishment, apparently."

"Instructed by whom?"

"Cult leaders. Only a select few even knew their identities, so I don't think the police ever figured them out. The leaders ruled with an iron fist."

"Sounds like it. What about the victims themselves? Was there evidence of some kind of . . . I don't know, cult ritual, at the crime scenes?"

Terry hesitates. "I would've said no until last month's victim was found—the day-care provider was cut open. It could have been an animal that got to her before she landed in the river, but it seemed to me like someone got carried away performing some kind of . . . procedure."

He winces, watching my reaction. "You know, maybe I shouldn't be telling you all of this."

The first two victims were physically assaulted—strangled, plus bludgeoned in Geri Hauser's case; I knew that. But this detail about last month's victim hasn't been made public yet. It seems that Terry is in good with someone investigating the case this time around.

"No, it's fine," I say. "It's what I asked for. I need to know." I lift my glass and down the rest of my chardonnay. Warmth slides along my chest, giving me the reprieve to gather myself, to blink back images of a woman's body opened wide. The way a taxidermist might ready a specimen for preservation.

"You said that you turned to forensics after Tatum died," I say, choosing each word carefully. "How do you think Tristen handled the loss of Tatum? How did Aggie?"

Terry heaves another sigh, then checks his watch. His wineglass is empty. "Our mom didn't speak to anyone outside the family and the police for about a month after it happened. She barely spoke to me. Mostly, she scrapbooked. I think it was her way of trying to make sense of everything, if she could just get all the information in front of her and contained in a single bound book, you know?"

I nod, understanding that desire well.

"And Tristen." He pauses to stare at the polished wood of the table. "Well, I think she chose death in an effort to control it. The art of it, the way an organism might live on after it. She once said if someone could take away our family member, she could give back someone else theirs."

He checks his watch again. "I got to get going. More work to do before I head home."

"Do you believe that? What Tristen said?"

Terry stands. Slowly, he pushes the chair back into the table. "Ivy, the moon is in waxing gibbous. Do you know what that means?"

"Yes," I reply, startled. "The full moon should be here in two days."

A smile hits the corner of his mouth. "Correct. If I were you, I would stick close to Lottie for the rest of your visit. Family is everything."

His parting words, "Family is everything," are something my own parents would have said to me.

In this context, however, the phrase sounded more like a warning.

———

Stepping out of my car, I peer up at the great Victorian that is the Caine house. Light from the third-story attic catches my eye; Lottie must be home. I should have called her to let her know I'd be back later than expected, but I needed time to catalog the new information Terry had provided.

As I enter the foyer, the house is quiet. Eerily so.

Shuddering from déjà vu after yesterday's discovery of my letter, I climb the staircase to the second floor and call out, "Lottie? You here?"

The garage door was closed when I drove up, and I didn't check to see whether Lottie's Civic was parked inside.

Steely fear slips over me like a plastic bag. My chest constricts as I recall the One Family code of ethics that Tristen shared with me, the blackmail that was employed against their members, at least until Tristen left, and the secrecy with which the cult has operated, preserving the identities of their elders even from the police. They could be anyone. Anywhere.

On the way here, a car drove behind me for a good mile. I thought that part of the road was too narrow to pass me, but what if, instead, I was being followed? What if it was the same car that followed me when I ran out of here after finding the newspaper clipping?

Floorboards moan above me, the only answer to my calling Lottie's name. I shuffle to the end of the hallway, past Lottie's bedroom, then mine, to the narrow set of steps leading to the attic. A light is on above.

Clutching the thin iron railing, I reach the landing at the top of the stairs, then open the door. The haunting, metallic sound of eighties music whispers from across the attic, long ago carpeted and organized with shelves and plastic tubs. A woman sits with a gauzy white veil cascading down her back. I suck in a breath.

"Ivy?" Lottie turns her head. "Hey, you're home."

"Hey. You're . . . playing dress-up?" I rub my elbows, surprised at my frantic heartbeat.

She stands to face me. The opaque material swirls at her hips, and a sheepish grin spreads across her full cheeks. "I got a little carried away. My mom wore this when she married my dad, and Grandma Aggie wore it to her own wedding. I was thinking it could be fun for us to dig through this stuff together. You have all the photo albums, but maybe we could flip through the yearbooks? You know, after you've been out sightseeing all day."

Lottie waves at two cardboard boxes with labels I can't discern from here. Only a desk lamp sitting on the floor beside her illuminates the space, along with moonlight spilling in from a set of curtainless windows at the far end of the house. The attic stretches behind her, covering almost the full length of the second floor; a creepy, child-size door in the corner must lead to the sunroom located in the tall, south-facing turret of the house. I won't be confirming before tomorrow's daylight, in any case.

Guilt scrapes a jagged nail along my temples—I didn't want to tell Lottie that I intended to question Terry again, so this morning I did a quick search for attractions in the region, then texted her I'd be visiting a national park a few hours away.

"Lottie, I really appreciate you going to such effort—"

"It's no problem. I enjoy it."

"—and I'm sorry, but I'm exhausted. I have a ton of emails to catch up on for work. I've been ignoring them for days now." After spending a month's rent to extend my trip, I'm going to need the income. God knows what medical bills are in store for me.

Her smile fades. Blonde hair sits askew on her shoulders, and her green khakis appear creased, as if she's been up here for hours.

Suddenly, Lottie rips the veil off her head, as if to throw it to the floor. She pauses just short of doing it, and we both stare at the quivering fabric.

"You know, Ivy, I've really enjoyed our time together. It's almost been like . . . I don't know, call me sentimental—like having a sister." Her normally airy voice hardens. She meets my look of surprise. "But this is not how you treat sisters—I know that much. Maybe that's what you do with your brother, but family doesn't just use each other like this."

"Oh really?" Her dig at me sets me off. "Isn't that what One Family did to your mother, and maybe to mine? Why did you take me to a One Family party?"

"What are you talking about?" The veil slaps the air.

"Yara's grad party. It was a One Family event. Did you not see all of the weird shit going on there? The handshakes, the flirting, the trawling older men and women?"

Lottie shakes her head. "I seriously have no idea what you're talking about. My mom was in One Family ages ago, and yes, it was a messed-up cult back then. But now it's some kind of social club. Some nonprofit organization, like the Freemasons. Yara's dad is a member. The Rock Island mayor is a member, and he's hosting some event for our family next month." She frowns. "Is this why you've been avoiding me? Because you're getting caught up in stories my mom told you? Did she also tell you she was on a lot of drugs back then? She did awful things to people she loved, including my dad, Aggie, Terry—"

"Because One Family blackmailed her. They forced her to."

"Look, Ivy, I appreciate you deciding to stay longer, but I thought it was to spend more time with me. To learn more about our family, not One Family."

"Lottie, that's not—I haven't been—I thought you were busy at work all week?" I stumble through a defense but can't find my footing. Seeing her disappointment snaps me out of my burst of temper. It's been years since I've allowed myself to get this close to anyone, and my lack of practice is showing. Panic tightens my chest at the thought of Lottie writing me off, and losing someone else. "I'm sorry."

"Yeah? Ditching me and going off-grid doesn't seem like it." Her jaw grinds as she lays the veil on top of the nearest box. "No, it's fine. I can catch up on Netflix shows anyway. Good luck getting all your work done."

Lottie shoulders past me, stepping wide of a creepy mannequin—cringe—that I didn't notice while I was staring at the ghost bride sitting on the floor.

Back in my room, the evening hours disappear quickly. Twice, I stand to go talk to Lottie, to apologize for unloading my stress on her, to ask her if she ever found Grandma Aggie's scrapbooks detailing Tatum's disappearance and death, then sink back down to the bed. The third time, I muster the courage to open the door and step into the hallway but see that the light in her room is out.

I need air.

Tiptoeing down the stairs, I head toward the dim night-light in the kitchen. I slip out the back door. Blades of grass tickle my bare feet and ankles, and the air is cool now, the heat of day doused by the moon. Crickets chirp somewhere close by; then an animal howls. I raise my head toward the sky and admire the black canvas with twinkling cutouts.

A round shape rises from the hillside. The dome of the kiln.

Although it's fifteen feet away from the safety of the house, I carry forward as if compelled by gravity. Standing at its face, I can see that the kiln appears well used, its mouth covered in soot. Farther inside and surrounding a flat platform on which items are fired, ashes are steeped in piles in the crack between the wall and base. Something silver blinks from the back wall, facing the moonlight.

I find a branch nearby, no doubt knocked loose by the wind a few days ago. Reaching inside, I usher the shiny object and a mound of thick ash toward me.

A whistle, I think. Slender and narrow, like a miniature flute. Made of sturdier material, like something that might be army issued, or that professional survivalists use. Hunters, maybe.

I poke around with the stick a bit more. Something else glints in the semidarkness.

A tiny piece of metal. Gold.

A gold tooth.

Cold terror roots me to the ground.

It takes me a minute to realize the crickets have all gone silent. Then branches crack from the forest to the east, as if someone is watching me from the shadows.

I tear back to the house, lock the patio door and the front door, then scramble upstairs and into the guest room.

An hour passes while I lie awake in bed, tensing at each shift of the house's structure, every howl of wind that rips through the rafters, the crack of branches replaying over and over again in my head.

I fall asleep.

In my dream, I'm a child again. Around five or six years old and playing at the park. Pigtails slap at my face as I spin in circles by myself. The skies are gray, not unusual in the suburbs of the Bay Area.

A man approaches from over a grassy hill. His figure seems to loom forward, although he remains far off. I look over at my mom and dad, sitting on a bench, bandaging Carson's knee from some fall he just took, then back at him; the man remains, staring. I can feel his eyes. Slick, silvery fear jump-starts me from my daze, and I break into a run, skipping, jumping over the teeter-totter back to my mother's arms, where she catches me, surprised.

When I turn back, the man is gone.

I wake up. I pull the lamp cord and flood the room with light.

Indented onto the skin of my palm, the silver whistle seems to blaze with heat.

Twenty

IVY

When morning finally came, I said hello to Lottie as I passed her in the kitchen and returned to the kiln. The same branch I used last night was flung to the side where I left it. Nothing else seemed disturbed.

Was someone watching me out there? Was that what made the nightlife stop chirping and cooing? Or was I becoming paranoid, on top of everything else?

When I returned, Lottie asked me what was wrong, as if she could see it on my face. I didn't tell her. I was too scared to push her further away than I already had with our fight in the attic.

Besides, Lottie had shared that she was an avid user of the kiln, that everyone in the family had had a phase with it, and that the kiln was unlocked and available to anyone on the hillside. I no longer knew whom to trust.

The moment Lottie left for work, I looked up the number for the *Wenatchee Gazette*. Liam Weathers didn't seem surprised to hear from me, but there was no missing the excitement in his voice when I said that I wasn't calling to ask questions, but because I'd found a piece of evidence that might be tied to the Full Moon Killer. Clearly, he could smell the possibility of a scoop, because he went out of his way to drive over and pick up the baggie with the gold tooth. He promised he'd have a friend of his in the police lab examine it.

I didn't know if I could fully trust Liam, but given that I still wasn't entirely sure of Terry's involvement, enlisting someone outside the family seemed like the smarter choice.

In front of a converted barn at the far end of Main Street, I pass a hand-painted sign announcing a summer sale on mixed corn feed. Bells twinkle as I pull open the door to the shop, reminding me of the whistle I carry in my jeans pocket. Although a unique find, I decided not to mention it to Liam.

Dust mingles with the smell of hay, and a large air-conditioning unit whirs from the corner of the store. A half dozen aisles of shelves are stocked with products on animal nutrition, opaque barrels marking the beginning of each section.

I approach the young woman behind the counter. Purple hair dye contrasts with dark-brown roots as she pops her head up from a stacking game on her phone.

"Welcome to Hermann Feed," she says.

"Is Hector Hermann here? I need to speak to him."

"Just a sec."

While she lifts the receiver of a landline, I scan the thick plastic covering the counter. Beneath it, notices, coupons, and handwritten ads form a checkerboard of dark and light cards—accidentally, I think. A navy-blue real estate broker's card sits beside a yellow piece of lined paper, which is next to a black square with white ink advertising swimming lessons in the next town south.

When Terry first mentioned Tatum's boss, back in his high-rise apartment, I made a mental note to look into Hector. Then at the winery, when Terry shared that most of the people who interacted with Tatum on her last day did so at her part-time job, I made speaking to Hector Hermann a priority.

The cashier hangs up the landline, then resumes clutching her cell. "He's coming. Are you shopping too? We're offering half off on sacks of grain."

"No, not today. Thanks."

A man emerges from a door marked HERMANN FEED ASSOCIATES ONLY, wearing a plaid button-up shirt tucked into jeans, tucked into cowboy boots. Sun spots dot his temples, and deep-set eyes appear weary at 10:00 a.m. Tatum's former boss and the previous owner of Chic Threads.

"Hi there. Can I help you?"

"I'm Ivy Hon. My mother was Tatum Caine." I cast an eye at the cashier, whose head is bent over her game. "Is there somewhere we could talk?"

Hector's demeanor, while friendly and professional at first, shifts to tense and concerned. He looks past my shoulder to the front door. "Are you with the police?"

The cashier lifts her head.

Odd greeting choice. "No. Tatum is my birth mother, and I'm just looking for more information about her."

He leads us to the gravel parking lot adjacent to the store. When he reaches the very back of the lot and the abutting field of tall grass, not yet transformed yellow by the heat, he turns to face me. I pause a good six feet away, aware that I've just isolated myself with a stranger, and I've told no one of my plans or whereabouts today—aware that someone, maybe the Full Moon Killer, trashed my car the last time I approached an empty parking lot like this. They could be anyone. Even a reputable feed-store owner in plaid.

"Ivy, right? What do you want to know?"

"I want to hear about the last time you saw Tatum. From what I understand, she worked a shift at your clothing store."

"That's right."

"What was her mood like? Upset? Calm? Anxious?"

Hector strokes his graying goatee. A layer of dust and straw coats the underside of his forearm. "Not any more upset than usual. She had been depressed for months, in hindsight. I was too wrapped up in making the store a success to notice then. That last day, she was withdrawn but still did her job and helped customers. She was a good one, Tatum. I was . . . it was really hard, when I learned he got her."

"Who did?"

He raises dark eyebrows. "The Full Moon Killer. Everyone had been freaked out about it after the two girls that died the summer before. And the bastard came back about a month ago and got sweet Katrina Oates too. My grandniece was in Katrina's day care. It's all so eerie."

"Did you see any men hanging around the shop the day Tatum died? I heard she had some romantic encounter that day." Not my birth father, apparently.

Hector toes the ground with a cowboy boot. "I didn't know anything about my employees' love lives. Still don't, and try not to get involved. Mal would be the best person to ask about Tatum's. Mal Ngo. She was the other salesgirl on the floor that day."

"Do you know where Mal is now?"

"No clue. I haven't spoken to her since she quit about six months after Tatum died. Said she was going to do big things but never said where."

"Do you think . . . Would you say Tatum's death affected Mal?"

"All of the deaths did. Everyone was affected. It was awful. It still is now, if you've seen the curfew mindset everyone has these days. No one out after dark, especially close to the full moon. My buddy Ross lost his little sister to the killer. He never got over it."

"Really? Who was his sister?"

"Stacey Perez. The first victim."

My neck tingles beneath my french braid. "That must have been devastating for your friend. Did he ever mention One Family to you?"

Hector glares. "I thought you were here to talk about Tatum. What's this about that cult?"

"I am here for . . . I'm learning that One Family was pretty entrenched in this area during the first murders. Geri Hauser was a member, the second victim. I'm wondering if you think Stacey was involved in the One Family organization too."

He takes in my hopeful expression, then grunts. "One Family isn't a club, like a sporting league or a gun-owner association. It's a cult. A sex cult. A woman I was seeing invited me to a meeting once, and I went. Once I was there, it was hard to get out. I never officially joined, but I was pursued like a dog for months."

I nod, hearing echoes of what Terry shared about his experience with Geri Hauser. Recall the way in which good-looking young people seemed especially interested in attendees of Yara's graduation party, and the *True Crime of Washington* chapter on women and cults. "Flirty fishing. I read about that. An attractive woman entices you to join One Family through sex."

Hector juts his lower jaw. Crooked, yellow teeth bite his upper lip. "Yup. Tristen was a very convincing representative."

Blood drains from my face. "Sorry, you said . . . Tristen? As in Tristen Caine?"

He nods. "Yeah, not my finest moment. She started coming around about a year after Tatum passed. When I wouldn't join, I think One Family got people to boycott my shop, because I went under a little while after, and the Caine family name has a lot of sway even without the cult behind it. I had to team up with my dad and his dream of maintaining the family feed shop. Check me out now."

I stare at him, not knowing how to reply. At his pained expression and the clipped way he speaks Tristen's name, as if she's responsible for the subsequent hard years he lived. Tristen was this man's introduction to One Family.

Tristen is linked to Geri Hauser through One Family; Tristen's own little sister was another victim of the killer.

Hector's eyes narrow, watching me. He clears his throat. "You all right, Ivy?"

"Yes, sorry. Do you know of any connection between the killer and One Family? Any rumors?"

He shakes his head. "Until last month, the killer was only a ghost that haunted this area for far too long. But the cult has been kicking around in pockets of the region the whole while."

Disappointment simmers in my throat as Hector returns indoors. The information he shared—that Tristen tried to get him to join the cult, that flirty fishing worked for so many other men, and that he didn't know of any connection between One Family and the killer— all smashes together in my head like letter tiles in a Scrabble bag. Everything I learn feels partially obscured without the full picture accessible—without some resource that contains all the information in one place.

Taking out my phone, I dial the number that Lottie gave me in case of emergencies while I'm in town. The call rings twice; then a woman's voice answers, warm and exactly the way a grandmother should sound. A television laugh track erupts from the background.

"Hi . . . Grandma Aggie. It's Ivy. Hon," I add with a wince. "Would it be okay if I dropped by this afternoon? I was hoping to check out your scrapbooks."

———

Aggie's gray two-story Colonial appears the same as when I visited with Lottie last week, the rose bushes that line the walkway deepening into a vibrant red. If Lottie wasn't able—or willing, after our fight—to find Aggie's scrapbooks in the Caine house attic, then I can go to the source.

As I take the woodchip-covered path, the front door creaks inward, and Aggie greets me with open arms. Ash-blonde hair is pulled up in a ponytail, wisps framing her square face. A paisley print button-up is rolled to her elbows.

"Ivy. C'mon in."

I cross the threshold, and the smell of cookies washes over me in a sugary cloud. Aggie leads me to the sitting room. Three scrapbooks are stacked on a dark coffee table. Next to them, a plate of chocolate chip cookies, a pitcher of water, and two glasses occupy a serving tray.

"Thanks for having me over on such short notice," I say, sitting on a deep, navy sofa.

Aggie takes a seat. Her cheeks are slightly flushed, or she's wearing makeup. Ever the beauty queen. "Pleasure is mine."

When I explained over the phone that I was searching for more clarity around Tatum's death, I expected Aggie to balk at the idea of strolling down memory lane—of picking at the scabs of wounds that would never heal. Instead, she invited me to come by right then and there.

She reaches for the book on top. Bound in white leather, the first page displays a professional portrait of Tatum, taken for her sixteenth birthday. The words *Always in Our Hearts* are written in a looping cursive arc above Tatum's head.

"She's beautiful," I say.

Aggie smiles. "She was. You have her forehead, I think. Your eyes must be your father's, but you have her widow's peak along the hairline."

Warmth churns behind my ribs, and my throat closes, thinking again how I'll never be able to verify whether that's true for myself. Not in person.

I turn the page and come face-to-face with the very newspaper article I found loose in Lottie's photo album. The headline—FULL MOON KILLER'S LATEST VICTIM: TATUM CAINE—glares, stark, from the center of the page beneath a sticky plastic sheet.

"I collected everything I could find on Tatum for years after she disappeared," Aggie says, her voice soft. "Each news article, magazine column, and mention of her that I could find, especially once the internet rolled into use. These three books are basically my life's work."

I pause before turning a page. "What do you think happened to her?"

Aggie twists her lips to the side, a quirk I have when I'm thinking. "Tatum is gone. After thirty years, if she were alive, she would have found her way home to me—found some way to send me a message. I'm not close with a lot of people, Ivy. But I did love my youngest child."

I flip to the next article, preserved from the *Seattle Times*. Aggie's choice of words—she loved her youngest child, and not "all my kids"—strikes me. I wonder whether she's grown distant from Terry and Tristen over the years—after Tristen left One Family and her confessions were used against her? Against the Caine family as a whole? Or maybe Aggie never felt close to them. I'm not a parent, but I've heard enough times that there's always a favorite child in a family that I believe it.

Carson was my parents' favorite child. Wasn't he? But memories of my mom taking me with her on day trips, then of my dad saving me a seat next to him while watching *Jeopardy!*, with Carson sitting on the floor, flash to mind as if in answer.

"Your husband, Richard—were he and Tatum very close?"

Aggie's closed mouth smiles. "I'd say Tristen and he were closer. They were very alike. Always testing society's proverbial walls for weakness. But he had a soft spot for Tatum. He made her anything she desired. A dollhouse, then a coatrack for her winter coats. They were always hiding things for each other around the house. It was a game they played, leaving something of meaning for the other person to find in unexpected places. After he died, she searched for months, hoping to find some remainder of him—just for her—behind."

Sadness swells in my chest. The thought of thirteen-year-old Tatum wandering their home, yearning for one last gift from her dad.

After an hour of turning pages and Aggie sharing memories of the months both following Tatum's death and preceding it, I stand to leave.

"I really appreciate this. Thanks for the cookies," I say.

"My pleasure, Ivy. Why don't you take one of the scrapbooks back to the Caine house?"

I smile. "You don't mind?"

She waves a hand. "Not at all. That way you can snap photos of anything that stands out."

As she escorts me to the door—me with the first scrapbook we opened, the most detailed one—a mix of emotions clutters my mouth.

———

Evening falls, and Lottie and I still aren't talking after our awkward fight in the attic. I tried apologizing again once I returned, but she brushed my words off. Instead, she noted the full pot of spaghetti warm on the stove and the bubbling meat sauce that she said was ready whenever I felt hungry. Then she went upstairs to her room.

It was quintessential cold-shoulder treatment—with a Lottie spin on it.

Night animals murmur in the darkness beyond the porch light, invisible from where I sit on the wicker love seat. Weeping willow trees shade this private cul-de-sac as if in perpetual mourning. Earlier at the kitchen table, I researched Stacey Perez's family and the whereabouts of her heartbroken brother, Ross, whom Hector spoke about.

Light internet sleuthing confirmed there are more than a dozen Ross Perezes living in Washington. I cross-referenced with social media and called a few phone numbers, but none of them led to the correct Ross, based on age and purported hometown. No mention of him in Aggie's scrapbook.

The killer must be linked to One Family, but it's not obvious how. Stacey wasn't a member, but her cousin was; maybe her brother was too, if I could just get ahold of him to confirm. Geri Hauser was a member. Tristen Caine was a member, and her sister, Tatum, was the third victim.

The first three victims could be connected to the cult in some way, and at least two of them were poisoned with an herbicide, but the next two women—Florence Yates, fresh out of college and killed in 1992, and Ashlee Drummond, a kindergarten teacher killed in 1993—don't display any links to One Family. Instead, fatal amounts of morphine were found in their bodies. The same goes for the next two victims, one of whom was found in Portland, Oregon.

Last month, Katrina Oates was killed only a few feet from the riverbank, cut open, and also discovered with excessive morphine in her system for her height and weight. If the killer's MO is to murder young women from the region by poison or morphine beneath the full moon and near the river, there are seven deaths from 1988 to 2006 that fit the bill. A new browser search confirms that paraquat—the herbicide used on both Stacey and Geri—and liquid morphine are each available online for purchase; anyone can buy multiple batches from various sellers, if they scroll long enough.

But what about male victims? The news has been reporting that the body found just this week bears similar marks as some victims of the Full Moon Killer—signs of strangulation, and found at the riverbank.

I pull up Google on my laptop. Five results in, I find what I need: a link to a public-records website displaying Washington crime rates, based on statistics provided by the FBI and its Uniform Crime Reporting Program. I filter deaths by sex and the word *poison*. Cross-referencing dates with the lunar calendar for each year is time-consuming, but I make a chart of victims who fit the Full Moon Killer's MO. Including male deaths, the list of possible victims increases to twenty during the years 1988 to 2006.

I rub my jaw. Try to process what I'm reading. In reality, the FBI may need to add another twelve bodies to their roster of Full Moon

Killer victims. Why has no one seen fit to include male deaths? Has the assumption been that the men committed suicide?

I set my laptop to the side, then rest my head in my hands. My temples pulse as if preparing to launch into a throbbing headache.

Which victim, long thought to be missing, did the gold tooth belong to?

As the only taxidermist in town, Tristen's occupation is more than suspicious when considering that Katrina Oates, the day-care provider, was, in Terry's words, "cut open"—almost as if an animal attacked her.

Most experienced hunters would know how to dress wild game. Tristen can't be the only person in the region who practices those skills. But Tristen also tried to recruit Hector, Tatum's former boss, to One Family. What else is Tristen at the center of that's been hidden all this time?

If Agent Ballo says one of my relatives could be the Full Moon Killer, Tristen might know how to do more with a carving knife than dress a carcass.

I head upstairs. Tomorrow is the full moon, and I'm not ready.

Inside the guest room, I pause at the oval mirror beside the door. Its ornate silver frame is like something out of a gothic romance series I binged a few months ago. My hair is mussed. Dark rings shadow my eyes.

Feeling the fatigue of this whole experience, I lean a hand alongside the mirror, peer closer at the freckles dotting my nose. The wall sinks inward.

Startled, I release my hand and a small, square panel pops ajar. As I pull it open, a dusty bracelet catches the light.

Twenty-One

Tatum

August 17, 1989

The river appears angry when I approach the north bank, white tips crashing against a rock protruding from the center of the rushing current.

Leaving the list of inventory, Hector's complaints, and Mal's teasing grin behind, I breathe in the fresh air and try to shrug off the anxieties of work. I didn't intend to say yes, but Mal's acceptance of Dermot's invite on my behalf did one thing right: it got me out of work early.

Plus, it's Friday afternoon. And Tristen's party doesn't begin until hours from now.

I spot Dermot waiting for me at the river's edge with a bucket full of something in hand. A smile blooms on my face. He lifts it toward me, and the beer glass glints in the sun.

"Feel like happy hour?" Dermot asks, an impish grin dimpling one cheek.

"You're going to get me in trouble." I glance behind me to the storefront still in view.

"An easy fix." He shrugs, then strolls backward along the river's edge.

"Hey, don't fall in. Be careful," I add, watching him pretend to tightrope walk. A tree root trips him up, and he wobbles a moment before regaining his balance.

"Fair enough," he says with a wink. He turns around so we're side by side, facing forward. "How was work?"

"Lame." I sigh. "My boss is on me about stupid stuff and . . . well, you don't want to hear about him, do you?"

Dermot props the bucket of beers on a tan shoulder, then gives an exaggerated groan as if the six bottles are heavier than they look.

We come to a wooded part of the riverbank that backs up to the outskirts of Main Street. Definitely more secluded but still close enough to civilization—to help, if needed. The actual island named Rock Island seems to float across from us in the widest part of the river.

A memory from high school flits to mind: how some kids would take dinghies out there to drink, smoke, and have sex. They called it *Rocked* Island. A fresh blush warms my cheeks, and it has nothing to do with the late-afternoon heat soaking my skin.

Dermot swings the bucket down to his side. "Well, I did ask *you* to the river and not your boss."

"Pretty sure he's seeing someone anyway. Not up for grabs."

Dermot's free hand brushes mine. "Good thing my broken heart mends fast."

We come to a stop beside a checkered picnic blanket, nearly hidden beneath a weeping willow and complete with an open metal lunch pail containing two sandwiches. A single rose pokes from the aluminum.

Mischief glints in Dermot's eyes. "Hungry?"

My stomach flutters as I realize this guy went to a lot more effort than I did. I peer down at my outfit, which must smell like musty clothing and faux-vanilla body spritzer after standing in the shop for the last six hours. I definitely could have freshened up. Added some lipstick, at least.

I absorb the thoughtful scene again, impressed by the show of chivalry. A hard, mean part of me wonders how many times he's created this exact setup for other girls. Another thought interrupts my masochism to wonder whether Tristen would remember him from high school, since she's four years older.

Dermot takes my hand. His touch is smooth. Butterflies thrum in my stomach as I meet his curious gaze.

"Ham and cheese okay?" he asks.

I release the breath I've been holding, ready to give this—to give normalcy, an invite for a day date—another try. "That's great."

We settle down on the soft blanket. Dermot hands me a sandwich, then pops off the top of a beer, offering the sweating glass to me. The air is dry, as it always is in mid-August, but the easy breeze from the river makes it comfortable.

"Thanks." I take a long pull, allowing the beer to relax the tension between my shoulders, to carry me into the weekend, away from Chic Threads. I'll have to go back on Sunday afternoon, but at least I get the day off tomorrow.

"Did you play varsity football?" I ask between bites of the sandwich. He's added just the right amount of mayo.

Dermot shakes his head. "Track and field. Still don't believe we went to school together, huh?"

I almost choke on my bread. "Of course I do."

He rolls his cat eyes toward the clear-blue sky. "Right, because you give every old friend a blank stare when they come into the shop."

"Okay, I was a little unsure at first, but it's coming back to me now. You were friends with Mickey Sales, right? You guys did hurdles together?"

"Javelin. The stick you throw," he adds, when I do that blank thing with my face again.

"See? It's a locked safe up here." I rap my knuckles against my head for emphasis, and he laughs.

"Well, I remember how you were always hanging around the art room," he says. "And how a vase that you made in ceramics won a blue ribbon at the Wenatchee arts-and-crafts fair."

"Wow, good memory."

"It was pretty impressive. I read about it on the bulletin board in the quad."

We share a smile, then bite into our sandwiches. Being here, beside the river where the current is pushing leaves and fish and life downstream, I can almost recall the person I used to be—the confident kind who entered contests and won prizes. Before everything went to crap and I began receiving veiled threats from people I thought I knew. Staring at Dermot, I'm pretty certain I do remember him from school. Or recall Tristen mentioning him.

We cheers another beer, then another. With each successive empty bottle, I feel released from my self-imposed chains, so consumed was I with maintaining appearances on account of the great Caine family name. Screw that.

When Dermot leans in for a kiss, I meet him halfway. I let the taste of his beer and my happy full stomach dictate my next move and do what feels good for a change, instead of what's right.

When he pushes my sweater down around my chest, revealing the tank top underneath, I pull it back up and over my head. Let the cotton fabric fall to the picnic blanket.

I reach for his jeans, then pop the top button open. His lips are soft, warm, and as I press his hand to my breasts, Dermot moans. "Tatum, I've thought about this for so long . . ."

Instead of answering—wondering what that could mean—I turn my head, and he kisses my neck to the skin behind my ear. His hand glides along my thigh to brush between my legs—a feathery touch that grows into delicious pressure applied at just the right angle. My breath hitches, relishing the moment.

As he climbs on top of me, I lean back until my head finds the blanket and my vision fills with lush green leaves and hanging branches—willow trees drinking water from the river and bearing witness to our tryst. He fondles my backside, my breasts, kissing them as I strip down to my bra and underwear, and I hear rustling in the bushes behind us, farther up the hill. Likely, from near the footpath we broke away from to arrive here, but I don't care. I'm done caring. I cared so much before, and it cost me everything.

He slides out of his jeans, then lays his full weight on top of me—a dense, pleasurable warmth. We maintain eye contact as he wraps the blanket around us.

It's the first time I've behaved so freely, or—as my family would say if they only knew—promiscuously, embarrassingly, immorally.

Peering above me, seeing foliage, sky, and thick, dirty-blond hair, I know that nothing worse can come of this than already has.

With an arch of his body, he pushes into me, and I curl around his figure, gasp from the instant, trembling pleasure, and accept the consequences, whatever may come.

Twenty-Two

IVY

Full Moon

Across from the steepled church, I stand frozen on the pavement in front of the diner where Uncle Phillip suggested we meet. There's a shadow occupying the stained-glass window directly facing me beneath the church bells. Staring at me.

My phone buzzes with a message from Carson. A video of Onyx playing with a charger cord on my living-room floor. Carson has checked in twice, asking where I store the catnip and extra kitty litter, but I haven't offered any new details about my trip, and he hasn't asked.

Glancing back up to the stained-glass window, I find the square empty; the shadow is gone. I brush back a strand of hair that's fallen from my crown braid, and the bangle I found in the secret compartment—neither of which Lottie had any idea about—dangles from my wrist. Was I imagining the shadow overhead? Or am I simply on edge, with today being the full moon?

Inside the diner, Uncle Phillip occupies a booth along the rear wall, stirring a spoon in a white ceramic mug. He wears the same pair of overalls he was wearing at Yara's graduation party. A large industrial fan on the floor blows his thick white hair to the side—prime location, given the sticky heat outdoors.

I hadn't planned on seeing Phillip again, not after he tried to break into the guest room the first night I arrived or his bizarre behavior at the graduation party.

Then I thought about Tatum's disappearance, the loss Aggie still feels, the guilt that Tristen harbors, and my own unexplored grief. When I first walked into the Caine house, I had every intention of learning my medical history, then leaving a week later; but the more I pull the thread of the story surrounding Tatum's presumed death, the more I feel certain that details about my own life are related.

"Ivy," Uncle Phillip says, scooting to the edge of the vinyl.

"Hi there. Please, don't get up." I take a seat across from him. No matter how often I hear Lottie call aunts and uncles by their first names, I feel my own mother's iron grip on my shoulder, reminding me to show respect. "Uncle Phillip" still feels too familiar, however. Especially given my suspicions surrounding his involvement.

He is the right age to have been an active murderer in the late eighties and nineties. He's a white male, never been married, and attractive, from what I could tell from old photographs. All the better to lure young women close.

Uncle Phillip slides back into the booth. "I will admit I was surprised to receive your invitation, grandniece. To what do I owe the pleasure?"

He grins a row of large discolored teeth as a server arrives at our table. She takes my order of a Diet Coke and Uncle Phillip's seltzer-water request. He makes a joke about having all the energy he wants. *No need for caffeine in these old bones!* The young woman leans in as she laughs, thrusting her cleavage forward in her low-cut shirt, and Uncle Phillip stiffens.

The server leaves to grab our drinks.

"I appreciate you meeting me. Since I only have a few more days here, I wanted to circle back to your understanding of Tatum's disappearance."

"Her murder, you mean."

I hesitate, caught off guard. This is the first time a family member has used such a stark term for Tatum's fate.

"Yes. Her murder. By the Full Moon Killer. I was wondering what you think Tatum has in common with the other victims—why she caught the killer's attention. Stacey Perez was a high school cheerleader about to start senior year, and Geri Hauser was a college coed home for the summer. They were all pretty normal girls, as far as I can tell. All young women from the same town—but that doesn't explain the other victims later on, Florence Yates and Ashlee Drummond, who traveled around the area and had a history of infractions."

Florence was caught stealing from a bakery at sixteen; then she was arrested for skinny-dipping in 1990 as a twenty-year-old. Ashlee Drummond was written up by both the Rock Island and Wenatchee police for trespassing in multiple homes before she was arrested for assaulting a man who she says tried to kidnap her.

Uncle Phillip rubs his chin. White stubble that could comb through cat fur makes an audible sound as he scratches. "They seem pretty alike to me. Florence was a young thing back in the nineties, but she was known around town for being . . ."

His voice trails off, and he stares at a framed drawing of two children eating ice-cream cones. "Florence was known for providing sexual favors to younger boys for money. If that's not a connection, I don't know what is."

"Sorry . . . sexual favors? What connection is that . . . Tatum wasn't . . . she didn't do that."

With a heavy sigh, Uncle Phillip lifts weary blue eyes to mine. "Ivy, how do you think you came about? I hate to be the one to tell you this, but your parents were not some star-crossed lovers. They were transactional acquaintances. You were . . ."

Tears prick from behind my eyes, and I work to keep my voice steady. "A mistake? I was a transaction gone wrong, and they weren't supposed to conceive. Is that what you're saying?"

Uncle Phillip shakes his head. "My friend in the police department told me, off the record, once he retired. A lot of young people were making money in strange ways then. I shouldn't have said anything. I'm sorry."

He watches helplessly as I fix my gaze on the same framed photo of the two kids—innocently enjoying ice cream and unaware of the hedonism of the 1980s to come.

Is it true? If Uncle Phillip learned this off the record, then it makes sense that Terry wouldn't have read in Tatum's case file about . . . whatever Uncle Phillip is implying.

What is he implying? That Tatum was an escort? A sex worker? The idea is so unlike everything I've heard about her, but I can't dismiss the sincere pity drooping his cheeks.

Inhaling a shaky breath, I try to remember who I am—my parents' daughter. Harold and Vivian Hon adopted me within days of my birth, deliberately and intentionally, as they had desired a little girl to round out their family for years. Lots of adopted babies are surprises to those who conceived them. All of them are ultimately wanted by the parents who choose to raise and love them. Even though this news hits me like a punch to the throat, I'm no different.

"Thank you. For telling me. But the sexual promiscuity or sexual manipulation you say Tatum wielded, and so did Florence, doesn't extend to Stacey Perez, Geri Hauser, or Ashlee Drummond."

Uncle Phillip sucks his teeth. "Maybe. Maybe not. I'm more internet savvy than I might appear, and there's been some speculation on each of those girls. Just trying to help you out on your quest."

He smiles, forming the last word: *quest*. As if I'm starring in one of the Netflix adventure shows I binge regularly. I don't know if he means it condescendingly or as a good-natured joke, but I grimace in return.

"What was Tatum like, as a young girl?" I ask.

"She was thoughtful. An introvert, often prone to reading in her room all day or doing word games—crosswords—while Tristen and Terry would run around the property until dusk."

At the mention of crosswords, my mind jumps to the one that's half completed in my bag beside me.

"I only saw Tatum once during her whole pregnancy, at Christmas, when she was around five months along apparently. She had her secrets," he adds.

I take a sip of my drink. "I think a lot of teenage girls do."

Phillip shares memories of growing up in this town. I learn that his and Aggie's father held two consecutive terms as mayor, and during World War II their mother single-handedly led the creation of Rock Island's victory garden, dedicating fifty acres of Caine-family land to the cause. After another Diet Coke and an exasperated sigh from the server, who probably hoped we would order more than drinks, I rise to leave.

"Have a good rest of your Thursday."

"Oh, I will," he says, matching my movements and getting to his feet with effort. "Each day passes the way it should, the way God wants it— and ends with a hard lemonade." Phillip flashes me another winning grin.

We exit the diner together; then he heads left while I go right toward my parked car. The sky is beautiful above downtown, blue with a hint of pink as the sun begins to dip.

As I reach my rental car, I continue past it. The bar is only a few blocks away, and I'm eager to see if Poe is there grabbing an early-evening drink.

Phillip seemed to genuinely grieve his memories of Tatum. But the connection he drew between the killer's victims and sexual impropriety still strikes me as faulty. Reaching. Maybe informed by some personal bias. What did he say about each day—it passes the way it should—the way that God wants it to? Phillip, Aggie's older brother by five years, could be more conservative than I realized.

Could I really be a transaction gone wrong?

The kitschy saloon doors are half-open. Inside the bar, a man I recognize slouches at the counter. Bass pumps from the speakers, louder than usual.

"Liam?"

His head wobbles up. We make eye contact, and it's obvious that the journalist is drunk. From the empty glasses lining the counter, he's been here awhile.

"Ivy." A smirk pulls his thin lips. Graying brown hair is swept into a ponytail, and his clothes seem to hang off his gangly frame. He takes a step toward me.

I look for the usual bartender, but there's only a guy behind the counter that I've never seen before, wearing a black apron and scrolling through his phone.

"The mystery child herself," Liam slurs.

I pause, taking in the empty bar around us. "Were you waiting for me?"

"Nah." He slaps a hand at the air. "I stop here on my way home sometimes. After long days."

"Was today a bad one?"

"Oh yeah. Worst in a long time."

"What happened? Did your friend in the crime lab examine the tooth?" I try to get the barback's attention to order a drink, but he's still looking at his phone.

Anger creases Liam's face before it crumples. "He did."

"Really? Well, what did he say?"

Liam sways to the left, then recenters himself. "Seamus Thatcher. The gold tooth belongs to him. He went missing in 1994, the day of the full moon. So there you have it. The Full Moon Killer has been offing men all along, not just women."

The smell of liquor rolls off him in waves. His anxiety makes sense—being the expert journalist seems to be his whole identity. The adoring glances, the reporters lining up to speak to him as the authority on the Full Moon Killer.

"I'm a fraud." He sniffles. "Everyone thinks I know everything about the killer, but look at Seamus. Poor Seamus. Just waiting to be identified for decades now."

"Can a gold tooth really survive the heat from a kiln, and over that many years?"

"Melting point of gold is higher than what kilns usually reach. Crime Lab Lennie told me that. So yes."

There's a photo of Uncle Terry in his twenties—longish hair, strong shoulders—standing in front of the family kiln. Lottie said that everyone has had a ceramics phase, but how long ago was Terry's?

"Well, we still don't really know if Seamus is a Full Moon victim, but this could be proof we're on the right track," I say, choosing my words with care. "If the Full Moon Killer didn't exclusively kill women, maybe there are more victims. The more accurately we understand what links them, the better we can identify the killer."

He looks over my shoulder, eyes glassy. "I thought I understood, back when I thought your mom was killed by the guy. Now, who knows who did it?"

"Liam, what are you saying? Are you backing off your theory that Tatum was a Full Moon victim?"

"Maybe."

"But who else could have gotten her? Someone in One Family?"

He snorts. "Probably."

I pause, absorbing the cavalier way Liam is speaking. Pop music seems to swell from the bar's speaker system. "Why do you say that?"

He glares at me. "You're too close to this, and you don't even know it. Phillip Caine was a member of One Family. But I'll bet you won't hear that from any of your relatives."

I stare at him, unable to muster a reply. No one I've spoken with has even hinted at this idea. If what Liam says is true, who else knows about Phillip? Does Terry? Or Tristen?

An image of Phillip and Tatum returns to mind—a photo from one of the albums. They were celebrating Phillip's birthday, for which a young Tatum had created a game of anagrams.

Liam seizes my arm and pulls me close. "But you know what? Even if the gold tooth proves everyone was wrong about the killer's MO, I can be the one to tell the world about it. About the great Caine family whose kiln contained a tooth—and what else? What else are you Caines hiding, Ivy?"

I try to shake him off, but he only grips tighter. "None of you has ever cared for the rest of us. You've only ever thought about yourselves and each other. Tristen Caine almost got me fired early on, and now here you are doing your little detective work and trying to be the new Full Moon Killer expert."

He twists my arm behind my back, spinning me into his chest. Foul, hot breath covers my ear, but I don't dare move, too terrified he'll break my arm.

"Hey!" shouts the bartender.

"I think it's time you went home," Liam sneers.

He pushes me to the floor, where I land with a hard thud. He darts from the bar, the bartender still shouting after him. When I lift my hands, blood dots my dirty palms, tiny pebbles of asphalt tracked in from outside sticking to my skin.

A different man crouches in front of me: Poe. His wide eyes take me in, notice my hands, then pause over the red marks on my arm.

"Are you okay?" Poe asks. Hearing his voice after I've been replaying our last conversation outside the winery in my head adds to my daze.

He helps me stand; then we shuffle to a booth. He had just parked his truck when he heard yelling and saw through the saloon doors that Liam was manhandling me.

"I'll get you some water," he says.

"Whiskey sour. I want that." Some additional balm, please.

He orders at the bar as my forearm begins to pulse. What did Liam say? *I think it's time you went home.* Phillip was in One Family, and the Full Moon Killer may have attacked men.

"Oh shit," Poe starts, returning with two glasses. He reaches for a cocktail napkin and presses it to my elbow. "You're bleeding here too."

He pulls back the white square to reveal a quarter-size splotch of red.

Concern etches his features. It might be the shock still blurring my judgment, but I suddenly want to curl into his canvas jacket and be held by him, cocooned.

"Pretty lucky you came when you did," I say. "I don't think that barback was paying any attention." I peer up from under my eyelashes, aware that I'm flirting.

He smiles, unleashing a thrill of excitement in my chest. "Not by the looks of things."

He slides into my side of the booth, then raises his glass to mine. "Cheers. To good timing."

We each take a drink. The whiskey soothes the tension knotting my frame, and I allow myself to relax.

The danger is over. Liam is gone. Poe is here.

"You sure you're okay?" he asks. "That guy pushed you down pretty hard. I could take you to urgent care."

"No, no—not the hospital. Going there will only make things . . ." My voice trails off as I catch his look of surprise. I haven't shared with Poe anything about my mysterious symptoms or the diagnosis that keeps eluding me. "I just don't like them. Any doctor will want to do some tests, and that's going to lead them to asking more questions and just taking up too much time."

Poe nods, probably sorry he suggested it.

"I'm . . . I'm not a fan," I say.

Another smile. "That's pretty clear. What did he want—that guy? Do you know him?"

I take a deep gulp of my drink. "Not really. He just kind of snapped."

"Seriously. Well, he better not come back. Or maybe he should, and then he and I can talk."

I swirl my ice cubes, watching Poe get protective of me. "So where did you come from tonight? Another client meeting?"

Poe shares the new campaign idea this company had for marketing some organic fertilizer. Apparently, his entire day was spent examining the product on-site—that is, at a dairy farm west of Wenatchee. I've never been to any kind of farm, but the way he describes it makes me feel like I was there too. Each time I pose a question, he provides enough detail that I can picture every bale of hay, flick of a cow's tail, and the vast open sky above, visible—as he put it—"no matter how hard you crane your neck around."

"You're very good with words," I say, meaning it. My eyes catch on his lower lip as he tips his glass to drink.

"You're a great listener." He moves closer to me. Our thighs touch. "Ivy, I don't think you should stay at your place tonight. Come to mine instead."

Rough, calloused hands, bearing a tattooed star on his left-hand knuckle, wrap around mine.

He leans forward so that he's only inches away. "It's a full moon tonight. And not safe outside for a woman alone."

I breathe deep, soaking in Poe's magnetism. "Yeah. That's true. What's the motel's name?"

Poe escorts me to my car. Both our heads are on a swivel, searching for Liam, but he doesn't turn up.

The drive over to Poe's motel grows increasingly dark—atmospheric, like something out of a sexy, romantic suspense drama. Streetlamps are spread much farther apart outside of Rock Island, adding to the sense of leaving behind the last chapter in favor of the next. Appropriate, as I think again about Phillip's sadness. About the journalist's tight grip on my arm.

Before driving off, I sent Lottie a text to warn her about Liam. He seemed to have it out for the Caines in general, and I wouldn't put it past him to swing by the house. How much of what Liam spewed is the truth, and how much is speculation rooted in his own fear? His resentment of the Caines? There is so much distortion of the past in this town, I don't know what to trust.

I suggested that Lottie lock her doors—and let her know I won't be sleeping there this evening. Although I haven't decided yet if the night will be romantic, I don't want to be anywhere near where Liam suspects I'll be.

Another thrill spirals down my neck and curls my toes. I hit the gas with more pressure.

When I arrive, the sun is nearly set. Poe's faded red pickup and an SUV are the only cars in the lot. I park next to the SUV and grab my bag from the passenger seat.

Excitement tightens my stomach. I tell myself to breathe as I approach room four on the first floor. The last time I slept with someone was years ago—a guy from a dating app—back when I never could have imagined the loss of my mother or the feeling of isolation that came afterward.

But Poe. In the hours that we've sat side by side, I've never felt anything like our connection before. I feel giddy, breaking through the barrier I've erected between myself and others, and the effect is exhilarating—terrifying, but in a good way.

Standing outside the chipped paint of the door, I smooth back a hair that's come loose from my crown braid. But I don't want to come off as put together, in control, and self-contained; I want to look how I feel—a little untamed and open for adventure.

I remove a dozen bobby pins and slip them into my bag, then run my fingers through the long waves reaching my elbow. Much better.

Feeling the consummate goddess—*Of confidence? Of sex?*—I knock firmly below the peephole. Poe calls to me from within.

Twenty-Three

SAMSON

The Present

On the drive to my motel, I'm blasting Bon Jovi, banging on the steering wheel to the beat, and just so amped about my meetup with Ivy. She was so sad that guy threatened her. Probably a prospective boyfriend, although she denied knowing him. Still, her honesty or their relationship didn't really concern me—or arouse me. It was seeing her knocked on the ground like an animal, waiting to be put out of its misery, and willing to comply with any request until the deed was done.

Maybe we'll have sex at the motel first. She wanted it. But that climax is always secondary to the real pleasure.

I drum a new beat on the dashboard as I take a side road to the next town over. Ivy said she would be just a few minutes behind, so I need to make this pocket of time count.

My copy of *The Complete Tales and Poems of Edgar Allan Poe* slides to the footwell of the passenger seat, beside my fold-up map. I swerve to avoid a pothole, and my lucky rabbit's foot swings hard from the rearview.

People my age are often confused by my rejection of technology, my obsession with the eighties. If they came from the boondocks of Fresno, where reception and internet is shit anyway, where we live and breathe cow crap and Reaganism, they'd understand. Ivy would understand if I ever told her the truth.

The highway exit for the motel sits past a blinking yellow light, the only one illuminating this part of the road. Brilliant colors tear the sky, the sun already disappeared beyond the sloping horizon of green spiky treetops.

Hanford Reach was a real thrill before I arrived in Rock Island. That hunter's wallet, flush with credit cards and cash, provided the necessary funds to get a roof over my head for a change, and a decent shower after skinny-dipping in rivers and beach showers for two months. No way he was living on the level with that much cash in hand. Likely a drug dealer.

I glide into the parking spot opposite my room and cut Sally's engine. The number four hangs askew, its bronze spray paint appearing dull in the setting sunlight and matching the feel of the motel as a whole. Layers of blue paint curl along the window, revealing shades of pink and a moldy green.

Light slices the darkness of my room as I turn the handle and step inside.

Ivy's thick lashes and big eyes, almost cartoonish in their innocence, were what first drew me to her. Forming a connection in public with someone isn't normally how I choose my victims. Then she started in on serial killers. The familiar stirring began in my chest, my stomach, and my groin. The one that demands I seize the moment set before me—one I wouldn't have considered if it weren't offered up on so shiny and golden a platter.

Ivy is different. Special. Alone, apparently, aside from some dubious blood relatives nearby. And I'm not the only one who's taken an interest in her, judging from the maniac screaming in the bar.

"Fucking loser," I say out loud, quoting the campers from last month with a smile. I close the door behind me with my foot and throw the keys on the nightstand. The motel is no prize pig, but the crisp sheets on the two queen beds, freshly changed by housekeeping, make it feel like the Hilton.

After I met Ivy last week and gave her that story about a sales conference, I thought I would leave a few days later. Seattle was waiting, after all. But when I went back to my truck that night and discovered that the body spray and deodorant I'd been coating myself in was finally empty, I decided to stay awhile. Enjoy some amenities that were undoubtedly cheaper than what I'd find farther west.

A bottle of Jack sits half-open on the dresser where I left it, but the room is otherwise spick and span. Maybe even inviting after the night that Ivy's had.

I hurry to the closet to retrieve the trash bags that I know I'll need before dawn. When I first began my hobby in the boonies, I let the elements do their thing—tossed evidence into the local river, used burn barrels, allowed animals an extra buffet in the middle of the night. Being on the road and less familiar with my surroundings, I've had to learn how to be tidier, more efficient, when an opportunity arises.

The annoying campers, the loud hunter, and the drunk hitchhiker I met by the river in Malaga were each pretty easy cleanups in terms of covering my tracks. I chucked the hitchhiker beneath a dock and went along my way. The police still haven't even identified the poor bastard.

The girl wearing a Chico State sweatshirt, roaming alone at night after I left the stoplight party in Chico, however, was an absolute mess of fluids once she died. Then somewhere around Mount Shasta, a homeless man who first tried to rob me barfed all over Sally's truck bed after I tied him up and threw him in the back. Lesson learned: buy trash bags in bulk.

A knock at the door. Two sharp raps. I glance around the room, still not ready for Ivy's arrival. The hunter's duffel bag with his knife, gun, and the cable ties is zipped closed on my bed.

"Coming," I say loudly. I chuck the duffel behind narrow folding doors, then shut the closet tight.

Moving to the door, I straighten my shirt. Smooth down my collar. The short sleeves strain at my biceps, and I've caught the swoony sighs women have thrown me; the nomad life and carpe-diem motto suit me well.

This is the space I'm meant to occupy—in plain sight, strolling just under the radar—culling back those idiots too dumb and trusting to recognize a threat when they sit down next to it at a bar counter.

No, Ivy will be my last bit of fun before moving on to bigger and better things in Seattle. Maybe I can get a restaurant job for more cash—and meet more transients like me, passing through without any family to bog them down.

I tuck back a hair as the air-conditioning unit beneath the window kicks on. Perfect timing. The sound should cover Ivy's cries when she sees the cable ties later. My groin hardens just thinking about it.

I plaster on a smile, then turn the handle. "You found me," I say, leaning into the doorframe.

Light glares from behind her, like a police spotlight blurring her features. Another bulb flickers from two rooms down. Then it burns out, leaving us in semidarkness.

I step back into my den. My safe space. My haven where I can be me. "C'mon in."

Twenty-Four

Ivy

Two queen-size beds fill most of the room. A nightstand wedges between them, opposite a small desk and dresser. The room is sparse, decorated in muted reds and taupes.

I offer a tentative smile. "Nice spot."

"No complaints here." Poe takes my bag, then drops it by the door. "How's your arm feeling?"

My tender skin pulses, a bruise beginning to form. During the drive, I worried that a flare-up of my mystery symptoms would occur after my brush with Liam, but I decided that's tomorrow's problem. "Fine, I guess. So strange to think that just happened."

"Totally. Very. Do you want something to drink?" He gestures toward a bottle of Jack Daniel's on the nightstand.

I smile, then shake my head. "I think I'm good for the night after the whiskey sour. Just feeling tired all of a sudden."

I glance toward the bed, wondering whether we'll sleep separately— whether I want to—when his fingers lock with mine.

He leans in—then bends closer still—and I hold my breath, fear overwhelming the excitement from moments earlier. I just got here. Does he mean to . . . Are we accelerating now? Is this our first kiss?

"Poe?" I ask.

"Ivy," he breathes, pulling me close. One hand wraps around my waist while the other snakes its way around my neck. Sharp mint reaches my nose as he leans down, his lips parted. A shiver traces my shoulders as he kisses me, stroking my cheek. I press my body to his.

Guiding me to the bed closest to the door, he lays me down. Climbs on top of me.

I curl beneath him, relishing his weight. This is fast. But it's also been ages—years—since I've felt this way. Despite the dull alarms beginning to sound in my head, that this is too much—too fast—and I should stop, I don't.

The kissing resumes. Softly, slowly. Then deeper. Harder. More intensely.

"Poe," I murmur.

He presses his lips to mine. Mashing them. I open my eyes, then see him draw backward.

Gentle hands caress my chest. Then lace around my neck.

And choke.

I'm so stunned that it takes me a moment to recognize the pain radiating from my throat. My lungs squeeze flat, straining for air. My adrenaline finally kicking in, I scratch and claw at his torso.

I find his forearms. Dig my nails into his skin. But his grip persists.

Thrashing, reaching for the nightstand, grappling, my fingers land on a pen, and I bring it sideways, hard, to stab his ribs.

He cries out, falling off me, then scrambles back onto the bed like a bear. Rage flashes in his blackened eyes.

He tears the pen from my grasp. Calloused palms press into the hollow of my throat. I scream—try to—as the air conditioner doubles its billowing noise, burying the effort.

Spots flash in my vision. I scrabble, scratch, scream, but nothing comes out.

I blink and black out for a moment. Blink. Black out. Wild eyes remain overhead.

Blink.

Black out.

Blink.

My lungs, my throat, my fingernails all burn.

The popcorn stucco ceiling above comes into focus. A twin to the ceiling material back in my apartment in San Francisco. Home. With Onyx and Carson.

Black out.

Blink.

Fire sears down my neck and chest. This time, I'm able to suck in a breath. I double over onto the side of the bed as coughs rack my body.

I twist my head and look up. Search for Poe's figure and ready myself for another attack.

But there's someone else here. I think. Stars continue to burst across my sight.

A blurry figure stands over a body that's writhing, contorting on the hard carpet.

The figure lifts their head to look at me—tall, different shape—but remains still. Staring at me. A jolt of new terror seizes my chest. Poe is on the floor. Who the fuck is this person?

I struggle to swing my legs off the bed and get to my feet. Limp toward the door as fast as I can. Don't look again, don't make eye contact and tempt fate. Grab my bag. Trot, jog, and stumble to my car.

In the driver's seat, I turn the ignition. I rub my eyes, willing my vision to right itself, then reverse anyway, panic fueling my actions. I turn toward Rock Island, back to Lottie's, as deep-belly sobs tear up my throat.

Tears soak my cheeks and the top of my shirt by the time I park in front of the Caine house. The windows are dark, like vacant eyes locking on to something in the distance. The full moon leers overhead, as if swollen with bloodlust—as if it knows what just happened. I call out for Lottie with someone else's hoarse, battered voice, but no one answers.

A handwritten note is on the kitchen table beneath an empty upside-down coffee mug.

Out with friends. Back later. Lasagna in the microwave if you're hungry.

When I reach the guest room, I climb straight into bed and pull the blanket over my head.

Poe tried to kill me in his motel room. On the night of the full moon. He offered me a safe place to sleep, and instead he tried to strangle me. Someone came into the room. Did something to him, then was standing over him on the floor.

Fresh tears pool on the pillow, the fabric growing cold.

Poe attacked me. My friend. My . . . what? Accomplice? Psychopath I dated?

I close my eyes. Wait for blankness to slide over me like a sleeping bag zipped high. Ambient wind whips outdoors, and everything feels peaceful for a moment as I wait for exhaustion to win.

Then hazel eyes turn to black in my mind, dead in all respects— cloudy irises, spidering veins, shadowed skin beneath—dead, but for the intensity with which they return my frightened stare.

Twenty-Five

Ivy

Sunlight, far too bright, filters through the mauve curtains.

The smell of coffee reaches my nose. Dark roast. Colombian, maybe.

What day is it? Do I have a deadline I'm supposed to meet this morning?

I stretch my body out of habit, and sharp pain pierces my muscles. My arms and my back cry out. My neck spasms where strong hands seem to squeeze like a vise all over again.

I sit up in bed.

I'm in the Caine house. No one bothered me while I was passed out. No one tried to kill me a second time.

Gingerly, I bring my legs over the side of the bed. Recognize that the throbbing in my head is more than a hangover.

I was attacked last night. And if another person hadn't entered Poe's motel room, I would be dead right now.

Fumbling for my phone, I tap the "Home" button. News alerts fill the screen. The first notification reads **New Victim of Full Moon Killer.** I don't bother reading the rest.

Stumbling to the door, I follow the scent of caffeine downstairs to the kitchen, where Lottie is watching television from the breakfast nook. A reporter's voice speaks from outside the Five Pines Motel; a body was discovered there early this morning. Lottie sees me lumbering into the doorway, then gasps.

"What happened to you? Your neck—are you okay?" She rises to her feet, but I lift a hand to stop her.

I gesture to the TV. "Tell me everything."

Lottie insists on getting me a cold pack from the freezer, which she places around my neck; then she sits down across from me. According to local and national news, which has been a flurry of interviews and wide shots of reporters "standing out front of some motel a few miles down from where that other body was found last week in Malaga," a new victim was discovered, an unidentified man. His death seems due to an injection with something that's still being determined. The police suspect (definitely this time) this may be the work of the Full Moon Killer. They're now thinking that the body found along the riverfront could be someone else's victim. Given that revision, the police are asking that anyone with information about either male victim come forward.

Against the bright grass visible through the window, Lottie's skin appears pale. Her eyes are ringed with red as she continues to stare at me.

"Ivy," she says, her voice quivering, "what happened to you? I think you should go to the hospital."

I lower my gaze to the gingham tablecloth. I'll break down in tears—in shock—and turn to a puddle of trauma if I keep seeing her horrified expression. "First, tell me if the police have any leads."

Lottie clears her throat. "Not that they're sharing. They've only said they're searching for a person of interest. Someone the victim was last seen with, leaving a bar."

Chills skate across my shoulders, and I allow myself a full, uninhibited shiver.

Me. The police are searching for me. Poe's attacker—who saw my face—probably is too. Did the killer mean to save me because I'm his relative? Or is he simply saving me for later?

When I look up, Lottie's eyes are wider than before.

"Ivy?"

"Nothing happened. I'm fine. I just fell—slipped outside on the porch stairs getting in last night."

"Why did you text me you were staying somewhere else?" she asks, her voice small but determined.

"I was drunk. I wasn't paying attention. I'm sorry."

"Where were you drinking?" Lottie pauses, then looks behind me to the talking heads on the TV. "Were you at a bar? The same bar as the victim?"

Shit. I rack my brain against the headache and overall pain pummeling my sore body. I can't logic this out yet. What am I supposed to say?

Telling Lottie the truth is not an option. Not before I know who was standing over Poe on the floor of the motel room. Any answer I give won't be enough to satisfy my cousin—or the authorities when they finally locate me.

"Lottie, I just . . . I can't talk about it. I'm sorry. Do you have any painkillers? Anything stronger than aspirin?"

Lottie goes upstairs, then returns a few minutes later with a nearly empty prescription bottle of Vicodin. I pop two into my mouth, ignoring my cousin's quiet surprise.

Facts race in my head, trying to make sense of this before the morning spins too far out of my control. Sweat breaks across my forehead, and I know the beginning of a mystery-illness fever is underway.

Poe tried to kill me, to strangle me. Someone attacked Poe. Poe is dead, likely by the Full Moon Killer's hand.

The reporter on the TV gestures to the weathered, blue motel, the stationary maid cart outside of an open room door, an RV that takes up five adjacent spots, then resumes facing the camera. The woman exudes confidence, her dark hair sleek and controlled in the morning humidity.

"If you're just joining us, this is Whitney Cruz coming to you live outside the Five Pines Motel. We've just learned that the young man who died here is the latest to be considered a possible victim of the Full Moon Killer—the second in under a week—despite the killer historically preferring to target women. Local residents are being asked to observe the curfew tonight."

I swing my attention to Lottie. "Curfew?"

She types on her phone. Pauses. "Wow, yeah. I guess I missed that when you came downstairs. The mayors of Rock Island and Wenatchee just announced a nine p.m. curfew tonight. Everyone has to be indoors by then."

My head is spinning. The Full Moon Killer is supposedly related to me, but I'm starting to realize that before last night, I'd really only considered that in the abstract. Now that I know just how close the killer is physically, it's impossible to ignore the fact that someone here in Rock Island, someone I've interacted with, is a serial killer.

"Are you sure I can't take you to the hospital?" Lottie asks, standing beside me.

Heat flushes my cheeks. The dimmer switch on my pain level is ratcheting up with each minute that passes. My shins ache. My bones beneath them throb. Another flare-up.

I wince, and my cousin eyes me harder. Despite what I know are her good intentions, I can't go anywhere. For several reasons.

"Yeah, I'm sure. Thanks. I just need to lie back down." The grandfather clock begins to chime at the front door. It's nearly nine o'clock.

"What about food? Can I make you something?"

I smile, recognizing Lottie's love language: feeding people. My stomach rumbles, and I recall that I didn't eat dinner last night, but I shake my head.

"I don't want to bother you." We still haven't talked about our fight. The last thing I want is to impose further and strain our tenuous peace.

She pauses before an open cupboard. "Well, if you won't tell me, I'll make you an omelet. You seemed to like that last week."

While she removes a pan from a lower cabinet, I can't shake the feeling that I'm missing something. My head feels cloudy, and there is still so much I don't know and haven't been efficient enough to grasp. My life-long lack of direction never seemed like a true handicap until now, when I need certain skills I don't have—patience; the ability to think of the big picture; self-preservation skills, apparently. How can I uncover years of misinformation and lies when I can't even manage my body's health?

The news program returns from a commercial break, and Whitney Cruz is standing in the same spot before the open motel-room door. Poe's room. The imagined scent of floral air freshener tickles my nose, and I gag.

"You okay?" Lottie freezes with a steaming plate in hand. She sets it before me. "Do the eggs smell all right? I can make toast if you want."

"No, eggs are . . . they're fine," I say. "Thanks."

She clucks her tongue, putting away a carton of milk. "Oh shoot. I'm late. I told my office manager I'd be in by now. There's a shipment of specially made washers coming in that I need to do QC on. Are you going to be okay here alone?"

"Of course," I answer quickly. Lottie peers at me a moment longer. "Really," I add.

"Okay," she says slowly. "Just lock the door. This whole thing is wild, and I don't like—" She points a finger at me and waves it around. "Whatever happened here that you can't tell me about."

She runs upstairs to change. Using my phone, I frantically scan for other news reports. Was anyone able to identify me from the bar?

Lottie pauses in the kitchen doorway on her way out. "If you're feeling up to it . . . I mean, if you want company, feel free to drop by the shop. I'm just twenty minutes away, Ivy."

After the bizarre story I gave her to explain my appearance—one that, clearly, neither of us believes—my cousin is still offering me a lunch date.

"Thanks, Lottie. I appreciate it."

As she closes the front door, the dead bolt turns behind her for only the second time since I arrived. My arm throbs—reminding me that Poe's violence wasn't the only thing I escaped. Liam Weathers attacked me yesterday.

I pause beside the mirror at the front entryway, still wearing the jeans and blouse I wore to meet Phillip and later passed out in. The skin above my collarbone is beginning to yellow, and black spots are already forming the pattern of a handprint below my jawline.

Behind me, the grandfather clock chimes, jolting my nerves to the ceiling. I peer around, as if someone might be waiting behind one of the thick fabric curtains. Watching me. Holding their breath for the moment I turn my back and head upstairs to lie down.

———

Wenatchee's city center bustles with afternoon traffic. A sign I passed on the highway said the population is only thirty-four thousand, but compared to the calm comings and goings of Rock Island, Wenatchee could rival Oakland. The dog walkers, joggers, and people ducking into smoothie shops and grocery stores all seem on edge, glancing over their shoulders, as if they too have local news streaming on their phones and have heard about the deadly reason for tonight's curfew.

After I napped, then lay in bed all morning, I finally dragged myself out the door for a late lunch. The sun feels good on my skin. My fever has dialed back a few degrees, and my muscles only feel tender now, thanks to the ibuprofen I combined with Lottie's Vicodin.

I pull the metal handle to Lottie's hardware store just as she breezes in from a back office. Delight brightens her face, spotting me. Her hair is in a topknot, and her green apron reads THE HELPFUL PLACE. A clerk smiles at me from behind a counter to my left. Two tall carousels holding painter's tape, duct tape, package tape, and tape measures stand opposite rows of home-improvement products.

"Hey, you came," Lottie says, breathless.

"I thought it might be nice to . . . to get out. Are you able to step away now?" My jacket collar is popped up to hide my bruises, but I want to leave Lottie's place of business as soon as possible. The shower I took helped return me to feeling halfway human, but nothing can reduce my resemblance to a boxer whose career has tanked.

I should be regrouping. Not hiding in my cousin's shop.

"Now's fine," Lottie says. "Let's go grab a sandwich at Tony's around the corner. Give me five minutes; I'll finish up what I'm doing."

I exit to the sidewalk. Across the street, a child jumps up and down in front of a frozen-yogurt shop, begging her mom for a sweet treat.

"Ivy."

I turn, expecting to see one of the Caines, but it's the most out-of-context person possible: FBI Agent Ballo. His thick black hair appears grayer at the temples, but his suit jacket and trousers could be the same outfit he had on in San Francisco. He stares at me in disbelief, then casts a furtive glance behind him.

"What are you doing here?" he asks. "In Washington State?"

I whip my head toward the glass window of Lottie's shop. The clerk bends over some kind of ledger. Lottie must still be in the back, getting changed. Frenzy swirls in my throat, choking my ability to think.

"I'm . . . I'm visiting my cousin," I stammer. This morning, after Lottie left, it crossed my mind to call Ballo. He'd asked me to stay in touch, after all, and there was no better reason to reach out to an FBI agent than to share that I'd been attacked and almost killed. I'd even pulled out the card he gave me with his phone number written on the back, but I was so tired and felt so feverish that I fell asleep instead. I drove to Lottie's shop still in a daze.

Agent Ballo sucks in a breath. "Well, I'm here with a team of special agents. I just got done meeting with the Wenatchee mayor because the Full Moon Killer took another life."

"I'm up to speed there."

"That's great, because we have a lot to discuss. Now, ideally. When did you get here? Have you learned anything about your birth family?"

"I can't . . . I can't talk right now. I'll meet you later," I pant, embarrassed at my panicked response, but resolute. I want to ask more questions—ask if the police have me pegged as their person of interest—but my thoughts are spiraling.

"I don't think you're grasping how important this is," he says, frowning.

"I am. I am, I swear. But can you please go?"

What will Lottie think if she finds out I believe one of her family members is a serial killer? That I've been taking copious notes on each family story she's shared while searching for a serial killer among the details? How will she react if I'm right and there *is* a murderer embedded in her life? She's been so loving and generous with her time, energy, and hospitality, allowing me to stay an extra week without any deadline to get back to the Bay. She's always saying how important family is. If I'm wrong and baselessly accuse someone close to her, I can forget about ever returning here.

Agent Ballo lurches toward me. "Ivy, I'm sorry if this is inconvenient for you, but I doubt I'm going to blow your cover as an FBI informant when you haven't shared anything about your birth family with me."

A string of bells clangs against the glass door as it opens. I turn over my shoulder to find Lottie standing at the entry to her shop. Blood leaches from my face as I meet her shocked expression for the second time today.

"You're an informant?" Lottie no longer wears the apron. "Ivy?"

Agent Ballo turns red. "I'll be in touch." He walks away, crossing the street.

"Who was that?" Lottie peers at me. "Who are you informing on?"

I exhale, feeling the vaguely woven story around my excuse for visiting begin to unravel. "Can we go somewhere to talk?"

We pass a line of people waiting on the sidewalk for coffee a few doors down, past the sign that points right and reads City Hall, and beyond the parking lot allowing access to Old Wenatchee, a part of town preserved from its days as a trading post. A bench overlooks a stretch of grass that ends in an artificial pond.

Once we take a seat, I begin my confession. The details I've stored up over the last two weeks are a relief to speak aloud, even as I watch Lottie's face drop with each revelation. I emphasize how I wanted to meet her and learn more about her family for my own understanding of where I come from—that I took the genetics test originally to learn what illness might be causing my myriad symptoms.

When I finish, still without sharing the truth about last night's assault, Lottie stares straight ahead. Stern disappointment replaces the stupor she wore upon catching me with Agent Ballo.

"Are you okay?" I finally ask.

She inhales through her nose. "I'm sorry you're sick. I had no idea about that, and really, I wouldn't wish that on you. But let me be clear about two things. One—there is no serial killer in my family, and certainly not one that's been living undetected for decades. Honestly, Ivy, I really thought you had come to form new bonds with us. Not try to break what you found."

Her nostrils flare, and I see a flicker of Tristen as she might have been in her youth. The wild child who told the world to disappear when her sister was declared dead.

"And two—you're no longer welcome at the Caine house. You should go home, Ivy."

Lottie rises without another word, leaving me alone to stew in the shit-covered bed I made for myself.

When I return to the house, it takes less than fifteen minutes to gather up my toiletries and clothing. I double-check that the newspaper clipping announcing Tatum's death is tucked inside a zipper pocket of my suitcase, ensure my letter is beside it, then load up my rental car.

I find a motel on the outskirts of Wenatchee, passing the Five Pines on the way. The parking lot is still packed with news vans, reporters, police officials, and civilian onlookers trying to get a peek inside room four.

A few miles north, I pull into the lot outside the Travel Host Suites and a fast-food restaurant. My phone pings with a text from Carson.

Hey. I just saw the news. Wtf are you doing up there with a murderer loose?

I start to reply, then pause, realizing I don't have a good answer to that question.

Three little bubbles blink across the screen. His follow-up message appears. I don't know how useful a lawyer may be, but if you need me, just tell me. I'll take the next flight up. No matter what, we're family.

Warmth spreads across my chest as I reread his words. His offer means more than either of us could unpack in the space of a text message.

And although my sensible older brother would lose his mind at the thought, the last known location of the Full Moon Killer is exactly where I need to be.

Twenty-Six

Ivy

Waning Gibbous

All night I tossed and turned, likely due to so many tragic details of my life converging at once. Around 4:00 a.m., I jolted awake in a sweat after dreaming that a man was standing at the foot of my queen-size bed. I thought at first it was the person who stood over Poe's writhing body. But he had the same shoulders, the same immobile frame, as the man from that day at the park when I was a kid—watching me but not approaching. Finally, when the green analog clock clicked over to six o'clock, I turned on the light and sketched the man in my notebook.

The current Full Moon Killer investigation remained sparse on details. I turned on the television, and the same footage of the Five Pines Motel was rolling, followed by more of the riverfront over in Malaga, where last week's victim was found. It's taken the police several days, but they finally identified the riverfront body as Tim Scheel, a hitchhiker who often set up his tent in that area. Based on the time frame—not during the full moon—and the lack of any poisonous substance, the police are officially ruling Scheel an unrelated death. Whether it's a homicide, suicide, or accidental drowning that killed him, the police are still determining.

Poe's name hasn't been released yet. According to the news segment, guests in the room two doors away heard a loud thump around 10:00 p.m., but that's it. No noise the rest of the night. No one, apparently, saw me arrive or run out battered and terrified. No one saw Poe's killer.

Lifting the corner of the thick blackout curtain that shields the window, I check the walkway. A maid's cart rumbles right past my room on the second floor, and I wince against the vibration. Yesterday's fever gave way to a headache that's currently trying to pickax my skull. These symptoms are worse than when I found the newspaper article declaring Tatum a homicide victim—and about on par with the episode I had after discovering that saved voice mail from my mom.

Shades of dark blue and patchy black cover my neck and collarbone. My arms, where both Liam and Poe gripped me, have turned yellow, green, and brown—my skin, an artist's palette of colors.

I reach for my phone and dial the number from Ballo's business card. Although my brain is screaming at me to hang up, some gut feeling keeps me on the line.

Agent Ballo picks up on the third ring. "Ivy, hi. I'm glad you called."

"Yeah, I thought I should."

"Was that your cousin outside that DIY shop?"

"Hardware store, but yes. She's . . . we're . . . things have gotten pretty bad."

Agent Ballo pauses. "Go on."

I tell him everything. Everything that I know, at least. I share how Poe attacked me before he was killed by someone else. I mention the sales conference that Poe was in town for, his nagging boss, and the colleagues he complained about over a whiskey.

As I'm telling Agent Ballo all this, the image of my destroyed rental car snaps to mind, and the fact that someone—Poe's killer—was standing over his twitching body on the floor. Did that person spare me deliberately? Why would they attack my car, then allow me to escape a week later?

The police have only publicly shared that they're searching for a person of interest who left the bar with Poe—me—not that they're closing in on his suspected murderer. Knowing that Liam Weathers probably wouldn't think twice about giving up my name—especially if he's eager for renewed credibility—the police will also want to question me about the deceased owner of the gold tooth.

Tears—fatigue, physical ache, stress—burn my eyes while I talk through these details with Agent Ballo. Even though I'm hesitant to spill everything to the authorities, if the person who killed Poe remembers my face or knows who I am, I might not have another lunar cycle to learn their identity—maybe not another night before they come for me.

"I see," Agent Ballo says in the least comforting response possible. "That's quite a confession. Have you sought medical care?"

"No. Not yet."

"Okay. Well, I can accompany you to the hospital and get a statement from you in person there."

"I . . . I don't really want to go. I have . . . an unusual . . . I have a medical condition that's complicated."

Agent Ballo is silent for a moment. "Ivy, we're going to need to document your injuries one way or another, especially if the Wenatchee police are looking for you as a person of interest. Have you spoken with them yet?"

"No, I haven't."

"Okay. Well, they have historically botched Full Moon Killer investigations, so that's good for us. The FBI is anxious to gather facts ourselves." He pauses. "Do you have other information to share about the Full Moon Killer—any information you discovered from your birth family? Because we're close, Ivy. I know it. I can feel it. Can you?"

"I . . . I don't know. I didn't come up here for this. I've screwed up so much in flying here, hurt a lot of people. I just wanted to find out what's behind my sickness. Maybe learn who my birth father was."

"I know, Ivy. And I'm sorry for what's happened to you," he adds. "But the FBI has been hunting this monster down for so long, and your presence here seems to have shaken him. Why else would he have spared you?"

"Honestly, I don't know."

"I'll tell you what. I'll give you until the police can catch up to you and question you before I'll take you to the hospital for an examination and a formal statement. As long as you can outrun those morons, you can keep searching for medical answers. But you'll need to take photos of your bruises now and send them to me after we get off the phone. Do we have a deal?"

I suck in a breath. Agent Ballo touched on my exact fears in coming forward. He's intuitive enough to know I don't really want to spend the next day, or several days, giving statements to varying branches of law enforcement, especially when my birth family is likely to completely shut me out if I do—if they haven't already. The possibility of getting names, phone numbers, more anecdotes, and scrapbooks that might lead me to facts about my health narrows to zero. And Ballo seems to believe that somewhere among those anecdotes are details that lead to the killer.

"Deal."

We hang up. I walk into the bathroom, then take photos of my neck, my arms, and my upper chest, where Poe's fingernails scratched my skin.

Once I send the photos off to Agent Ballo, I stay weighted to the squeaky bed.

I just bought myself another day or so, however long I can elude the local badges, but have no idea what to do next. Lottie has cut me out, rightfully—and the only way to heal the rift between us, ironically, would be to prove my suspicions about our family. Without anyone left to pester in Rock Island, I'm a sitting duck.

Unless I expand my search. Lottie confirmed that Yara's dad is a member of One Family, right? Liam had said Phillip was also once a member, and Terry mentioned that Yara's family, the Sanchezes, used to be rivals of the Caines. Is it possible that someone else in One Family had a grudge against Phillip and could have attacked Tatum—his favorite niece, who made him anagram games for his birthday—as a form of revenge? Accessing Yara or her dad without Lottie's help will be difficult, admittedly. But maybe Phillip would be willing to speak to me again, somewhere less public. I only wish I had known of his previous involvement before our diner meetup, before the Rock Island police began searching for me.

I lean back onto my elbows and the mattress groans. Emotion closes my throat. Poe tried to kill me in a motel room similar to this. I almost died less than forty-eight hours ago. How am I supposed to move forward from that?

I blink away tears. Take a deep breath.

If you want to get to your destination, you need a map. My dad's words linger in my memory.

Next to my laptop on the quilted bedspread, the scrapbook I borrowed from Aggie lies open. I flip to the last Post-it note I placed, days ago, it seems. An article clipped from the month of Tatum's death lies center on the page.

The press was thorough in working their way through Tatum's relatives and close friends, each of whom shared their hope that Tatum would be found alive, then their increasing resignation to her death as the weeks carried forward. This particular article included quotes from Tatum's coworkers. Three women employed at Chic Threads were off during Tatum's last shift; the fourth worked with her for the four hours that their shifts overlapped but said nothing seemed out of character for Tatum.

I need to get out of Rock Island, away from the police and whoever killed Poe. Just for today.

"Mal Ngo of Seattle," I say out loud, scrolling down the website of her acupuncture practice. "Maybe after thirty years, you want to talk."

———

Salty air fills my lungs three blocks from the Puget Sound, as I trudge up a hill as steep as any in San Francisco. Seagulls caw overhead, filling the sky with their cries.

I step inside the lobby of an old brick building, quaint among the surrounding modern glass and concrete structures. Noise from the street dims as the door swings shut behind me. Between a chiropractor and a makeup artist, I find Dr. Mal Ngo, DAOM, in the building's directory.

I exit the stairwell at the fourth landing. Framed photos of Pike Place Market decorate the hall. At Mal's office, I reach for the door handle, and my stomach twists, so close to answers.

It's locked. *Shit.*

Without knowing whether Mal will return or if I'm missing some break in the killer's case back in Rock Island, this whole trip might have been a day wasted.

The elevator chimes. A woman files forward from its parted doors and stares at the phone in her hands. Her gray slacks and white button-up could make her a business owner in the building or a client getting a spinal adjustment on their lunch break, but as she approaches the office door I'm standing beside, she sees me and starts. Natural hair balances bright eyes and a narrow chin. "Hi. Can I help you?"

I turn to the bronze plaque on the door, then back to this woman's questioning gaze. "I'm here to see Mal Ngo."

"That's me. Do you have an appointment? Happy to have you walk in, but I'll need to check the schedule."

Warmth flushes my cheeks—relief that I did something right. I touch the scarf I tried to wrap stylishly around my neck. "I'm Ivy Hon. Tatum Caine's daughter. I was hoping to ask you a few questions."

Her lips, coated a deep purple, part. "Let's go inside."

Mal unlocks her office, and we enter a cozy waiting area: a love seat, two chairs, and a clear-plastic water dispenser. Above the love seat hangs a black-and-white image of two people bent over a rice field.

"My grandparents in Vietnam," Mal says, watching me. "Can I get you anything? There's water, but I also have tea in the session room."

I shake my head. "I'm fine. Thanks."

As Mal disappears into an inner office—or session room, from the peek of a long red table—my thoughts charge forward. Who is this woman? Tatum's former retail coworker-turned-acupuncturist, sure—but why rush me inside? Did she not want anyone to see me?

Mal emerges, then crosses to the front door. She turns the dead bolt. Fear skitters across my bare arms.

"Just don't want anyone interrupting us," she says. She takes a seat opposite me in a wooden chair. "So you're Tatum's daughter. Little Aimee. That's what she called you, at least. And you've come for answers."

My heart flutters. *Aimee.*

"You don't seem surprised," I reply, still tense after she locked the door.

She lifts both eyebrows. "Don't I? I guess I'm not. I always thought if I were you, I'd want to know what happened."

"What did happen?"

Mal tilts her head. "Do you not know . . . ?"

"No, I'm aware of . . . I know she's gone. I mean, what happened before? How did Tatum come to give me up? What did my birth father say about the adoption?"

Mal takes a deep breath. She looks up as if to examine the paneled ceiling, the rice-field photo behind me. With each passing second of her silence, a part of me shrivels in fear that this woman will confirm what I've always suspected and what Uncle Phillip implied: I was a mistake. Unwanted. Doomed to screw up whatever I endeavor.

"I'm sorry to surprise you like this. Did Tatum talk about me with you?" I struggle against the emotion that tightens my chest. But then— I'm not sorry. I need answers. I recall Aggie's kind admonishment back in her garden, that I really should stop apologizing.

A sad smile replaces the tension on Mal's face. Fine lines around her mouth and eyes melt away, and I can picture the young woman who would have folded clothes with Tatum.

"She did. I was the only one she told about her pregnancy at first."

"Okay. What was she feeling—was she excited, or . . . ?" My voice trails off in time with the pity that slides down Mal's face.

She inhales a slow breath. "Tatum loved you, Ivy. I know that. But it was a difficult thing to wrap her mind around. Your father was excited, though."

I perk up. "Really? You knew him?"

"I didn't, but Tatum always said that Bowen wanted you. When she gave you up, she said that's what broke them. He wanted to keep you, and she said that couldn't happen."

My mind spins at the details Mal so coolly tosses out. "Bowen? That's my birth father's name?"

"Bowen Lam, I think."

Electricity zaps through my body, touching the end of each limb, as I search the name for meaning or some similarity to the name of anyone interviewed in the articles from Aggie's scrapbook. *Bowen Lam.* Questions I haven't thought about in days return with ugly promptness.

Is *Bowen Lam* the name of a concerned father and boyfriend? Or a sociopath who angrily turned on a young woman when she disappointed him?

"And he wanted to keep me?" I press again.

Mal drops her eyes. "I'm sorry, Ivy. I know how painful all of this must be. I've tried not to think about Tatum all these years, because it's just too hard to remember that she's gone, and she was taken in such a horrible way. And she was only my friend at a part-time job while I saved up for college—not my mother. I'm sure this is awful for you."

Her words should strike me in the heart and tempt a sob from me, but I stifle it. "What did you say about Bowen? Was he angry with her?"

"Oh, furious." Mal's eyes sharpen. "Tatum said she had never seen him as upset as when she said she meant to adopt you out. Everything kind of devolved after she got pregnant, which is why I never met him. They met at a Nirvana concert over in Wenatchee, when the band was just starting touring in Washington. Bowen was from Tacoma—or Seattle. Somewhere on the west side of the state."

"Why does no one in Rock Island recall him? It doesn't seem like the area had a lot of diversity in the late eighties. I would think a young Asian guy dating a white girl would have caused people to talk."

"Well, he would drive to Wenatchee on weekends and stay with his uncle. Wenatchee had lots of cultural communities then because of the plastics plant nearby. Good wages and consistent work. So no one really gave Bowen and Tatum a hard time there. They would hang out after Tatum's shift ended, and I guess her mom was working long hours and didn't notice."

"Okay. But the case file showed that Tatum saw someone romantically the day that she died. Dermot McCoy. Do you think that was Bowen? Did you see anyone?"

Terry leans forward in my memory, sharing confidential details.

Mal purses her lips. "I did. Tatum met up with Dermot after she finished her shift, but she seemed excited about it. Earlier that day, however, she ran back from her break into the store, terrified. Said that some guy was watching her outside from down by the river."

"Do you know who that was? Was it Bowen? Or Hector?"

"Our boss? I doubt it. Tatum didn't know the guy. Or she wouldn't tell me. I always suspected it was Lino."

"Another coworker?"

"No, he was the older brother of one of Tatum's friends. Stacey."

My mouth goes dry. "Stacey Perez?"

Mal nods. "That's it. Lino was her older brother—half brother."

The office space behind Mal blurs into a white canvas, and all I can focus on is her slender frame floating against a blank backdrop. Hector Hermann, Mal's former boss at Chic Threads, mentioned that his friend Ross was Stacey's older brother.

"Why would this guy—Lino—be harassing Tatum?" I ask in a small voice.

Mal places her hands in her lap. "Lino always blamed Tatum for Stacey's death. He thought that if Tatum had gone with Stacey to the movies the night that Stacey was murdered, the Full Moon Killer wouldn't have found her alone. Lino was pretty obsessive. Violent."

"Would you have a picture of him? Did he have a brother named Ross?"

Mal shakes her head. "I don't know. I'm sorry. If I think of anything, I can let you know."

I leave my phone number with Mal, promising to contact her if I learn anything new about Tatum's death.

On the drive home, the mystery of Ross and Lino Perez takes the back seat to another name: Bowen Lam.

"Bowen Lam" dances through my head in different combinations. My cheeks hurt by the time I exit the Seattle city limits, I'm smiling so hard at finally having a solid detail about my birth father—the person who can tell me what medical anomaly is screwing with my immune system.

When I reach Snoqualmie Pass, I'm singing the name out loud and reveling in the sound.

Aggie said that I might have my father's eyes, and it's obvious to me, based on photos of Tatum, that I have Bowen's coloring.

Bowen Lam is the name of my birth father.

Lam Bowen. Able Mown.

Blame Won. Amble Now.

Bawl Omen. Mean Blow.

Twenty-Seven

TATUM

August 17, 1989

"Marmie? You home?" I enter our house, holding my breath. I told her I would be back an hour ago, but that was this morning before Dermot came to the shop. Before the best afternoon I've had in over a year, spent lounging under willow trees and enjoying a few beers and the touch of someone who doesn't stare at me like I'm a leper. That's got to count for something, right?

I step into the foyer, mentally preparing my defense. Her shift at the hospital would have ended about the same time as mine, but she often stays late when needed. Nerves around town have been strung taut, and she's been working longer as more folks are getting sloppy in their fearfulness, drinking that extra beer, kayaking, or—worst of all—swimming in the river.

Dermot tried to walk me to my car, but I thanked him and said I would go alone. Not because I didn't want him to. But because everything about our interaction was perfect, including the impromptu picnic-blanket sex. A year ago, the idea would have made me blush a bright red;

today, I was grateful for the physical distraction from my worries. Dermot asked if he could call me tomorrow, and I agreed with a shy mumble, despite baring every part of me to him only an hour before.

The phone trills from the kitchen. I pause, waiting to see if Marmie comes barreling down from the attic to grab it, but I'm alone. I shuffle down the hallway to the small bulletin board of notes Marmie updates every week and reach for the phone with a shaking hand.

A tiny part of me is eager to lift the receiver—the sliver that hopes it could be Dermot already missing the sound of my voice. The rest of me tenses as I check the clock—five past seven. Just enough time for word to have gotten around that I disappeared with a boy along the river's edge and emerged later hand in hand, cheeks flushed and carrying a bucket of empties.

"Hello," I answer. Heavy breathing greets me, and I stiffen, now certain of the caller. My shoulders prickle as if he's standing behind me. I snap my head to where the front door has blown ajar. The coats on the rack flutter in a tunnel effect.

"We need to talk," he says. "You can't keep behaving this way. The whole town knows."

"Knows what? That I'm depressed? That I'm desperate for connection, thanks to you?" I surprise myself with my own anger. Rage fills me, thinking about the last year and all that I've lost, thanks to this person who was supposed to care about me.

More silence. Someone coughs in the background. "I warned you about what would happen if you didn't fix your life."

I hear a click and the line goes dead. The rage evaporates from my frame until I feel only sadness. I replace the receiver, then cross the foyer to close and lock the front door. As I trudge upstairs, a light is visible in Marmie's arts-and-crafts room; she must have left it on when she went to work. On a desk within, a photo album is open to blank pages, an envelope with Polaroids wedged beneath. Marmie always says how important memories are to the Caines—one of the oldest families in Rock Island.

I used to agree with her before all this mess happened—my mess. Now I yearn for the ability to forget everything. To erase the memories haunting me, dragging me backward.

Staring at the open photo album, at the rows of albums lining a shelf behind the table, I have the sudden urge to douse them in kerosene. Toss them each into one of the burn barrels on the outskirts of town—or the kiln—and get rid of all the Caine family's *precious memories*. Finally free us of the expectations that name places on us.

With a sigh, I turn away from my fantasy of destruction and take a long, hot shower. The reset button is exactly what I need after another shift at work, trying to stay afloat against the regret that threatens to pull me under every week. When I emerge, all fluffed and buffed, I feel less anxious—or at least, more confident that I can fake normalcy at Tristen's party tonight. I wish I could invite Dermot.

The Santorini house is owned by another old family in Rock Island, who made money in shipping in Seattle before they bought land in Central Washington. I didn't realize the Santorinis were fans of Tristen's new network, One Family, but they love touting the latest craze. Last year, rumor had it they bought equity in Koosh balls, and the year before I heard they were urging local farmers to invest in wheatgrass crops.

I pick out a flowing dress, trying to mimic Tristen's attire. Instead of a white, gauzy garment like my sister's, my green cotton wrap dress will be more forgiving of the changes in my postpartum body.

"Do as the Romans do," I murmur.

The bangle Marmie gave me dangles from my wrist. I slip it off, then press my hand against the wall to the right of the mirror. When my dad was alive, he was always finding something to improve in this old house. During renovations of the bathroom, he made me my own secret compartment in the connecting wall, to match the one he had in the sitting room where he stored his cigars.

The wall pops open, a cube just big enough for my secrets and prized items. I place the bangle inside. Wouldn't want anything to happen to it tonight. No telling what lies in store at Tristen's party.

I head downstairs, grabbing my father's whistle by the door. Considering Marmie was right and someone did surprise me today at work, it can't hurt to wear a different accessory.

In the garage, my plain red bicycle is propped against my father's pegboard of tools. Marmie's Ford pickup is still absent.

I often wonder if my life would have turned out this way— friendless, boyfriendless, babyless—had my dad not died from a heart attack while on a hunting trip when I was thirteen. Would he have protected me somehow? Spared me the loneliness that drove me to reach each of these dubious distinctions?

Tristen drives up in a standard Ford four-door that our dad insisted on when she turned seventeen: "The safest model out there, and American-made." She emerges wearing the same white, gauzy robe she wore in the shop earlier, holding a jug of what I assume is alcohol, and a grin on her face like some hillbilly goddess. A current of air from the river sways the fabric of her robe, completing the image.

"Ready, new blood?" She stands with one hand on the car door, allowing Michael Jackson's falsetto to spiral out from the interior speakers.

I break into a smile. "I think so?"

Returning to the porch, I grab the extra beer that Dermot sent me home with, then slide into Tristen's passenger seat.

We drive down the hill and onto the main road. The closest house to ours, the McKinleys' farm a mile down, is dark this time of night. The Jeffersons' house farther on is awash in lights illuminating each window of the first and second stories, as if they too have a big night ahead.

It's been a year since I went to a social gathering, just before I found out I was pregnant. My stomach ties itself in knots, anticipating tonight with a mix of terror and thrill.

We turn right onto a dusty road that leads to the river, and Tristen drums her hands against the steering wheel to the fierce tempo of "Bad." But as I watch my sister's erratic movements—not on beat and the way she swerves to overcorrect when we clip a pothole—it's apparent she's more than enthusiastic. She seems high.

"Do you want me to drive?" I ask.

"What?" she yells above the music. She jerks the steering wheel to another drum solo and makes us veer across lanes.

"Do you want me to drive?"

She shakes her head, then does a full-body shimmy. "Nope. I'm good."

We turn right again, past a thick copse of trees, then onto a dirt road with a direct view of the Santorini house. Backlit and glorious before the glinting current of the Columbia River, the house is a beacon in the night. Parked cars form three rows on either side of the driveway and demonstrate the allure of a One Family gathering for miles.

Tristen parks at an angle, taking up twice the space of other cars. She jumps out, then says something I don't catch. I reach over and cut the engine.

"What?" I step from the passenger side, straightening my dress. Tristen bounds toward the house, jug in hand. She turns back to offer me a sip.

"You want?"

"No, thanks."

"Cool. More for me."

My sister lifts the jug to drink with both hands. A full moon looms overhead, lower than usual. I can almost make out a face—two eyes and a mouth agape, staring in our direction. A lunar voyeur.

The creepy feeling traces the back of my neck. Somehow I know the moon is watching us, waiting. Eager to see how else we might mess up our lives tonight.

I follow my sister as she dances up the path, telling me whom to watch out for among the more aggressive boys, and listing the women she wants to introduce me to. Light twinkles from the downstairs windows, music and laughter enticing us closer like a siren song we can't resist.

Indoors we find people sitting on every furnishing available. Women drape men's laps on sofas, armchairs, and tables, laughing and throwing their heads back, exposing their chests to the men's curious eyes. The music penetrates my skin as we venture past the foyer and into a kitchen twice the size of ours, with glass windows enveloping the space. The river twinkles below.

Men huddle together in groups while the women disperse among them, like predators on the hunt. Drinks pass from hand to hand above a pool of heads, shoulder to shoulder in the hub of the renovated Victorian, and I watch as a man adds a pill to his cup, then shares it with a male friend.

I clutch my unopened beer tighter against my ribs. "Tris?"

My sister either ignores me or can't hear my meek voice above the din. A woman with wavy auburn hair cascading down thick hips sweeps Tristen into a hug. They pull apart, and the woman nods downstairs to the basement with a knowing grin.

Tristen says something in response, then tugs me forward toward an open door.

Alarms peal within me and I pull back. My sister clutches my hand harder, no doubt growing impatient.

"Tristen," I say again. She yanks me forward, knocking me into a man who doesn't seem to register the impact. I apologize, but no one hears.

Tristen is already two steps down, following her friend, when I freeze in place.

Glistening skin undulates below in a sea of writhing bodies and red-hued lighting. Long hair, short hair, wavy, curly, and natural hair mingle together as heads turn and necks arch in pleasure with their partner. No. Not one partner. All the partners. Open mouths part midkiss, then shift to find another willing and open mouth waiting to be tasted. Searing moans swell from the basement's floor. Tristen's friend reaches the crowd down below, then removes her sheer T-shirt, and it's my turn to yank my sister's arm.

"Tristen!"

She turns back to me, blue eyes dilated to black spheres, and I know my sister is somewhere else. "Loosen up, Tater. Don't be such a drag."

"I . . . I forgot something in the car."

Without waiting for her response, I whirl on my heel, then slam into the torso of the man I knocked into. He grips my shoulders, and I falter, moving a step below, closer to the orgy. "Wrong way," he says, his face backlit and blurry.

He massages my arms, pushing me down another step. Then another.

"Get off me!" I shout, but my voice is lost in the thumping bass.

His thumbs hook beneath my shirt, then my bra straps, nudging them off.

I look behind me, searching for my sister, while this man pushes me another step. Tristen has disappeared.

I lift my foot and slam it into this guy's shin; he jerks to the right, falling against the wall.

Fighting the swath of One Family members and their friends, I tear back through the kitchen, back to the front door, as my stomach seizes in roiling nausea.

Outside, I gulp the crisp night air. Expel from my lungs the cigarette smoke and pheromones that were so dense inside the house. I keep walking until I'm nearly level with Tristen's car at the far end of the driveway.

"Tatum."

My heart still racing, I stop short. Goose bumps ignite the skin of my arms at the familiar voice. The same voice that threatened me only two hours ago. I turn toward the tall silhouette. I can't see his face, but I know every feature creased in disgust, the tensed fists hell-bent on punishing me over and over again for something that I can't and won't take back.

"You've avoided me long enough, Tatum. Come with me."

I search behind him, try to see whether anyone else has come outside. Tristen? Voices in animated conversation carry over the booming hook of a popular song, while the loudest noise of all clamors in my ears and against my ribs in a feral tempo, like a trapped rabbit trying to escape.

He sees me looking for help and bares white teeth, then opens a palm—waves it forward in some perverse show of chivalry. I stare at it a moment before realizing he wants me to go first, forcing me to trek ahead of him into the dark field.

As I place one unsteady foot in front of the other, my mind races, searching for a way out, a means of getting someone's attention before he snaps my neck in two. But none comes to me. Instead, I focus on my breath—a restricted cadence of inhales—and continue forward.

In through the nose. Out through the mouth. Just like the nurse taught me in the delivery room.

The easy slope of the field sharpens to a stronger decline. This far from the house, the music gives way to the sound of water lapping the wet earth of the riverbank. Another hundred yards ahead, something else shines in the stark moonlight: a handsaw.

I gasp, then whirl back to my captor. He grips the cold steel of a handgun pointed at my heart. "What is this? What are you planning to do?"

Frantic, I fumble for the whistle and bring it to my lips. He snatches it from my neck, breaking the thin fabric rope and yanking me forward.

Another broad smile. This time, facing the moon, I can see every feature of the face I once thought I knew so well.

He adjusts his grip on the gun, then takes another step toward me. "Well, Tatum. That depends entirely on you."

Twenty-Eight

IVY

A dog barks somewhere from the valley below the Caine house. The sound is curt, as if alerting anyone listening that I'm lurking out front.

Lottie has already gone to work this morning, much too far away to heed the dog's warning. And she never locks her door.

I climb the steps of the porch, continue past the potted plants and love seat that formed the scene of so many evenings for me, then reach for the brass door handle and push inward.

The latch doesn't give, so I push again.

She locked it. Seriously?

"And all it took was a new murder," I grumble.

Around the side of the house, the kitchen is visible through the lace curtain covering the back door's window, and I cross my fingers before turning the handle. With a click, the door swings inward. Releasing the breath I've been holding, I step inside, then make my way up the stairs.

Although Lottie said I was no longer welcome at the Caine house, I can't stay away. Not when I recall the box of photo albums and year-books she was sitting beside while playing dress-up in the attic.

The narrow door is already ajar when I reach the final steps of the spindly third-floor staircase. It falls open with a moan. Avoiding the naked mannequin, I stride toward the boxes on the floor, eager to put my question to rest.

Spines of photo albums occupy the closest box. The second crate contains yearbooks from 1989, 1985, and 1980. I pluck the spine embossed with 1980, then pass over Terry's senior portrait to scan the last names that start with *P*.

No Perez.

This morning, I spent an hour searching for online records of Bowen Lam, with zero returned possibilities. None. Yes, there are other people with names very similar to his, but when I did a double click and found images of those people, they either weren't Chinese, or they were years too old or too young.

Although Mal said Bowen was from Tacoma and I don't know Bowen's age, I check among the *L*s of the senior portraits section anyway. No one that fits.

I flip to the front. Terry is nine years older than Tatum. Stacey would have been Tatum's age, and I'll guess her older brother Lino would be Terry's age or younger.

I search the freshman-year photos for a Perez. No luck. The next year, the sophomore students don't have a Perez either, but following the official class photos, there's a landscape image of everyone together on a field trip to Seattle.

Out of due diligence, I scan the paragraph of names in tiny print below the photo and pause in the middle. Perez-Ballo. Rosalino Perez-Ballo.

I flip to the sophomore-class photos and scan with a shaking fingertip until I find him: a thin, bright-faced fifteen-year-old from Rock Island who grew into a man that approached me in a coffee shop in San Francisco. Agent Ballo.

Someone bangs on the front door below. Muffled words reach my ears. "Rock Island Police. Open up."

Panic surges in my throat, recalling I broke and entered someone else's home. And the cops seem to have a name for their person of interest that the news reporter mentioned yesterday.

"Ivy Hon? We need to ask you some questions." Another knock, harder this time.

"Shit," I breathe. I hold still, apart from the hummingbird beat of my heart, praying that the officers leave.

Radios sputter downstairs on the porch, then recede. An engine starts outside. I gather up the yearbook and tiptoe to the ground floor.

Mal suggested that Stacey Perez's older half brother had it out for Tatum. The understanding now ripples through my chest, touching everything I thought I knew about why I came here. I recall Hector's story about his buddy Ross—Agent Ballo must have gone by both "Ross" and "Lino" at different points in his life.

Did Ballo lie to me about the DNA results linking me to the Full Moon Killer? To get me interested in my family and lure me to Rock Island? But why? To further punish Tatum postmortem by drawing me to the scene of her death? If he's the brother of the first victim, I would think he'd use that common link between us to his advantage somehow—not hide it. Ballo seemed genuinely surprised to see me in Wenatchee, but he's an FBI agent. They're probably all trained in deception.

Coming here alone was a mistake. A stupid, idiot mistake, and I have to wonder how long Agent Ballo has been in Washington— whether he just arrived as a result of Poe's murder or if he's been up here since last week, when I discovered the whistle and the gold tooth in the kiln. Has he been watching me since before he approached me outside of Lottie's store?

I inhale three breaths through my nose and peer through the stained glass of the front door. I grip my phone, wishing I had someone to call to help me make sense of all this.

Days ago, I would have gone to the bar searching for Poe. My neck throbs, as if emphasizing what a poor judge of character I am.

Picking my way back through the house to the kitchen, I pause beside the breakfast table I'm no longer allowed to occupy.

My skin turns cold in the morning sunshine that slants through the window as an entirely new thought occurs to me. Agent Ballo flashed me a badge in the coffee shop, but I never examined it up close for myself. Maybe Agent Ballo isn't an agent at all.

The fresh scent of lemon lingers in the kitchen. Lottie's coping mechanisms for stress have seemed to be baking and cleaning; judging from the pristine counter tile today, she must have pictured my face in the grout.

Onyx's lemongrass kitty litter pops into my head, and I can practically smell its citrusy, dusty aroma. I haven't thought about her in days—there's been so much that's happened. Carson sent me pictures and told me that she's accepted him as her human and now curls up next to him on the couch. The best place for me is undoubtedly back home with my cat and my brother. But I think I knew that when I purchased my plane ticket.

Ballo lied to me. What is his real motivation in asking me about my birth family and, just yesterday, striking a deal with me on the phone to delay interviewing me?

His sister was the first Full Moon Killer victim. He held a grudge against the third victim, Tatum, and decades later sought out her daughter. Could Ballo have some connection with the most recent victim?

I sit at the table, then search "Katrina Oates murder" on my phone. The search results run the gamut from official declarations of her death, sound bites from neighbors, and journalists describing the now-public gory details, to an interview from an old high school classmate in Des Moines.

While reading about her evisceration is disturbing, what sticks out to me is the absence of friends. Her aunt provided a tearful interview after Katrina was found—several, in fact—to the reporter I saw outside of the Five Pines Motel. She shared how beloved by the kids Katrina had been ever since she moved here a year ago. But unlike the articles I read about Tatum, no friends made any kind of statement of grief that I can find, official or otherwise. No anecdotes about what a good friend Katrina was or how deeply she'll be missed. The poster board and teddy bear I saw by the river's edge were a part of a vigil independently held by a local church jarred by the violence.

I think if I died, Carson would at least give me a Facebook memorial post.

My phone's map shows that the day care is only a few miles away. I take a quick look out front for police cruisers, then slide out the back door of the Caine house. Katrina Oates is the first victim of the Full Moon Killer in thirteen years; there must be a reason why she was chosen.

The drive passes quickly, taking me through downtown and into a residential area. Outside a small building with a slanted roof, a young woman wearing yoga pants and a zip-up exits the front pavement. She passes a sign erected on a patchy green-and-yellow lawn that reads, How Does Your Garden Grow Childcare, Se Habla Español. Conspicuously absent, to my mind, are any flowers. Posters. Drawings or signs of a once-held memorial. It hasn't even been a month, and from the aunt's interviews, I doubt she'd remove them so soon after her niece's death.

"Excuse me," I call to the woman. She pauses but looks past me to several cars parked along the road.

"Yeah?"

"I'm new to the area. I have a baby."

The woman waits for me to finish the sentence in any way that might be convincing.

"And I need day care," I add. "Do you have a kid enrolled here? Do you like it?"

She shifts her weight from one sandal to the next, then looks behind me to her car again. "It's okay."

"It's got great reviews online, and it's cheap, which helps a single mom." I offer a commiserating smile, hopeful she's who I've pegged her as.

She takes in my unwashed jeans and wrinkled blouse, which I should have cleaned before leaving Lottie's house with its washer and dryer. Then she nods. *One of us.*

"Yeah, it's cheap. The care was all right if you knew who to schedule with. I think things are getting better now, though."

"Now? Like, was there a change in management recently?"

She hesitates. "I've got to get to work. I only stopped by here because my kid had a poopsplosion and needed clean clothes." She comes up to my window but glances toward the day care's front door before speaking. "Let's just say some parents complained. The kids who were in full-time care started showing bruises, and one kid last year got a broken leg. Supposedly, he fell from the playground out back, but other kids said one of the teachers pushed him after he bit her."

"That's terrible. Did someone report it?"

The woman shakes her head, already backing away to head to her car. "I don't think so. A lot of parents are just struggling to get by since that plastics plant closed over in Wenatchee last year. I didn't report it either, because I wasn't there—you know?"

"Who was the teacher who pushed the kid?"

She tilts her head. "Not good to speak ill of the dead, is it?"

I drive back to the motel, not sure where to go next or what to do with this new information—Katrina Oates may have injured children in her care.

As I pull into a parking spot, then cut the engine, my phone buzzes with a text. Part of me hopes that Lottie has reached out, willing to make peace. To accept that my pursuit of our family history isn't a betrayal so much as a deep, panting need for the truth of my diagnosis and the reality behind Tatum's death.

When I open the message, I suck in a sharp breath. It's not Lottie's name—but Carson's—across the top.

Seems you are in over your head, moi moi. I'm texting from midair somewhere over Oregon and I'll arrive at Spokane shortly. Onyx is with your nosy—I mean, helpful—neighbor. See you soon.

Seeing the Cantonese word for little sister—*moi moi*—and reading that Carson is flying here, unprompted and less than a day after he offered, fills me with such relief that my throat closes. My eyes burn with tears as a boy runs past, calling dibs on the front seat of the family car.

Carson. Here. My big brother and protector when we were kids, traveling across two states to join me on my quest to learn more about my biological family and, essentially, everything that marks us as different. His coming to Washington is an act of such pure love and support that I stare ahead at the passing maid cart, absorbing the gesture.

My phone buzzes, and I'm eager to read another midflight message from my brother. But it's from a number I don't recognize.

The reporter told you to leave. Your cousin told you to leave. Now I guess I have to convince you.

Air skates across my neck.

I scan the covered walkway of the motel, the concrete fountain of the courtyard and the iron stairwell leading to the second floor and my room. No one is watching me break into a sweat in my driver's seat. With trembling fingers, I text: Who is this? What are you planning to do?

Three blinking dots pulse across the bottom of the message.

Five seconds. Ten seconds. Then the dots disappear, and I read the response.

Well, Ivy. That depends entirely on you.

Twenty-Nine

IVY

The Full Moon Killer. That's the only person who would care about me remaining in town with the goal of uncovering his secrets.

I lock my car doors and turn the key in the ignition.

Leaving is the smart thing to do, even if it is in line with my own MO to never follow through on anything. The Full Moon Killer has my number and has been watching me—that's reason enough for any sane person to hightail it back to California without a diagnosis.

Sweet Ivy, you can do this.

I shake my head, fighting the memory of my dad's voice. As painful as the truth is, maybe I can't. Maybe I should accept that instead of throwing myself farther down the deep end.

I cut the engine.

My stomach is a tight ball by the time I reach my room, but I wear the knowledge of my dad's fervent support like a parka against my mounting panic. Although terrified to stay here and see this through—on so many levels—it's clear I'm making progress.

Why else would the killer care about me—why follow me—if not because I'm getting closer to the truth? Maybe closer than anyone has yet.

My motel room smells different when I return. Not simply clean because the house staff came through and made the bed and spritzed some air freshener. Sharp. Lighter.

I breathe deep and recognize the scent with a choking cough. Eucalyptus. The same as when I returned to the guest room at the Caine house and found the letter removed from my suitcase. Someone has been in my motel room.

How did they find me—know that I've relocated to this new motel? What was this person searching for this time?

Vulnerability grips me, and I want to stack the end tables against the doorway and pull the bedcovers over my head. Hide away from the danger that's crawling closer with each ticking second.

On the floor lies a stiff take-out menu for a local pizza restaurant. The only tool needed to interrupt the door's lock mechanism.

What if Ballo isn't an FBI agent but does have FBI connections? Is that how he knew I'm here and how to jimmy open my door?

My entire frame itches, knowing I'm trapped. This person has been harassing me since I landed in Washington. And if that person has a way of entering my room, I need to work harder. Faster. It's already four o'clock, and dusk will roll in within hours, and then what will happen? Will I fall asleep, then hear some pizza-parlor menu struggling to flip up the security bar at three in the morning?

I lie on my belly on the floor—cringe—and search under the queen-size bed, but the boxy frame extends to the carpet. Searching in the shallow closet and the tiny-but-clean bathroom confirms that the intruder isn't hiding here.

My muscles cry out as I get to my feet, still sore from Poe's and Liam's attacks and the aftermath of another flare-up. I settle onto the bed, find a position that's comfortable, and pull over my laptop.

Between the Rock Island Library, local newspaper archives, and the internet, I've made a solid list of everyone who fits the victim bill:

young, male or female; killed in the nineties or early aughts; show-ing signs of poisoning, drug overdose, or strangulation; whose murder or unsolved disappearance occurred under a full moon in the Pacific Northwest. Many of them, as reported by news outlets and confirmed by the police, appeared to be innocuous or indeterminate deaths that were ultimately ruled suicides or left unsolved.

I click the final tab of my web browser to bring up my latest search results. The photo of Quentin Eriksen, a twenty-eight-year-old killed in 1991, exudes confidence as he stands beside a giraffe during a trip to the zoo. A young teacher who doubled as Malaga's swim coach, Eriksen was found on the riverbank, beneath a full moon, and dead from a morphine overdose.

Scanning for headlines that leap out as something useful, anything that counts, I find a hyperlink three pages in. Allegations were made against Eriksen—of abuse. According to five different families, during private lessons Eriksen made swimmers do laps naked, assuring the boys that he was testing the hydrodynamic drag of their bodies.

I'm not grasping something. I can feel it. Some detail that links all these victims.

I lie back on the bed, ball my fists into the thick fabric of the bed's comforter. Focus on the ceiling's smooth surface. A cobweb strings across the top-left corner of the room.

My mind sidesteps to the person who texted me this afternoon. Well, Ivy. That depends entirely on you.

What was I thinking allowing Carson to join me with a serial killer nearby and targeting me?

Panic rises from below my ribs. The sound of cars on the main thoroughfare outside reaches my ears, and for a second I imagine Liam-the-journalist among the cars, following me, or Ballo or someone else creeping along in secret—someone from One Family—maybe hiding where the motel property line meets the forest.

My phone vibrates beside my hand. A blocked number. Anxiety wars within me, desiring to answer and meet whoever is behind these murders head-on, and wishing this would all go away.

Go away. Go away. Go away.

I shut my eyes tight, then pick up the phone. "Hello?" But the call has already gone to voice mail.

The clock on my phone reads five thirty. My gaze drifts to the motel door, so easily picked with a piece of cardstock earlier. I cross to the small desk opposite the bed and try to lift it—see if it can serve as a barricade tonight—but it's bolted to the floor.

My phone vibrates from the beige bedspread. A voice mail.

A sick feeling spreads in my gut as I hit "Play."

"This message is for Ivy Hon. My name is Special Agent Hanover with the Federal Bureau of Investigation. Please return my call as soon as possible at the following number."

I lunge for the pad of paper and pen on the nightstand, then jot down the digits. With shaking fingers, I dial the number, then stop short. What if this isn't the FBI? What if Ballo got someone else to call, posing as the FBI, just as he did?

Footsteps clamor outside, followed by a man's and a woman's voice. I remain frozen.

Whoever attacked and killed Poe saw me—my face—I'm sure of it. If Ballo is the killer—and why else would he have lied about so many subjects?—why hasn't he come for me? I can't just sit around waiting for him or someone else to strike. I need to do something. To confront Lino Ballo the way I have each person who saw Tatum on her last day. Right?

Agent Ballo picks up on the third ring. "Ivy."

"Hi. I have some updates for you. Are you free now?"

He sucks in an audible breath. "Yes. Yeah, let's have them."

"Not on the phone. Can you meet me in Wenatchee? The coffee shop on Main."

"Definitely. I'll be there in ten."

The line goes dead. I stare at the blank screen another moment; then I leap toward my sneakers and grab my bag. Spinning on my heel, I tuck my laptop and the scrapbook that Aggie let me borrow under my arm, then trip over the take-out menu in my path. I check my back seat—empty—as I get behind the wheel of my rental car. I've just exited the parking lot when flashing red-and-blue lights appear in my rearview. Police cars cut across traffic into the motel, and my thoughts jump to the letter from 1994 that I left behind in my suitcase. Ignoring the desire to go back and get it—to protect the relic of my past—I accelerate.

Liam must have given them my name. It's been three days since he said he would tell the world about the gold tooth, and I don't know where he found the restraint to wait this long. That, or the bartender finally found one of my recent credit-card receipts and identified me as the person Poe left with. Either way, the police know where I'm staying and who I am.

Inside the coffee shop, Ballo is already seated at a wooden table for two along the back wall, away from the window. He's got a cup filled with black coffee, same as in San Francisco. Déjà vu climbs my neck as though it's free-soloing.

A glance around confirms we're alone, and even the barista seems glad when I don't approach the counter for an order. Everyone is tense before tonight's curfew. Popular, happy music pumps from the shop's speakers in a contrast that makes me grind my teeth.

"I'm glad you called, Ivy," Ballo says with a smile. "I hope this means you found something."

His excitement dips as he eyes my neck. "Are you sure you're okay?"

Tugging my loose hair forward to hide the bruising, I reply, "I'm fine."

So annoying that I can't seem to drop the people-pleasing, the knee-jerk reaction to tell people what they want to hear, even now. "I've learned a lot since coming up here."

"And? Did your birth family know anything about the Full Moon Killer? Anything that can help the investigation?"

"Well, no." My hand shaking, I take a seat facing the wall.

"Then I don't understand." He frowns, flicking a sugar packet with his thumb and forefinger. "Why did you want to talk?"

"I found some old high school yearbooks in the attic. An older family member's yearbook, actually, that neither of my parents were in. But you were."

Ballo stops moving. "Oh?"

I nod. "Only your name was listed as Rosalino Perez-Ballo."

His gaze flicks behind me. "You sure it was me?"

"You're Stacey Perez's older brother. Her half brother. I know that. What I don't know is why you would omit that, why you would hide your history in Rock Island from me. I don't know if you're really an FBI agent, or if the people who called me today are."

Ballo's eyebrow flicks up. "Other agents called you?"

"They did."

"Did you tell them anything?"

I hesitate a second and he has his answer.

"Good," he says. "This is not what you think it is. I'm just looking for answers, same as you."

"But you were angry with Tatum. Why were you harassing her that last day at her job?"

"Who says I was harassing her?"

"Answer the question."

Ballo peers at me as if sizing me up. "I'm not ready to share those details, Ivy. We need to be focused on finding the killer."

The forceful part of me, which I've kept shuttered out of a fear of being abandoned since my mom died—the flash of temper I show only to Carson—rumbles in my chest. I look Ballo square in the eye, emboldened by the public setting. "What if I already have? What if I'm sitting across from him right now?"

"Ivy, this is dangerous. What you're suggesting could lead to—"

"If you don't tell me—everything, why I should trust you—right now, I'm going to the police."

His jaw shifts back and forth. "Okay, then. Grab your stuff."

"What?"

He reaches into his inner jacket pocket just as he did during our first meeting. Instead of a business card, he withdraws a gun, black and shiny in the artificial lighting overhead, and points it at my chest.

"Because we're going on a drive."

I blanch. I've never seen a gun before, let alone up close. A sheet of cold passes down my body. "Where? What do you want?"

He locks dark eyes on me. "Resolution."

"Ivy?" a voice—one I'd know anywhere in the world—calls from behind me.

Carson. My brother. I turn and find him standing two tables away, a mirage of safety. Black sweater sleeves are pushed up to his elbows, but his face matches the pallor of mine. A duffel-bag strap is slung across his chest. The barista has disappeared, probably into a back room.

"Stay where you are," Ballo says.

Carson lifts his hands to chest level.

"He's my brother," I whisper, finding my voice. "Carson, what are you doing here? How did you find me?"

"Your—your rental car," he stammers. "Pea-soup green stands out. Plus, the bar codes all over the windows. I had my Uber drop me here when I saw it. Ivy, what is going on?"

Ballo pauses. Then he tucks the gun back into his jacket. "I guess we're all going on a drive."

At my rental, Ballo shoves Carson into the front passenger seat; then he slides into the back seat. He points the gun at Carson's headrest.

"Get in," he says to me through the window.

He directs me toward Rock Island, and I steer wide of potholes, terrified the gun will accidentally discharge.

I turn when he tells me to, not computing his directions or where he's leading me until I peer up at the gray two-story Colonial with the beige woodchip path. Aggie's house.

Thirty

Ivy

We exit the car. I stand, feeling the tension knotting my muscles all over, then take in the countryside surrounding Aggie's rural home five miles outside of town. No FBI agents began tailing us around the church, and no police cars flipped their high beams as we passed. No one knows we're here.

Above the idyllic scene, night has begun to fall. Stars dot the sky like tiny punctures in a canvas. Wounds in an otherwise whole piece of skin.

"Up to the door," Ballo says, gesturing with the gun.

"Sure," Carson replies, the first word he's said since we got in the car. He takes two steps forward, then whirls behind and throws himself at Ballo's waist, a wrestling move I recognize from our childhood. Ballo digs his toes into the ground and throws a punch that connects with Carson's head. Carson lists to the side but lunges forward, clocking Ballo on the chin before Ballo brings the handle of the gun down onto the back of my brother's head.

"No!" I scream. Carson collapses to the grass. I lift my eyes to Ballo, feeling my face crumpling, imitating Carson's body. "You didn't have to do that."

"Open the trunk, Ivy."

"What?"

"The trunk. Open it."

I hit the button on the key fob.

"Now put your brother into the trunk."

"What?"

"Ivy." The gun makes a clicking sound, and I know he's released the safety.

Carson is six feet tall, but he's lean. Although the last time I picked him up I was probably fourteen and he was sixteen, I manage to get his body into the trunk without hitting his head.

When Ballo shuts the lid and takes the keys from me, tears fill my eyes. Regret, disappointment, stress. My only family left. Carson bought a flight and flew here to help me even when I hadn't asked him to, and now he's in the equivalent of an overhead-compartment bin because of me.

"I'm so sorry," I whisper.

Ballo motions for me to start up the woodchip path. "Let's go."

"Ivy, hi. Who's your friend?" Aggie greets us at the door, the blue cotton of her sweatsuit damp across her neck.

Ballo answers by shoving me directly into her arms. Aggie and I fall backward, and I knock into the banister of the staircase. A loud crack cuts through the foyer, and I hope it's the railing and not my grandmother's hip.

As Ballo steps forward and begins to shut the door, I throw a glance at the closest neighbor's house a quarter mile away and up the hill. Too far.

"Who are you?" Aggie backs into the hall across from the living room where we opened her scrapbooks. Tension lines her face, eyes wide with outrage and fear at the home invasion.

"I'm here for answers," he says. "Someone in your family has been terrorizing this region for decades, and you know who. Don't you?"

"Wh—what are you—why would—"

"Mothers know all the horrible things their children do, and they always keep their secrets. But you can't keep protecting them forever. Especially when one of them is a murderer."

The color drains from Aggie's already pale face. "What are you talking about?"

"Or maybe both of them are. Maybe it's a family affair. Or, hell, Oregon isn't that far—does your brother-in-law come visit at the end of each lunar cycle? Just tell me who it is!"

"Ivy, you and your friend must be thirsty. Go into the kitchen and grab—"

Ballo shifts the gun to my head and cocks it. "Don't move."

I stand still. Frozen in place. I chance a quick breath, then hold it.

Aggie lifts a hand, slowly. "Ivy has nothing to do with this. She's just a visitor. You can let her go. I'll help you figure out who in my family is the killer you're talking about. Let's start with your name. What is your name?"

He slaps at the air, dismissing her grab for control. "I'm looking for the Full Moon Killer. One of your family members, according to Ivy here's DNA."

"What?" Aggie's mouth drops.

"We don't know that," I start. "She never met my birth father; no one did. Harassing us the way you harassed Tatum isn't going to give you any answers."

He stares with a blank expression, as if reliving those months. "You sure? Because I don't remember any Asian guys in Rock Island, growing up. Whereas the Caines have been here since before Stacey was killed and afterward, when others were killed too."

Ballo turns his attention back to Aggie. "So I'm going to ask you again: Who are you covering for? Which child or cousin are you going to tell me you were with last month when Katrina Oates was murdered? When my sister was attacked before then?"

Aggie's expression is blank. "I'm sorry—I'm very . . . I can't think straight with that gun. I don't know what you mean."

"Oh no?" Ballo leers at her. "Well, let me explain."

———

My heartbeat is the first thing I hear. *Tick, tick, tick, tick.*

I open my eyes and continue to see blackness. Lifting my eyebrows shifts the blackness a little, this way and that. A blindfold. I'm wearing a blindfold. Bile rises in my throat as a quick inventory confirms my hands are tied, and so are my feet. The restraints cut into my dry skin and elicit images from recent internet searches I've memorized of cadavers tied up—kills attributed to various serial killers. Am I about to be next? Will my image one day show up to some other jackass of the future getting in over her head?

My pulse quickens, begins to beat faster than its audible *tick tick tick*, and I recognize the actual source of the noise—a clock. There's an analog clock close by.

Someone coughs across the room. I'm not alone.

Two quick breaths through my nose do little to calm my nerves—to reassure myself that I'm okay—since each inhale causes a sharp stab to my ribs. I must have fallen harder than I thought against the staircase. The cuts in my hand from the floor of the bar—barely healed—pulse, as if threatening to split open.

It's cold. Although I can't see them, I'm sure my fingernails are blue, tied to the armrests of some wooden chair, and unable to rub together for warmth.

Turning my head to the right, then left, I find more light seems to emanate from the left. Smaller breaths, a few sniffs, tickle my nose. A twinge of antiseptic mixed with lemon. Thick dread hits my stomach as I realize the scent here can only mean a cleanup was performed recently. Recalling the way I laid Carson in my rental's trunk, helpless and vulnerable, I press my lips against a scream—bite back the crawling fear slithering up my throat that my brother might be nearby and might have undergone an act that required industrial-strength sanitizing.

He still could be. The person who coughed hasn't made another noise.

My hands jerk against the restraints but have no effect. Panic, panic, panic. Whimpers seep from my lips like the animal I am, waiting for the slaughter.

Agent Ballo must be close. He did this hours ago, after he tied up Aggie with rope in some elaborate knot, then herded me downstairs to the basement. Once he returned to Aggie's kitchen, I must have passed out alone in the dark.

I was so dumb, playing directly into his game plan.

Wooden boards creak from several feet away.

"Hello?" I whisper to the room. "Who's there?"

A muffled noise answers—someone gagged across from me.

"Carson?"

Footsteps reverberate in the house, approaching. A doorknob rattles. Then the basement door moans inward. Each step down the wooden stairs is as ominous as an executioner's gait. I breathe deep and taste the scent of aftershave. When my blindfold is untied, revealing Ballo, a primal urge rises in me to bite him.

"I'm sorry about this, Ivy," he says, though his expression is hard. The black cloth shakes in his hand as if there's a basement breeze.

Vision restored, I whip my head to take in the scene. Behind him, Aggie is gagged and strapped to a chair identical to mine, hands behind her back. I meet her wide eyes and recall the sound of her muffled response. Not Carson.

Boxes, old bicycles, framed photos, and discarded furniture line the walls. A glass multishelf curio cabinet stands opposite the staircase and, in the corner reaches, a narrow, landscape-style window covered in blackout paper.

Jars, vials, and cartons are stacked on each shelf; the bottom shelf is the exception, displaying a handsaw similar to what I saw in Tristen's workshop. Chains are coiled beside it. The walls are concrete, naked of decoration. Two plastic tubs with rope handles hold sporting equipment.

"Where is Carson? Is he still in the trunk?" My voice trembles, unable to hide my fear. "Why are you shaking?"

Ballo doesn't answer. Instead, he examines my hands and feet to make sure they're still secured. He bends down so that we are level; then he peers at me with determined, veiny eyes. "I haven't slept in two days. I'm going to need your help, Ivy. I tried talking to Aggie, but she refuses to tell the truth."

I wait, still unsure what he wants from me.

"Your grandmother knows who killed my sister. Now, I don't want to hurt anyone, but I need answers. You can't expect me to believe that one of you doesn't have a name already in your head. I've waited too long, Ivy."

Taking note of the dim light at the edges of the blackout paper and of his frenzied fatigue, I wonder how much time has passed since he corralled Carson and me into my rental.

"I'm sorry, I really don't know."

He scowls. "Sure you don't."

He glances over his shoulder to Aggie. "So which one of you is lying, and which is telling the truth? Ivy's DNA says the Full Moon Killer—my sister's murderer—is on some wack-job family tree branch of yours. Aggie says the opposite; the killer isn't one of yours."

"You can't keep us here because you *think* we're hiding something," I say.

Ballo folds his arms. "You'd be surprised. FBI agents have a pretty long leash with the law."

Aggie is silent, watching the spectacle.

"I don't think the law allows vengeance crusades. How do we know you're with the FBI? You barely showed me your badge."

He shifts his weight, then gets to his feet. He paces to the left, then to the right, before he stops again.

"I'm a systems administrator for the bureau—technology. The field agents I overheard—their intention was to contact you once they had approvals from leadership. Instead of waiting for them to get their shit together while someone else could die, I hoped you'd dig up something useful—papers, photographs. When I learned you'd flown up here, I thought: even better. I decided to let you lead me to your relative, the killer. Only problem is the FBI learned I contacted you and placed me on administrative leave. I came up here on my own, and I've been watching you since I landed, the day after the full moon. After all that, if you're not going to help now—"

"What? You're going to . . . hurt me, like you did my brother?"

A fire sparks in Ballo's eyes. "Your brother attacked me—*me*—Ivy."

"After you abducted us. The whole reason you're doing this is to get your revenge on whoever took your sister. Right? So what's your plan now? You're hoping to identify the killer when they come to save us—to come check on their matriarch, Aggie, when she doesn't reply to calls for a few days?"

Ballo scowls. For some reason I think of my conversation with Mal, Tatum's former coworker. About Stacey's controlling and violent brother.

I make eye contact with Aggie. Her arms shift behind her back. She nods.

"Maybe," I say. "Maybe the reason that you'll do anything to find this killer, even stalk and abduct people . . . maybe the FBI placed you on leave because you killed your sister." Recalling Phillip's words to me in the diner, I lean forward. "Maybe you killed Stacey because she was an embarrassment to your family."

My accusation rings in the basement. Ballo flushes red. He grips the skin of my forearms, and I wince. "If you're going to point the finger at me, that escalates things, Ivy. You're forcing my hand."

"Did you?" I say, cringing beneath him. "Kill Stacey? Is that why you still feel so guilty?"

"Shut up!" He slaps me across the jaw. Lights break across my vision, and I taste blood. "Those rumors after Stacey died," he seethes. "They ruined life up here for me and forced me to move states. I narrowly escaped a formal inquiry when the cops were looking for someone to blame."

He aims the gun at my chest. New terror spikes in me, and I lick my lips, regretting that I provoked him.

"If you hurt me," I begin, "you'll only reinforce that idea. You'll never escape being suspected as the Full Moon Killer yourself."

"Isn't that what I've already done? Made things worse?" His voice breaks. "You're right—but only if I let you leave to tell someone. I've lost everything. My job, my reputation, my little sister."

He lifts the gun to my head. His features are ragged, drained, but determined in the way he meets my defiant gaze. "Everyone said all these years that I was the murderer, with no evidence but a sullen attitude. Well, maybe I don't need your help, Ivy. Maybe harming someone related to the killer will be enough."

"It won't be." Aggie's deep voice rings out from behind Ballo. We both turn to find her sitting upright, the gag down around her neck, although her hands are still tied behind her.

"The police will track you down and put you in prison for life, for crimes you didn't commit. Do you really want that? Put down the gun. Leave Ivy alone. Let's talk this through."

My chest tightens. Shallow breaths are all I can manage, waiting for Ballo's reaction.

He keeps the gun at my eye level but turns to Aggie. "Where were you the weekend that Katrina Oates was killed? Which of your relatives were you with?"

Aggie doesn't blink. "I wasn't with anyone in my family. I was over in Spokane for the Spokane Squash Festival. Mine are award winning, and I was hoping for another blue ribbon."

I suddenly feel frayed. Even more on edge. Like if I touched a wall socket, I might burst into sparks.

The Spokane Squash Festival. The largest squash expo on the West Coast, according to the rental-car company employee who was complaining about losing business when it was canceled. I might misrecall something that was said, but the banner's extra-large typo remains stark in my mind: *Spokane Squash Festaval.*

Sweat forms under my arms, watching Aggie's innocent expression fix on my confused one.

"Ivy?" she asks.

I shake my head. "That conference was canceled. You weren't in Spokane that weekend. So what were you doing?"

Aggie glances from me to Ballo. Then to the stairs behind him and the loaded weapon he holds. She straightens her back, taller and more athletic than the usual way she carries herself—bent, tired, as an afterthought—and reminds me in a burst of millennial meta-clarity how frequently older women are overlooked. She takes a deep breath that swells her senior citizen's chest like a lion about to roar.

"I was rooting out the weeds."

Thirty-One

IVY

The gun whipsaws away from me.

"You." Ballo is breathing heavily, his shoulders rising and falling. He steps to my right between Aggie and the staircase. "Tell me everything."

Gray-blonde hairs, mussed from her struggles when Ballo tied her up, create a crown around her square-shaped face. She stares him down, at the pistol aimed at her head, with a calculating mien. Then she meets my gaze, her expression softening.

"Ivy, I never meant for you to be caught up in this—for anyone."

I take in this woman's light-blue eyes, the bump that we share on the bridges of our noses, and the blunted chin she passed on to Tatum. Could she really be a murderer—my biological grandmother—not just once in self-defense or due to circumstances out of her control, but twenty times, if my estimates are correct? The memory of watching Aggie in her garden, her toned forearms that had me questioning whether weeding was an aerobic activity, fills my mind.

"I don't understand," I say to her. "You can't be the killer. That person killed Tatum."

Aggie narrows her eyes. "I didn't touch my child. Someone else did. Because of Tatum's death, I began consuming all the news I could in the Pacific Northwest, trying to find the clue or criminal that would lead me to her murderer. I don't feel strongly for people, generally. But I love my children. The hole the death of a child leaves in a mother's heart can't be overestimated."

Ballo snorts. "Bullshit. You killed her like you killed Stacey and Geri. You didn't start up after Tatum, you began before her. They were all killed under the full moon. You don't have any code that you murder by."

Aggie—the picture of calm, sitting tied up in a chair—shakes her head. "I'm the opposite of impulsive. Unlike yourself, I watch my victims. I make certain they are who I think they are—then I act."

"And who are they?" I ask, the start of a fever rising in my cheeks.

"Sadists," she replies. "True psychopaths. Malicious individuals who hurt others out of some sexual or primal pleasure. I find the ones that the police let slip through the cracks and deal with them my own way."

Ballo sneers. "So you're doing us all a favor, huh? You're saving us from some future loss? Some superhero? Wake up, Grandma. You're the villain."

"If the police had found the person who passed through town and attacked my Tatum, she would still be here. I wish someone had seen what that man was capable of, and done something about it!" Her voice goes hoarse, and she coughs, although I'm not sure I believe it.

Malicious individuals who hurt others out of some sexual or primal pleasure. The memory of my easy conversation with Poe returns to emphasize the point—he was luring me in, only to attack me later when we were alone. My throat closes, remembering the moment his touch turned aggressive. Although I don't know whether Aggie's good intentions make decades of murder okay, I'm positive I would be dead if she hadn't entered Poe's motel room.

"You killed Poe. You showed up when he was . . ." My voice trails off, and I can't finish the sentence. *Strangling me.*

A sneer crosses Aggie's face, and I have the sense that I'm witnessing the Aggie her victims meet.

"In 1993, after Ashlee Drummond began torturing children she deemed antisocial in her kindergarten class, I didn't want to work anymore in our town. I wondered whether it was worth it to have to endure the public mourning, then heightened vigilance by the police, that would always follow. But the wrong people continued to visit our region. Later, I avoided watching Rock Island closely for years, successfully, before Katrina Oates moved in. When she began abusing babies at the day care, I couldn't stomach it.

"I swore that was it last month, but then that man you call Poe took up residence here, stalking and wooing my newly returned granddaughter—Samson Truman was his real name, if his driver's license is correct. I'd been running an errand in town when I saw him leave the bar after speaking to you, Ivy. Call it some intuition, but I followed him to the pickup truck that he was sleeping in over by the river in Malaga. I watched him for an afternoon and evening, and saw when he attacked that hitchhiker who was later found beneath the dock. Lottie was on the phone with me when she received your text message telling her you were staying with a friend on Thursday. I knew Poe meant to kill you, Ivy. And I couldn't allow it. Even if it meant I had to leave the body instead of disposing of it the way I normally would—not with all those security cameras at the motel."

I shake my head. Wish desperately that my hands were free to rub the mounting ache away from my temples. "He seemed so normal."

"The good ones do. I've watched people like him for years now."

Poe's spectral voice returns from the bar. *I've been watching people all my life. That's why I'm so good at sales.*

I apply that to Aggie, watching her closely. Gone is the effusive warmth of the Caine family matriarch who served tea and gourmet crackers on her back porch. All those homemaking skills—the broad smiles and easy banter—were a useful front in maintaining the image of a benign grandmother. Here, she doesn't need any of that. In her base-ment, despite the gun still pointed at her head, the mask is dropped. She can be the cold hunter she truly is.

"Aggressors believe small towns are easy prey," she continues. "Women were frequently targeted during the eighties and the nine-ties. When hitchhiking and drug parties became less common, preda-tors showed up less frequently in the area, and I acted more sparingly; but when people like Katrina and Samson come around, I can't stop myself—and I don't want to; I stifled those urges for so long. Now, the full moon always tells me when it's time to strike."

Ballo cocks the gun, startling both of us. "You think you're Central Washington's savior? What about my sister? What about Stacey? She didn't do anything. She wasn't some evil person. She was an innocent seventeen-year-old, and you poisoned her, strangled her, and left her to be found in the river."

Aggie shakes her head, gray flyaways catching the air. "I didn't. I didn't begin working until after Tatum disappeared, and my choice of weapon was always morphine or another drug. Wholesale batches that could be easily obtained, or stolen from the hospital."

"Bullshit!" he shouts. "If you didn't kill Stacey, who did? Who else would have done the same thing to Geri Hauser and Tatum?"

His hand quivers, his aim less steady, and Aggie doesn't reply. As much as my stomach twists, thinking about my biological grandmother as a murderer, I believe her when she says she didn't hurt Tatum. And judging from Ballo's frenzied thirst for vengeance, I'm not sure I'll make it out of here without her.

I brace myself, then pull against my restraints as hard as I dare.

Carson was obsessed with professional wrestling when we were growing up. He tried for days to show me how to throw my body, then break my own fall, the way that The Rock did in the ring. I never learned how to do it right, but I recall his voice walking me through each step. Swing my shoulder forward, then down. Tuck my head and roll.

Ballo's skin flushes red. He removes the safety latch from the gun, but it takes two hands to do it. "I've waited thirty years for this. Nothing you say will get you out of the *justice* you've been heaping on others. Finally, you'll get your own dose."

I lunge toward him, taking the chair with me and fall two feet from where I was. Instead of knocking him backward against the shelf behind him, I smash into his knees, making his legs buckle. The gun goes flying across the room as he falls on the chair and shatters the wood.

He crawls across my chest, reaching for the gun.

"Ivy," he grunts, "you're not thinking clearly. She's a murderer. She killed her own daughter."

"No," I manage, stretching forward, an inch closer to the firearm than he is.

"Ivy! Wake up!" Ballo punches my underarm, and a jolt of pain corkscrews through my bicep, my chest, my shoulder. I can't speak. I can't move. "There are *two* serial killers in this town? If you do this—if you help *her*—you are as big a disappointment as you think."

I fold into a ball, groaning through the agony radiating down my side. His words strike me in the heart.

But Lottie compared me to a sister before Ballo outed me. Carson flew up here just to be with me, for moral support. And though the memory of my parents dims with each day, the way they made me feel never has: loved. Wanted. Despite our differences.

I grit my teeth. "You don't know me." I jerk my knee into his belly, and the air whooshes from his chest. He rolls to the side, cradling his stomach.

Something clatters to the floor near Aggie's chair. A penknife. She dives over us, grabbing the gun. Ballo leaps to his feet, but she whips the barrel toward him. I grapple for a broken chair leg, then bring it sideways to connect hard with his knee, and he topples to the floor, hitting his head with a thud.

We stare at him, unconscious on the concrete. I hold my breath. Finally, his torso rises, then falls.

I meet Aggie's gaze. For a moment, fear grips my heart. I'm a witness to her confession, even if I'm technically family.

Aggie, as if sensing my unease, relaxes her war posture.

I gather my courage and ask the only question that counts right now. "Did you kill Tatum?"

"No."

"Do you believe that she died?"

Aggie startles. As if there was never any doubt. "Yes. There's nothing that would keep her from coming home for over thirty years."

Her sincerity is bright despite the dim lighting of the basement. Ballo continues to breathe shallowly, a raspy sound beside us.

Something else squeezes my chest—not fear, not love, exactly. Quiet appreciation for Aggie's intentions, despite her horrifying methods.

My mother always warned me against believing strangers too quickly in a big city like San Francisco. What if the strangers we know carry the greater risk of breaking our hearts—betraying our expectations?

"Aggie . . . what if Tatum is alive?" I'm as surprised as anyone at my words, but I realize it's what I've been thinking ever since Liam said she might not have been a Full Moon victim. What if she doesn't want to be found?

She sucks in a breath that she holds for several seconds, searching my face for something. Evidence of a joke. "I know that's not the case."

"Why is that?"

Aggie's attention scatters to the ground; then she hugs the elbows of her sweatsuit. "Because someone took her from a party, then led her to the river."

"How do you know that?"

Aggie's recounting of the facts is consistent with everything I've read and heard. It's long been accepted as the truth, but I know from

Liam Weathers that presumption and guesswork can morph into "truth" over time.

"The police said so," Aggie insists. "Phillip and others told them they saw Tatum walking with a man toward the river."

"Phillip did?" There's a roaring sound like waves in my ears.

She nods. "He was there that night."

I know Phillip was a member of One Family, thanks to Liam.

"Aggie, when did Phillip leave One Family?"

She meets my eyes, and the concrete wavers beneath me.

"He never did. Now he heads the local chapter."

Thirty-Two

IVY

Running up the stairs and through Aggie's kitchen is a blur. As I reach the lush potted plants that flank the sliding glass and lead to outdoors, a thump sounds from down below, and Aggie and I pause.

She has smoothed the gray flyaways back into her ponytail. A fresh pink colors her cheeks. "He's awake," she says.

Tying Ballo to one of the chairs in the basement took Aggie less than five minutes. Her hands deftly knotted the ropes, and I wondered how many times she had completed the same routine with other men and women.

I follow her, ignoring the pain in my ribs, as she steps onto the porch where we ate sandwiches and iced tea, past the impressive vegetable garden with its prizewinning squash that she didn't take to Spokane.

When I told her my suspicion that One Family was involved in Tatum's death and that Phillip may have had a role to play in it too, she snatched up the rope and went to work. Phillip lives on the property, she explained, down the hill and out of sight of the main road. Anger shook her hands as she finished the knots, but her face was pale.

"Wait." I stop dead. "Carson."

I whirl on my heel, then round the side of the house in the early-morning darkness, back to where Ballo had me park my rental. Fumbling for the keys that I took from his pocket, I mash the buttons on the fob until all the doors are unlocked—except the trunk. I jam the key into the trunk's keyhole and stop abruptly; the blade is bent.

"Carson, can you hear me?"

"Ivy! Get me out of here! What's going on?"

Relief floods me. He's okay. "Hold on, the key isn't working."

Aggie remains on the concrete pavement, watching. Waiting for me.

I slide into the driver's seat, then feel around at my feet for the trunk release. The hood pops up, but none of the latches I pull or push unlock the trunk.

I climb into the back seat. Paw at the leather headrests and search for a manual knob—something to pull or twist in order to lay the seats down and access my brother—and land on a recessed button. I push down but nothing happens. "Ivy?" Carson calls. His voice is wary. Strained, as if he spent the time I was passed out in the basement shouting for help.

"Shit."

"What?"

"I'm . . . I don't see a way in. I think the trunk release is broken. I need to call someone."

"And that can't happen before we speak to Phillip," Aggie says.

"Carson." I don't take my eyes off my grandmother. The Full Moon Killer. "I need to take care of something else. Can you hang tight?"

He groans. "I guess I don't have a choice."

Aggie and I march down the sloping hill and through a grove of trees nearly invisible from the back of the house. Less than the length of a swimming pool, the verdant barrier serves as a marker between Aggie's two-story house and the single-level ranch house occupying the valley beneath. No birds—no other signs of life—make an appearance as we crunch through twigs and leaves. Several hundred yards away from Aggie's home, I wonder if the wind has ever carried the sound of screaming—toward Phillip's house or away from it.

A rain-rusted chair in the unfenced yard faces the river—the infamous body of water that's been responsible for so much transition and death over the years. Aggie strides up the front walkway, a worn dirt path, then reaches for the brass doorknob, not pausing to knock. I follow her into the house and find Phillip standing at a kitchen counter, armed with not one but two handguns that he's loading with bullets.

He sees us and blanches. "Aggie. I was just about to come over there. Are you okay? Who was that man who shoved his way into your house?"

He motions to three square screens presenting black-and-white images of Aggie's front door, her back door, and his own front yard. "I just got home and was skimming footage from the last few hours. I saw a man drag Ivy into the house."

Phillip places both hands on the counter, next to his guns, then hangs his head. He releases a deep breath from between his shoulder blades. When he lifts his head, his mischievous grin returns. "So what happened?"

"You tell me, Phillip. What have you been up to the last thirty-plus years? What kind of sick and twisted activities in One Family have kept you busy all this time?" Aggie seethes, staring at her brother. "You told the police you saw someone following Tatum to the river the night she disappeared. Why should we believe you?"

The grin wipes clean from his long face. "What's going on? What is this about, Aggie?"

I step forward. Try to ignore the loaded weapons by his hands. "When did you decide to get rid of your niece?"

Phillip's gray-blue eyes flit to Aggie's. "What kind of nonsense—"

"She knows," Aggie says. "And I don't know why it took me so long to piece together the obvious before. I guess I thought, as my older brother, you would care for Tatum like she was your own. Stupid, really, when you've never cared for anyone but yourself."

Aggie continues to speak in the same matter-of-fact way that she did down in the basement. Phillip squints past us at the door.

"I'm not following what you two girls are up to." He offers a casual smile, probably trying to defuse the tension, but he doesn't move from the beige laminate counter, inches from the guns.

Girls. As if we're wearing training bras.

I let the moment slide to focus on the facts. "Phillip, you told the police you saw a man pursuing Tatum toward the river and away from the Santorini house, right? A story that a reporter caught wind of and began to tout as fact. Another presumed death under the full moon."

Phillip shakes his head, shadows drawing across his weathered skin. "Other people at the meeting saw the pair of them walking away. Others confirmed it."

"You were in One Family the night that Tatum died," I say. "One Family has extreme views on member behavior and their families' behavior. You'd been harboring those ideas so long, there wasn't even a question when you did it."

Phillip's upper lip twitches as he fixes two angry eyes on mine. "Did what?"

"Killed your niece. When I learned you were a member, I thought you were like the others who got swept up in One Family's world, then cut ties later on—who returned to reality, before the nonprofit guise. Instead, you were so entrenched in the cult that you became an elder. You killed Tatum to align with the One Family code of ethics."

Aggie sucks in a breath beside me, as Phillip stares at me like a cornered dog, hackles rising ceiling-high, and takes me in—my straight black hair, tawny skin, the round eyes that kiss at the edges—everything that marks me as different from him. Likely, he hates it all the more that I—the adopted-out grandniece he tried to forget—am the one who's come to shout his crimes.

"You were ashamed of Tatum having a baby, unmarried, and were probably embarrassed at her disregard for One Family rules," I continue. "So you killed her, then threw her body in the river. Or dismembered her with one of the tools from the Caine garage."

"That's ridicul—"

"You were supposed to protect her," I say.

Phillip slams his hand on the counter. "Everything I did was for this family. For the Caine name! Something you wouldn't know anything about, Ivy Hon. You are not one of us, and you were never meant to be in this world. I tried to get you to leave too, but you were too stubborn to take a hint."

Something tickles my nose. A sharp, minty scent—eucalyptus. The same aroma found in my bedroom at the Caine house and my motel room. Phillip's aftershave. It's the first time I've been close enough to him, in such still air, to smell it.

"You destroyed my rental car," I say to him, my voice rising. "You broke into my motel room, then sent me that threatening text message. You've been following me."

"What did you do to Tatum?" Aggie growls.

"I didn't touch Tatum!" Phillip roars. "First, she delivered a baby, with no husband by her side; then that final day, she was seen fornicating with a man on the riverbank. No niece of mine would behave in such embarrassing ways, and the One Family elders believed she deserved death like the others—but I *saved* her. I convinced them that Tatum should leave and disappear, taking her ruinous conduct with her. She didn't adhere to the One Family ways, but I made it so that she was spared. You know why, Aggie?"

Aggie stares at him, mouth agape. He adds, "For you! That's why. Out of affection and sympathy for my sister, after she lost her husband only four years before. Then Ivy here began nosing around, threatening to ruin everything. The mayor is holding a ceremony next month to honor our family. Do you think that would happen without me mitigating the family mistakes?"

His shoulders rise and fall, covered in overalls and plaid. Sweat gleams across his wrinkled forehead in the kitchen lighting, and for a moment he appears like the old, meandering man he's been pretending to be all this time.

"What do you mean 'she deserved death like the others'?" I ask. A clock ticks somewhere in the house, counting down to whatever is about to happen next. Phillip peers at me, as if surprised by my words. Confusion gives way to disbelief—then resignation that the admission came tumbling from his own chapped mouth.

"Stacey Perez. Geri Hauser," I add. "They were always thought to be the first two victims of the Full Moon Killer, but that's incorrect. They were killed by One Family, weren't they? You all—the elders—were so hell-bent that members and their families follow the One Family code. Stacey was the cousin of Yolanda Underwood, a long-time member, and Geri Hauser was a member herself. You must have told each of them to stop their bad behavior, and they refused. Then you killed them."

"They had more than enough chances," Phillip says, sneering. "We begged them to reform their wild ways, but those girls ignored us. I told Tatum she would meet the same fate as Stacey and Geri if she didn't clean up her act, but she also refused."

"How did you get Tatum to leave?" I ask. Aggie hasn't moved beside me. I can only imagine what's going through her head.

Her brother drove her daughter away, out of her life. The presumed death of her youngest set Aggie off on a path of—in her mind—vigilante justice. How much death has occurred because of Phillip's malicious arrogance, his compulsion to control? How much of that compulsion has been encouraged by others over the years, reinforced by his role as an elder in a cult, and as a member of a founding family in the region?

Phillip ignores me, turning to his sister. "Aggie. I did it for her own good. For the family name. For all that we've worked for, and Mama and Daddy worked for."

Aggie lifts red-rimmed eyes to his face. "How did you get her to leave?"

Phillip grinds his jaw. "I told her that if she ever returned, I would go after her baby. I knew where the baby was because I insisted on placing it for adoption. She asked me for a pregnancy test, thinking I wouldn't tell you, but then it was—"

"You. It all comes back to you," I interrupt. "She didn't want to give up her baby for adoption, but you forced her to—falsely telling her the town would never accept her marriage to an outsider or the product of their relationship, me—forever rendering the baby illegitimate. Despite the orgies and drug use, One Family had strict rules about propriety outside of the cult. Image was everything."

Phillip's shoulders pull back, away from my summary of his misdeeds. As if he still stands by his actions. "It was that reporter that began running with the idea that Tatum was a victim of the Full Moon Killer, although we both, apparently"—he gestures between himself and Aggie, the real serial killer Liam Weathers built a reputation on—"always knew the truth."

"But why sacrifice your niece for One Family? She was your real family."

Phillip sneers again. "My *family* worked to build up this community, this life that you've benefited from too. My parents and grandparents were tireless in lifting up the Caine name, before my niece began to tarnish it. One Family understands the power of that name and respects it to this day."

Aggie lurches forward, as if his words snap something inside her. "You did all that to Tatum—to me—because you needed an ego stroke? Because you miss the glory days?"

She levels a punch at his jaw. He stumbles into the darkened hall beside the kitchen, and she follows him. Aggie delivers blow after blow, but Phillip begins to fight back, landing a punch on his sister's cheek with a growl. Photo frames shatter on the floor as they smash against the wall.

They fall behind the counter, landing with a thud. Another strike of skin on skin sounds; then a drawer is opened in the kitchen, and cutlery spills across the floor in a chute of aluminum.

I fumble in my pockets for the slender whistle I've been keeping on me. I blow into the mouthpiece, and a sharp note slices the air.

But they keep fighting. I move forward and catch Aggie slam Phillip's head against the drawer. I blow again. "Where is Tatum now?"

Both Aggie and Phillip turn. Recognition slides across Aggie's face.

"Ivy," she says slowly. "Where did you get that?"

"The . . . the kiln. I saw the whistle inside, stuck toward the back."

She reaches toward me, and I instinctively take a step away. "That's a high-heat-resistant, titanium survival whistle. That's my husband Richard's whistle, which disappeared the night that Tatum did. She was wearing it."

Her fists clench across her knees, curling and uncurling. "Phillip, you forced her to leave, then tried to burn the evidence."

Phillip stares at me, black eyes visible from the floor. "Leave no stone unturned, right, Ivy Hon?"

He lunges for me. I slap the whistle on the counter, grab both guns. Fire a shot into the ceiling. Plaster and insulation explode from above, showering us in particleboard.

Aggie and Phillip freeze. I point a barrel at the pair of them, entangled on the laminate flooring. For a moment I can see them as brawling siblings instead of the cold killers they are.

My ears begin to ring from the gunshot.

No. From the police sirens. The horns wailing outside. Distant at first. Then drawing closer.

"Ivy," Aggie breathes, "I never meant to . . . to take anyone's life. It was Tatum's death that made me go down that path. Everyone I killed was inflicting pain on someone else—an innocent. I stopped more heartache that they would have caused, and I always made sure to research my targets. But the police won't see it that way. I need to leave."

Neither of them blinks, waiting for my reaction.

"Whose gold tooth did I find in the kiln, Aggie?" I ask. "Beside the whistle."

She doesn't hesitate. "Seamus Thatcher, an elder-abuser who worked in a convalescent home. In the beginning, I left my victims at the river-bank. Tried to make it look like they drowned with morphine in their systems—suicide—so no one would ask questions or look too closely. But when the news started linking them to the Full Moon Killer and logging my kills, I began obscuring their deaths in other ways: cremating them in the kiln or making their deaths look like animal attacks."

Horror flicks my shoulders. "You can't just get away with all that."

Aggie stares me down. "Ivy. I also saved your life."

Before I can respond, she gets to her feet, then opens the door opposite the kitchen. A pantry. From it she withdraws a rain chain and a bungee cord. She turns to Phillip and begins to tie him up while I refresh my grip on his handgun.

"Where is Tatum?" I ask Phillip again.

He only glares.

"He's not going to tell. Not now at least," Aggie says. She crosses to me, and I stiffen, anticipating her touch. She lets her palm fall to her side. "What matters is Tatum didn't die that night. And neither did you that year."

Sirens continue to swell, nearing our location in the backwoods behind Aggie's expansive property.

Aggie and I share another look, and we both understand that I'm not going to stop her. She strides behind me, and without turning, I hear the front door slam shut. She takes off running, sprinting toward the grove of trees.

Phillip refuses to make eye contact, bound and chained in his own house. Another minute goes by, then two, and the sirens are at his doorstep. Tires crunch along the outside gravel while car doors open and shut. More footsteps run forward, several pairs, followed by shouting. The front door flings open, and I brace myself for commands from the police to drop my weapon.

"Ivy!" Carson's breathless voice booms from the entryway. Police officers swarm behind him, telling him to move, to get down, and he steps sideways, bumping into the armchair, knocking a folded blanket loose.

"How did you—"

"Every rental car has a GPS location, and when the police didn't find you at your motel, they began tracking yours. They found me, then heard the gunshot go off down the hill."

As blue uniforms bark their orders, I lift my hands above my head.

In the dim lighting, amid the aggressive pace of officers spreading throughout the house, I focus my hazy vision on my brother. Wide eyed and probably in shock at finding me bearing not one but two guns, he scans my torso, then my face, as if taking inventory. Against all odds, I'm alive and in one piece.

A relieved smile spreads across his jaw. Gratitude fills my frame as I meet the gaze of someone I can trust across time and geography, no matter our fights or misunderstandings. I smile too. Carson nods, as if reading my thoughts: *family*.

Thirty-Three

Ivy

One month later

Light reflects off the Puget Sound behind her, sparkling at her shoulders and along the crown of her shoulder-length brown hair. Freckles dust her chest, visible in her loose linen top. Her eyes are a deep green, unlike anyone I've encountered in the family, but I find myself in the bump on the bridge of her nose and the way she gestures with her hands when she's excited.

Tatum is beautiful. She's exactly the way I always pictured her—her skin lined, but each wrinkle well earned, and exuding energy in every movement she makes—and yet my imagination could not have done her justice, seeing her in flesh and blood.

She pauses, then turns her head toward the sun. "You feel that? Those are some of the last summer rays we'll get around here."

Closing her eyes, Tatum breathes deep the salty air of the sound. I should probably mimic her and enjoy the sunshine before I return to the Bay Area, with its gray skies that will roll in soon too, but I don't. The sight of my birth mother, alive and at peace after hiding away in

Seattle for so many years, fills me with such warmth that I keep stealing glances when I think she's not looking.

In those moments, I pause in telling Tatum about life in the Bay—about my family and my brave brother who flew up here to be with me—and forget what I was saying. Usually, that's when Bowen, my birth father, dives in with an anecdote about how they redid the upstairs bathroom together last summer and how Tatum is a whiz with a drill.

Within thirty minutes of meeting him, I asked Bowen about his family's medical history—was there anything unusual on his side? Taking my clumsy question in stride, he volunteered that his mother had lupus, an autoimmune condition. She died at the age of eighty-seven, just two years ago, and he came out of hiding to celebrate with her. Tears formed in my eyes as he confirmed that my condition, although challenging, is not an early death sentence.

My doctor shared with me that lupus was one of her chief suspects, second to cancer. She said it's often considered the disease of a thousand faces because it can present in myriad ways, making it incredibly difficult to diagnose. Although I'll need to confirm the diagnosis with another battery of tests once I get home to the Bay, knowing I have a family history of lupus is a strange relief—the end of my search for answers finally in sight.

While sitting in side-by-side Adirondack chairs, Bowen often takes Tatum's hand in his. Wide palms that would be great at repairing crowns and applying veneers as a dentist, his original career choice, now dedicate their talents to creating dumplings and other dim sum items he sells from his gourmet food truck. From what they share with me, Bowen and Tatum lost touch after she fled Rock Island. It was in Seattle, where he moved several years later, that they ran into each other at another Nirvana concert, and decided to hide together under assumed names. He couldn't pursue dentistry if they wanted to stay hidden, so he turned to the recipes his parents taught him. He gave it all up for her.

According to Tatum, her adjustment was easier since she left when she was almost eighteen. No investment in nursing school yet, or debt, or preconceived ideas about what she would become to hold her back. She says her only motivator then was to survive. To escape her zealot uncle and his network of far-reaching cult members.

The night that she escaped, Phillip walked her to the riverbank and said she could either grab a bus that left in thirty minutes and disappear, or the hacksaw she'd seen glinting in the moonlight would make it so no one found a body, regardless. She chose the bus. Once she arrived in Seattle, thanks to the nineties grunge scene, she was able to get in good with concert venues as a roadie, and eventually graduated to managing the lighting board for the biggest stadium in the city.

I sip my iced tea. Late-afternoon sunshine slants overhead, countering the chills I get each time I make eye contact with either of my parents.

"Anyone hungry? We're near happy hour," Bowen says.

"Me, I could eat." Tatum pats her belly.

"Me too." I smile.

Bowen heads inside through the balcony doors that connect to their bedroom. Tatum tucks both legs beneath her in the wide chair.

"Oh, you found it," she says, nodding to my wrist. "I always wondered if someone did."

I lift my arm so the bangle I found in the secret compartment of the guest room catches the light. "It's yours?"

"A gift from my mother. The night I left, I had tucked it away for safekeeping. I guess it stayed there until you came to visit."

"Wow, I guess so. Another secret kept for thirty years." We share a smile at how unimaginable this all is.

"So, Ivy," she begins, and delight at her speaking my name floods my core, "there's something I need to say to you."

My stomach clenches automatically, fearing the worst. Is she angry I'm here? When I called earlier this week, she was reticent to meet me.

She was nervous that my contacting her was a trick by Phillip to get her to betray their deal after all these years: stay away from Rock Island, or he would track down her baby girl and end her shameful existence the way he'd promised he would.

Once I updated Tatum on everything that happened—Phillip's arrest for second-degree murder in the Perez and Hauser deaths, plus Aggie's evolution into the Full Moon Killer—she was silent for a solid minute. So long that I asked if she was still on the line.

Tatum swirls the last dregs of her glass, oblivious to my sudden anxiety, then sits it on the table between our chairs. "Hold that thought. Barkeep! We need another iced tea out here, please."

"On it." Bowen's deep timbre carries through the open door.

Tatum turns back to me. "So I should thank you. Again."

Relief flushes over me. She's not kicking me out. "No, I think it's the other way around. I literally wouldn't be here if not for you—twice over."

Tatum smiles, then shakes her head. "Well, it's one thing to go meet your birth relatives and discover the truth of your lineage—that your grandmother ended up leading such a . . . that she chose a . . ."

"Such a dark path?"

She purses her lips. "That's a nice way to put it. It's incredible that you learned all that and didn't go screaming into the night. But it's entirely next-level of you to then track me down where I've been hiding all this time. How did you find me, if Phillip didn't share what he knew?"

"Ah. Well, I guess I tried to think like you."

"But wasn't that hard? You'd never met me or known much of anything about me."

I set down my glass on the table and mull over her words. "True. Yeah, I guess. I didn't know anything concrete when I landed here. But sleeping in your childhood home, talking to your relatives, and meeting friends of yours, I started to form a picture of what your personality might have been. I learned how much you enjoyed puzzles and word games, which I do too. I thought, if I were trying to stay hidden but didn't want to totally give up my identity—especially if I was forced into hiding—I'd try and repurpose what I already had. Like, with a word puzzle. An anagram."

"You were on the money there."

"I mean, I stumbled, definitely. Over the last two weeks, I couldn't figure anything viable from 'Tatum,' but then I went to your middle name, Erica. Ciera was the only anagram that made sense and popped up in search results when I paired it with 'Lum.'"

She breaks into a grin. "So you knew Bowen and I had reunited, and I'd taken his last name?"

"No. Not exactly. I tried 'Lam' for a long time before finding a match that made sense with Lum—another way that Cantonese character is written in English. And I thought again of the people you loved most when you were forced to leave. I thought you taking his last name might be a way to honor that relationship. That pivotal moment that gave you a child, and I guess sent you on this spiral."

"Ivy," Tatum says, her face suddenly grim, "that's not what happened. Bowen and I were overjoyed about you. It was my uncle and One Family that messed everything up."

I have my doubts, knowing she was only seventeen and still in high school, but don't argue with her.

Dishes clang from the kitchen downstairs, the noise carrying up to the balcony. Footsteps climb the stairs.

"I return bearing gifts." Bowen emerges triumphant through the french doors. He carries a tray with another pitcher of iced tea, a bowl of berries, sliced cheese he says he loves from the local market, and three freshly steamed bread buns filled with barbecue pork—char siu baos, my favorite. He places the tray on a wrought iron table, then slides into the chair beside Tatum.

"Dig in," he says.

I grab a small plate from the tray, then pluck the closest bao. "Thank you. I didn't realize how hungry I was. Seattle has pretty good Chinese food, huh? Almost as good as the Bay Area?"

Bowen gives an exaggerated shrug, but Tatum smirks.

"*Someone* I know would say better," she says.

We each serve ourselves a plate of snacks, and Tatum tops off my glass. While I munch on the happy-hour spread, I catch Tatum peering at me, then at Bowen. I can't know what she's thinking, but I know I've allowed myself a few moments to pretend—just for a second—what life would have been like had we not been separated all this time.

Sunlight glints off the streak of gray forming along Bowen's temples. Tatum shared photo albums with me, and old pictures of the pair of them. Bowen's thick black hair is shaved close on the sides and cut short on top now, but at one point he kept it long.

He dusts his hands free of crumbs on the rooftop terrace. His eyes drop to the notebook poking from my handbag. "Keeping a log of your adventures?"

I smile. "More or less."

"Would you be willing to share?"

"Bowen," Tatum says, and gives him a light pat on the arm. "He's so nosy," she says to me with a wink.

He tucks his head. "I am. I know it, sorry."

"No, it's fine," I continue. "There's nothing interesting in here, really, aside from the anagram notes I made trying to find you, Tatum. Mostly, it's drawings and random facts I learned. The names of the Full Moon Killer's victims. Images that I dreamt and would try to get out of my head by writing them down."

"To exorcise them," Bowen says. He takes another bite of bao.

"In a way. Only it wasn't really successful," I add. "There's this one recurring dream I kept having while staying in Rock Island, from when I was a kid playing at the park with my family; I used to love this one park. In the dream each time, a man whose face I can't see would come over the hill, then stare down at me on the playground while my brother was getting a bandage for a scrape. I was left alone, and it would be just me and this shadowy figure—locking eyes—until I'd wake up. Probably, there's some kind of symbolism in there, but I don't know what it is."

Tatum coughs, as if choking on her bread. She casts a furtive look at Bowen, but he's frozen in his chair.

"What? What is it?" I stiffen. "Did I say something wrong?"

"No." Bowen exchanges a glance with Tatum, who only shrugs.

"It's just that . . ." Bowen takes a breath. "When you were a child— maybe five years old or so—I decided I had to see you for myself. Tatum finally told me everything when we found each other again, all that happened to make her adopt you out and why she had gone into hiding. I knew Tatum would never do anything to jeopardize your safety, like break her agreement with Phillip to stay hidden, but I hadn't made a deal. Her family was never receptive to meeting me, so no one learned my name or face either."

His voice becomes heavy, thick with emotion. Tatum drops her gaze to her empty plate.

Bowen clears his throat. "So I went down to the Bay Area. Hired a private investigator that might help me find a half-Chinese, half-white little girl around the age of five, who was originally born in Central Washington, then adopted when she was two days old. And he found you. I returned to that park every day for a week, hoping to see you. I didn't want your address—I thought I'd be too tempted with that information—so I just asked the PI to give me a location where I might see you. And I did. I . . . I'm sorry this caused you pain. But I needed to see you. To see the little girl I never wanted to give up."

He smiles, remembering. "It was the happiest and one of the saddest days of my life."

Tears burn the backs of my eyes. A thought occurs to me, and I open my notebook to where I tucked the envelope with my faded childhood address scrawled across the front. "Bowen, is this from you?"

Recognition lights up his dark features. "You did get it. I had the private investigator forward it to you, so I was never sure. I hope that wasn't too alarming for you as a kid. All I wanted was for you to know you were loved by us."

"Wow. Do you remember what you wrote? I can't read it, and only just found it a few weeks ago."

"Let me see?"

I pass the stiff paper to him.

Another smile. He clears his throat. *"Dear Ivy. You must know first and foremost that I love you and always will. I'm also sure your adoptive parents love you too. Second, my father used to say you never know what may be coming for you, but in this case I might. Make sure you have a good doctor watching you, because lupus runs in our family.*

"I just needed to tell you that. Of course, I wanted to share this news with you in person, but I wouldn't let myself. Especially if there was any chance a meeting would cause you harm. After all, your physical health is what's most important to me, and your mother. Anyway, now I'm rambling, but I thought you deserve to know. One day, in my dreams maybe, I will find you older and happy and we can be friends, maybe even family. Again, this letter is not meant to hurt you. You should never have been born without knowing how much your mother and I care for you. Yours always —Bowen."

Certainty replaces the previous doubt I felt whenever I read the fragmented sentences. An interest in my "physical health," after all.

"That must have been very painful for you, to write a letter that was never answered."

Bowen wipes his cheek, creasing the fine lines at his temples. "It was. But overall the experience was a huge relief—seeing you happy. It seems like you had a great childhood."

I nod because I'm afraid my voice will break. Then add, "Yes. Unequivocally yes—and in other ways, it was difficult. In hindsight, there was a lot that I had a hard time with, but that was never my family's fault."

Tatum mulls over my words. "Could you explain that?"

"Well, I grew up with a loving family," I begin. "I'll always be grateful for that. But there's a part of me that felt abandoned after my dad died, then my mother after that. Meeting you both, and all of the Caines, has led me to realize that although I lost my parents, it worked out for the best. I still have Carson, and now Lottie, and I found the pair of you. I'm more resilient than I thought."

"Right. And now that you've learned some of the good, and a whole lot of the bad?" Tatum asks.

I laugh softly. "I feel okay. Knowing where I come from, knowing what you two survived, gives me more confidence to . . . to try new things. And follow through this time."

Tatum's hand creeps into Bowen's. The two of them share a look—darty, and almost shy—and I imagine them as a younger seventeen- and nineteen-year-old flirting for the first time.

Watching them communicate without words, I feel calm. Peaceful. Or as close as I've come to it in I don't know how long.

The Ivy who departed San Francisco craved connection so deeply that she pushed everyone away. I couldn't handle close relationships once my parents died. My grief stymied any desire for personal connection in the same way that Carson's did initially—before he was able to resume normal work hours, participate in rec leagues, and begin dating only months later. For me, that never happened. Closing myself off was the only way to ensure I wouldn't be left behind again.

Now, as I steal glances at my birth parents, I wonder whether I just needed someone to say it's not my fault I was given up, even if it's irrational. That everyone genuinely did the best they could with the time they had with me. That no one wanted to leave, either my birth or my adoptive parents, but circumstances—life—required it.

I smile, catching the squeeze Bowen gives to Tatum's knee. "Have you guys ever been to Fisherman's Wharf? I think you'd really like it."

"We'll have to check it out," Bowen says. "Next month?"

"Oh, Ivy. I almost forgot." Tatum reaches behind her chair and withdraws a package wrapped in kraft paper. A corner has already been untaped. "I read your card, but I thought it would be nice to open the package you sent me together."

I stare at the brown cube, drawing a blank. "I didn't send you anything."

"No?" Tatum passes me the note. Slanting cursive not unlike my own hugs the bottom-left corner.

Thinking of you
and excited to meet again soon.

Tatum raises both eyebrows. She lifts the tape covering the other side of the package, then folds the paper open. Inside is a plain white box.

"You didn't send me this?" she asks again.

I shake my head.

Tatum glances at Bowen and lifts the lid. Nestled in a bed of tissue paper is a slender, nearly indestructible survivalist whistle, no larger than a finger.

After a long moment, Tatum raises her head. A tear catches on her cheek before she breaks into a smile.

ACKNOWLEDGMENTS

They say writing is a solitary process. However, drafting and editing a novel during a pandemic, while under sporadic lockdown with family, is anything but. This experience has been unexpected in many ways, and I am intensely grateful to everyone who helped make my third book a reality.

For starters, I am lucky enough to call Megha Parekh my editor. Your insight always steers me back onto the right path when I present my initially unruly plot points, and you remind me of the stories that I love most to tell. To the entire team at Thomas & Mercer and Amazon Publishing, including Sarah Shaw, Brittany Russell, Lindsey Bragg, and Gracie Doyle—thank you for supporting this latest novel and making another dream of mine come true.

To Caitlin Alexander, my developmental editor—thank you for your patience, clarity, and excellent knowledge across the gamut of subjects. You are a one-person dream team, and I am so grateful you edited my third novel.

To James G. and the rest of my copyediting and proofreading teams—I am indebted to your keen eyes.

Adoption is an incredible gift to give any child, and I hope this novel related some of my heartfelt appreciation for it.

Humble thanks must go to my aunt, Vicki Perea-McIntyre, who demonstrates that everything happens for a reason. I am so glad I sent you that Facebook message, now some eleven years ago.

Thanks to Trisha Arnold for your consistent friendship and patience with my research-related questions.

To my cousin, Tifany Lee, thanks for always being so supportive. Your kids are my favorite readers.

Stephanie Kurz, thank you for introducing me to Tim's Cascade potato chips and the whole of Washington State. While I was familiar with this beautiful state before we met, your anecdotes and friendship have brought it alive in my mind over the years.

Gail Campbell, you are an unsung hero of this novel in that I don't know how I would have written it without your support. Thank you for the many visits during the course of its drafting. "You got the cutest little baby face!"

To my mother, Joan Greene, thank you for entertaining my questions when I first learned what adoption meant at nine years old.

To my older sister, Liana Marr Mejia, to whom this book is dedicated, thank you for being a constant through this life's unexpected adventures.

Finally, Kevin and Caden, I must thank each of you for allowing me to hole up and write during these months of relative lockdown. The gift of quiet is a rare thing these days, and I know the effort that comes with it. Love you both as far as the Columbia reaches and with more fervor than its current could claim.

ABOUT THE AUTHOR

Photo © 2019 Jana Foo Photography

Elle Marr is the #1 Amazon Charts bestselling author of *The Missing Sister* and *Lies We Bury*. She graduated from UC San Diego before moving to France, where she earned a master's degree from the Sorbonne University in Paris. Originally from Sacramento, Elle now lives in Oregon with her husband, son, and one very demanding feline. For more information, visit the author at www.ellemarr.com.